CW00867621

Copyright © 2C

ISBN-13: 9798516352249
ISBN-10: 1477123456

Cover design by: Creative Solara
Editor: Kemely Parfrey at Under My Spell Proofreading

To everyone who has supported me with my writing from day one.
To all my readers who have been following me on this journey.

Thank you X

CONTENTS

TWO BROKEN SOULS

E.L Shorthouse

EMMA

HAPPY READING

CHAPTER ONE

Gracie

It was the last night of the summer holiday, and senior year is starting tomorrow—my last year of high school. When this is all over and I leave I will miss it, but I won't miss this damn town or most of the people that live in it. Everyone from our school year was having a party in the woods, a tradition of this town for many years. It was the one night of the entire year that we all get together before school starts when most of us won't even look at each other, let alone spend any time together. It was high school after all, what else can anyone expect?

The bonfire lit, the music blaring, and the drinks flowing. People were making out, taking photos and acting like they were all friends. This wasn't my scene. For starters I don't drink due to personal reasons. When your father is an abusive alcoholic, who takes all of his anger out on you, it puts you off drinking. I have that fear inside that if I do drink, I will act like him, and that is not who I am. I could never imagine hurting anyone or anything. But according to everyone else, alcohol doesn't agree with me as it makes me sick, which is why I don't drink.

"Gracie, will you be OK here alone? I promise I won't be too long?" Lola, my best friend, said.

"I am a big girl. I am sure I will be fine," I laughed, "Go and do what you need to," I added.

I knew where she was going. Someone has caught her eye, and

she was going over to him to make sure he knew that. Lola loves boys; she always has. I don't mean she screws around, I mean, she loves them in more ways than one.

"I will be right back, OK? Don't you move!" she warned, in a slight slur.

My best friend was slightly drunk, just the same as most of the people here except the odd few, including myself. I nodded, waving her away. I knew she wouldn't be "right back" as she put it, but I know she will come back eventually, once she has had enough.

Lola gave me a quick hug before heading off. I watched her make her way towards Harry, one of the sweetest and quietest guy in our school. I believe she has a massive crush on him, something she will not ever admit to anyone, even me. Lola doesn't do relationships as they cause too much drama; her words, not mine. I never minded sitting alone for a little while. I like my own company sometimes.

Suddenly I felt like someone was watching me, making me look up. I soon realised that I was being watched by some guy I had never seen before, not at school nor around town. Trust me when I say I would have known if I had seen him before, he stood out from everyone else. This gorgeous and mysterious guy had jeans and a leather jacket on while most of the other guys were in hoodies or their letterman jackets. I could also see he had a tattoo on his neck, but unfortunately he was too far away for me to identify what it was. His hair was dark and slightly messy, it suited him. The way he was looking at me was intense, and he didn't look like he was pulling away anytime soon. I knew I should but I too couldn't take my eyes off of him; he was drawing me in, and I have no clue why.

I see a smile slowly creeping onto his lips, or maybe it was a smirk. I wasn't a hundred percent sure, but it was something. I decided that it was my cue to turn away from him. I quickly pulled my eyes away from the gorgeous stranger, looking any-where but to the direction I knew he would be. I could still feel his eyes burning into me. I ignored the feeling, trying my best not to look at him again. It was not an easy thing to do. I stood from where I was sitting, walking away towards the lake. If I were away from him, I wouldn't need to be careful not to look at him.

I walked down the docks, sitting at the edge of it, letting my feet dangle over the water, thank God for my choice of sens-ible shoes, or they would be floating around on the water right now.

I closed my eyes, listening to the sound of the water. I loved the sound of the waves crashing, it relaxes me. I sometimes wish I could afford a boat to go sailing around the world. That would be amazing! Just me and the ocean, that is perfection to me. At least out there, no one could get me. Running my fingers through my long brown hair, I sighed to myself knowing this fantasy of mine will never happen, but that doesn't mean I can't dream.

"Why did you run away?" I heard from behind me.

I jumped, nearly falling headfirst into the lake, only just man-aging to stop that from happening. I did not recognise the voice, but still, I knew who it was. It was him, the gorgeous stranger that I was trying to avoid.

"I did not run away," I said softly, not looking at him.

A part of me is hoping that if I do not look at him and say as few words as possible, he may leave. I heard feet against the dock, silently wishing that it was him turning and walking away, only to be disappointed when a figure sat down next to me.

"I would call that running away," he said with a chuckle.

"Maybe, but what do you expect? I had some stranger standing there watching me. What was that even about?" I said, finally turning to face the stranger.

Bad idea!

A small squeak fell from my lips when my eyes met his due to the close proximity, and wow, aren't those beautiful?! I found myself getting lost in his almost emerald eyes. I swallowed hard, words unwilling to come from my lips.

"I couldn't help myself," he said, "You seem different from all those other girls. Why is that?" he added.

"You don't know me, how could you possibly know I am different from all those other girls?" I asked.

"This entire night I have not seen you drink, make out or take anything," he said without even pausing to formulate his answer.

The entire night? How long has he been watching me? Should I be creeped out?

"How long have you been watching me?" I asked.

"You caught my attention the very second you arrived here," he answered my question again so honestly.

"What? Why?" I said, confused.

"Because you did, simple as that." he shrugged.

There was nothing simple about it! Out of all the gorgeous girls here, he happened to notice me?! Yeah, I am calling bullshit on that one. I have nothing on most of the girls here tonight. And more to the point, why is he here? This is for the students starting senior year tomorrow, and as far as I know, he doesn't even go to our school.

"Who are you?" I said, sounding slightly bitchy. That was not the way I intended it to sound, it just came out that way. The handsome stranger laughed.

"You will know me soon enough, Gracie," he said, getting to his feet.

"Wait! How do you even know my name?" I asked.

"You will find out soon enough. See you around, brown eyes," he smirked before rushing off.

I didn't even get a chance to get up before he disappeared. What just happened? Who was he? And the biggest question is, how does he even know my name? I don't know if I should be flattered or scared. I sat there, confused and trying to work out what just happened. Right now, I wanted to find out who he was more than anything else in the world.

I jumped to my feet, rushing back to where everyone else was, hoping I would see him. If I never, it would annoy me for the rest of the night. So I looked around, and he was nowhere in sight. How can he vanish? He only left the docks a few minutes before me.

"Gracie, who are you looking for?" I heard Lola laughing from behind me.

"The strangest thing just happened," I said, turning to face her.

"What do you mean?" she asked.

And I told her what happened and by the time I had reached the end of my story, Lola seemed as confused as I was feeling.

"I don't know if the full thing should freak me out," I said.

"I honestly don't know," Lola said, "What did he look like?" she added.

"He has dark hair, green eyes, there is a tattoo on his neck, and he is wearing jeans and a leather jacket," I said, "Have you seen him?" I added.

"I think I did see him, only a few minutes before you showed up. He drove away in his car, though," she said.

"Damn it! This is going to annoy me all night," I said, "I don't even know who he is. I had not ever seen him around before tonight," I added.

"Me neither," Lola said, "This really is an odd situation," she added.

All I could do was nod in agreement with her. He said I would find out who he is soon enough, seriously, what did he mean by that? Ahhh! Who was he?

"I guess you will have to wait and see if you run into him again," Lola said.

"I guess," I sighed.

I tried to push him and the whole ordeal to the back of my mind, but it wasn't working. I was both annoyed and intrigued by what happened. Annoyed because he wouldn't tell me who he was, and intrigued because of the way he acted.

All I can do right now is hope that either I see him again or he disappears out of my head. I am OK with either, but I would prefer the first option, at least that way I could get his name.

"Come on, let's ask around and see if anyone knows who he is," Lola suggested.

I was not too keen on that idea, but she insisted. I let her do the asking, but anyone we asked had no clue who he was.

"I swear if you didn't say you saw him, I would be close to thinking he doesn't exist," I laughed.

"He might as well not," Lola said, laughing too.

I groaned, feeling a little frustrated by now. I think I should stop before I frustrate myself further. He is only some guy, and

I shouldn't be this adamant about trying to find out who he is. Maybe he will always be a stranger that I never knew. Who knows, time will tell. For tonight, I am going to try my best to forget about him.

We can be strangers who passed in a night of sorts.

CHAPTER TWO

-

Ryland

I have been staying in a hotel with my mom for the last couple of weeks, just until our house gets ready, which thankfully will be tomorrow. I must say I am glad to be having my own space back. Currently I am sitting outside the said hotel, thinking about Gracie. Tonight wasn't the first time I saw her. I had seen her a couple of times since we got in this town, however she never noticed me until tonight. I don't know what it was but from the moment I first laid eyes on her, I was drawn to her. I know I sound like a crazy assed stalker right now, I can assure you that isn't the case at all. I guess I was just lucky to see her around, and everytime I saw her, she happened to be laughing and smiling with her friends, though I knew straight away that it wasn't her, not the real her. I could see the sadness in her. I could tell she was keeping secrets. What secrets I do not know, but they are there.

How did I know? Because a broken person can tell when someone else is broken too. As for her name, I heard one of her friends calling her. She will see me again very soon. I stayed in my car for another twenty minutes, or so, before heading inside.

"Hey son, did you have a good night? Stay out of trouble?" she added, raising her brow at me when she said the last part.

"It was fine," I said, "And no, I did not get into any trouble," I added annoyed.

"Then make sure it stays that way, OK? We can't keep having to move because you can't behave," she said.

Yes, I get into a lot of trouble, I don't deny that, but it would be nice if my own damn mother had a little faith in me. In fact I don't ask to move, I mean I could go to another school if or when I get expelled, it's her who chooses to move to another town.

"I know mom, will you get off my back?" I said, rolling my eyes.

I didn't give her another chance to say anything. Instead, I headed into the bathroom for a shower. I stayed in there longer than I needed to, but I was hoping that would give her time to fall asleep. I loved my mother, she raised me practically on her own, but she can be a pain in my ass at times.

I got myself dried and dressed, heading back through and noticing she was still awake.

"Have you eaten? Or do you want to order in?" she asked.

"I am fine mum, go to sleep," I said, "We both have a busy few days ahead of us," I added.

"OK, if you are sure," she said, and I nodded.

She got herself into her bed, and I went to mine. The sooner I got my own room back, the better. I never understood why we didn't stay in our old house until the new one was ready for us to move in. My mother got told when she bought the new house that the current tenants weren't moving out for a few weeks, but she insisted we came to this damn town straight away anyway.

I hated small towns like this where everyone knew everyone's business. I got into my own bed, grabbing my phone and decided to see if I could find Gracie anywhere. I was curious about the life she lived. I started by looking at a couple of people on

Facebook from the party who added me earlier, seeing if any one of them had her. It took a little time but in the end, she came up on my friend's suggestion. That was handy. I won't add her, though, not right now.

I was hoping her page wasn't private, and luckily it wasn't. I clicked on it, looking through, even though there was not much on it, she doesn't seem to post often, which was unusual for someone our age. There were a couple of posts and about ten photos. I clicked on one of the images, zooming in, the same sadness in her eyes I have noticed anytime I had seen her.

"What is your story?" I whispered as I looked at it.

I knew from the moment I first saw her that she was different from everyone else. I don't know why, I just did. She was beautiful, though, even with the sadness behind those brown eyes, they were still beautiful. I am not one for getting pulled in by the opposite sex. I prefer to only have fun with them, use them for my needs, but with Gracie, there was something, something that was drawing me in, like a moth to a flame.

I sat my phone aside, making sure my alarm was set for the morning for my first day at my new school. I was dreading it, and I hated school. It wasn't for me, hence I am always getting expelled; three schools in the last two years, not so good. I don't know why my mom keeps insisting I go back; nothing is going to change. I told her I'd rather go to work, but no, she wants me at school.

It isn't like I can't do the work, I am not stupid. I can do the work very easily, but it just isn't for me, I hate school. There is nothing else to it. This new school wasn't going to be any different, apart from the fact that it is my last year, and I'm gonna be eighteen in a few months, which means If I want to, I can leave. As I will be classed as an adult, my mother or the school can't do anything about it.

Tomorrow is going to be just like all the other first days, pointless and a waste of my time. The only good thing about tomorrow is that we will be in our house and I will have my personal space back, rather than sharing a hotel room with my mom.

I am hoping to run into Gracie tomorrow, as I know she goes to the same school that I am starting at, why else would she have been at the Senior party tonight? Plus, there was only one other high school around here, which is a good few miles out of town and private. I have the feeling she isn't the type for private school.

At least with her around, I would have something to occupy myself. I wonder if she was still thinking about what happened, wondering who I was and how I knew who she was. I had a feeling she would be because it isn't every day you have an encounter like that with a stranger, is it? I will find out tomorrow when I see her reaction as she sees me at school. I don't know if she will come to me or run from me, the same way that she did tonight in the woods.

I knew I was getting to her too, that is why she couldn't take her eyes off me, that was why she disappeared trying to get away from me. I am just hoping that my behaviour around her hasn't freaked her out too much; that was the last thing that I wanted. Even if that were the case, I won't back off. I can be very persistent when I need to be.

I had to be at school an hour before classes started tomorrow, to see the principle and be told the rules. Someone telling me the rules is pointless because I don't follow the rules, I break them, and this isn't going to be any different. The principal wants to get me a "buddy" to show me around, someone who will be in all my classes. How old am I? Ten? I don't need someone to escort me around, I can find my way around, I am not that stupid, but apparently, it is what this school does. Trust me, whoever it is, he or she will not last the full day with me, I will put them off escorting me within the first hour. I know it is usually the good girl/boy type they get to do these things, but around me, that is a horrible idea. I would be a bad influence on them, and the principal will learn that the hard way. Unless I can request someone, now that is an idea. I knew the exact person I would ask if that is allowed... Gracie! Hmm, maybe an escort for the day won't be a bad idea, especially if I can get her to be that for me.

She may not like that idea, but I sure do. I smirked to myself, deciding that was the plan. I was going to tell them I would feel comfortable with someone that I already knew, even though technically I don't know her, and she doesn't know me. The principal doesn't need to know that though.

Maybe this first day isn't going to be as bad after all.

"Goodnight Ryland, I hope that you have your alarm set," she said.

"I do. Goodnight," I said, trying not to sound a little annoyed.

"Good, then get to sleep," she said firmly.

I rolled my eyes, not responding to her whilst getting comfortable for the night. Tomorrow was a new day, a fresh start. Yeah, right, it may be a different town, but everything else will be the same. The sooner I hit eighteen, the better, and then I can do as I please when I please without anyone moaning about it.

CHAPTER THREE

Gracie

I was sitting in my first class, tugging at the sleeves of my hoodie. I needed to make sure they never crawled up or people would see the bruises on my arms with the shape of my father's fingerprints. He was drunk when I got home last night and was rough with me, the way he always is. At least the bruising on my side is easier to hide.

"Are you not melting in that hoodie?" Lola chuckled from next to me.

"No, I am alright," I giggled.

The truth was it was way too hot, but I couldn't take it off. If I did, people would see and start asking questions. You can tell just by looking at them it was someone else's hands that made those marks. I pushed my so-called father to the back of my mind, trying to concentrate on my class, but there was something else distracting me—the stranger from last night. I was still no closer to working out who he was. I don't know if I would ever know who he is, or how he knows my name.

The class was interrupted with a knock on the door. It was the principal's secretary. Our math's teacher Mrs Holland answered it, and talked to her for a minute before closing the door as she came back in.

"Gracie, the principal would like to see you in his office," Mrs Holland said.

Why would he want to see me? I don't ever have to see him because I don't get into trouble at school; it makes life that more manageable. Some of my fellow students oohed, all wondering why I was getting called to the office. I nodded, grabbing my things and heading out. I was nervous, racking my brain, wondering what I could have done wrong. I couldn't think of anything. Maybe I wasn't in trouble. It could be for many different reasons; well, I will keep telling myself that.

I took a deep breath before knocking on the door, waiting for the principal to call me in. It only took one knock before he did just that.

"You want to see me, Sir?!" I said when I entered.

I looked up, realizing he was not alone. Someone was sitting across him at his desk.

"Yes, I would like for you to show our new student around. Ryland is in all of your classes and claims you two know each other," he smiled.

Do we know each other? How could I know someone who is new here? I looked at him, confused.

"We do?" I said.

The person whose back was to me turned to face me, a smirk playing on his lips.

"You have forgotten about me already, brown eyes," he said.

No, it can't be? What is he doing here? And why has he asked for me? The mysterious, annoying, gorgeous guy from last night.

"You," I said, the tone in my voice made it clear that I was surprised.

"I did tell you that I would see you again very soon," he said smugly.

Ryland stood up and came over to me, taking his place in front of me, only a couple of inches between our bodies. My breath caught in my throat, having him extremely close to me once again.

"It is nice to meet you officially, Gracie," he said, extending his hand to me.

The way my name fell from his lips was enough to send a shiver down my spine. I pulled myself together and placed my hand in his.

"Yeah, nice to put a name to the face," I said as we shook hands.

"Did you think about me last night?" he asked, sounding so sure of himself.

"A little, maybe," I said.

"I thought so," he said, still holding onto my hand, not breaking eye contact.

I couldn't handle the way his eyes were burning into me. The look was intense, it felt like he could see right through me. We heard the principal clear his throat from behind Ryland, reminding the both of us where we were, so I quickly pulled my hand from Ryland's, putting some distance between us.

"I would like you to stay with Ryland for the day. As I mentioned he is in all your classes, and if there are any issues you can report them straight to me, OK?" the principal said.

I saw Ryland roll his eyes while the principal instructed me. Issues? What does he mean?

"Issues?" I asked.

"Yes, he is referring to me not being the most well-behaved person," Ryland shrugged.

"Yes, remember this is your last chance Ryland," the principal pointed out sternly, and finished with "The two of you should get to class before it finishes,"

Great! That is all I need, a trouble maker.

"Yes Sir," I answered lowly.

Ryland didn't say anything; instead, he grabbed his bag and walked out. I sighed, heading out after him. He was waiting outside, standing against the wall.

"We could always ditch?" he suggested.

"No, that is not going to happen," I said, "I don't do that,"

"Good girl?" he asked.

"No, not quite," I said, the consequences for me if I ever ditched school would be dyer, and not worth it.

"Meaning?" he asked.

I didn't answer his question. I started walking away, making my way back to class. I heard him running to catch up with me, soon appearing by my side.

"I take that as you're not wanting to answer my question," he said, "But I will find out your many secrets," he made sure to add.

My many secrets? How does he even know I have secrets? I chose to ignore him when he suggested that too. He chuckled, finding me ignoring him amusing, apparently. I don't know if I can handle him all day, but I don't really have a choice.

****

It was close to lunchtime, needless to say the morning had been interesting. Ryland was an instant hit with the girls, not so much with the guys, some of which have said not so nice or welcoming things, but Ryland never took any of it from them.

He stood his ground, and they all soon backed off.

"Are you joining us for lunch?" Lola asked him as the last few minutes of class came around.

Now why would she do that? I was hoping he would have lunch with someone else; it wasn't like he lacked offers. Plus, I needed a break from him, even if only for a little while. I can't take his charm, wit and flirting with me much longer.

"Yes, if that is alright," he said, flashing his smile at her, "That OK, brown eyes?" he added, turning to me.

I couldn't turn around and say no, that would be rude of me. I smiled and nodded as it looked like he was joining my friends and me for lunch then. All I could think at that precise moment was how glad I would be when this day comes to an end. I don't know what it was about him. He got to me. He got under my skin too easily. He was driving me crazy, and I don't think he knows quite how much. I wish he would stop calling me brown eyes. My name is Gracie, not brown eyes!

The bell rang; everyone piling out. I sighed, taking my time. I think a part of me was hoping that if I took long enough, he would get annoyed and find someone else, but did he? No, of course he didn't. He waited for me, telling Lola and Brook to head to the lunch hall and get us a seat. I looked at my friends, begging them with my eyes not to leave me unescorted with him yet again. What did they do? They smirked and sauntered off, leaving me all alone with him!

"Come on, what is taking so long?" Ryland asked.

"I'm coming," I said, hoping to hide my annoyance from him.

"If I never knew any better, I would think you don't want me to join you for lunch, why is that?" he queried smugly.

I have seen that smug look enough today, it was starting to piss me off. I don't condone violence at all, but I found myself wanting to slap that stupid look off his handsome face!

"What gave you that impression?" I asked, sarcasm in my tone.

"Come on now Gracie, don't be like that," he said, pouting at me, "Admit it, no matter how much I annoy you, you are enjoying having me around, it brings excitement to your usual dull life," he added.

I let out a groan of frustration, throwing my hands in the air before storming out of the class. Yes, I was acting childish, I didn't mean to, but I can't handle Ryland around me.

Why can't he go find some other girl to annoy for the rest of the day? I am sure she would enjoy it better than I do. It's not like I don't like him, that isn't it at all. It is more that he gets kicks out of annoying me, and when he is around me, I turn into some sort of a pathetic nervous wreck.

"I'm sorry, I promise to behave for the rest of the day," Ryland chirped, catching up with me.

"Somehow, I don't believe that," I thought aloud, finding a small giggle falling from my lips when I said it.

"You are probably right, I don't know how to behave," he said.

I laughed, rolling my eyes. At least he is honest; I will give him that.

"I am curious, how did you know my name?" I asked.

I have been with him the entire morning, but I have not asked him that question and I was still wondering how could he know my name.

"Let's just say that last night wasn't the first time I saw you around," he said, "I have seen you a couple of times, you haven't seen me though, and I know your name because I heard you friends saying it," he volunteered a better explanation.

At least now I know that he isn't some crazy assed stalker. Though I had not seen him before last night, I find it all a little strange. He saw me, but I never saw him, yet the first time I officially met him, he drew me straight in. I must not have been paying too much attention to what was happening around me on those days that he claims to have noticed me.

"And there was me thinking you were some crazy assed stalker," I said.

"I still could be," he replied, smirking at me.

"Try it, I will not hesitate to kick your damn ass," I said firmly.

Ryland let out a loud laugh, the sort of laugh that drew attention. He did have such a beautiful and unique laugh. I can't blame people for getting drawn into it. He slipped his arm around my shoulder, pulling me close to him.

"With you around, maybe this school will not be as bad as I thought," he said.

I could feel people staring, wondering why the new sexy bad boy had his arm wrapped around me. I tried to ignore those stares, keeping my head down, and trying to hide my now red cheeks.

Why do I have a strong feeling that Ryland will not be leaving me alone anytime soon? I was not sure what I thought about that, but at least I only need to see him at school, right?

"If you say so," I said, stifling out a laugh.

"I do," he said confidently.

I too believe senior year may have just gotten a bit more interesting.

CHAPTER FOUR

Ryland

I was heading home after the classes were finished. I offered to give Gracie a lift home, but she had something to do after school. I was disappointed when she said she wasn't heading home right away, as I normally would have waited, if only I didn't have to rush to our new house to help my mom move us in. She had movers aiding her most of the day and I did offer to stay off school and help, but of course, my mother was having none of it. I couldn't wait to sleep on my own bed again. Those hotel beds are pretty uncomfortable.

I put the address into my satnav since I have only been to the house once before, which was when we viewed it, meaning I wasn't one hundred percent sure where it was without directions, and it turned out not too far from the school. I hated moving. It was too much work, and I hated getting new neighbours too. My mother was one of those people who tried to make friends with everyone. It works for her, but it annoys the hell out of me. I hate meeting new people because they are all the same; judgemental. Plus, we were not ever around long enough to truly get to know people; this place will be no different.

I pulled up outside, seeing the movers were still there I groaned as I was hoping everything would have been sorted already, that way I wouldn't have to do much. Call me lazy, but doing this moving malarkey over and over again, it gets very annoying.

"Good, you are here! You can help get the last of the things in," my mom said as I stepped out of the car.

"OK, mom," I said, trying my best not to roll my eyes.

"Thank you, son, and then you can get your room organised and get your own space back," she smiled.

"I can't wait," I returned with a smile.

I know I give my mom a more challenging time than she deserves. She works hard and has raised me alone, well, for the most part of my life alone. She has always done what is best for me, never blaming me, and knowing this can be overbearing at times. Having said that, my behaviour had nothing to do with her. That was down to my past, a lot of which my mother was never aware. But that is a story for another day.

I helped the movers with the rest of the things, meaning we were done within the hour which was much quicker than expected.

"Mom, I am going to get my room sorted," I said.

"OK son. Fancy Chinese for dinner tonight? Not quite equipped to cook yet," she laughed.

"Chinese is fine," I smiled, heading up to my room.

I made my bed up to start with, tempted to climb into it right now, but I had too much to do. I didn't have many things. I realised there is no point in owning too much. The more you own, the more you need to take with you or leave behind when you move on.

I decided to take a break, sitting on my bed and going onto Facebook, adding Gracie and hoping she would accept my request, except she may not, I think she has had enough of me today. Well, she acted as if she did, but I know secretly she enjoyed being around me, no matter how much she denies it. To my surprise, it only took moments before she had accepted it. I smirked, deciding to send her a message.

Ryland Connors: Hey, brown eyes. Are you missing me yet? X

Gracie Jackson: Hey, can you stop calling me that? And no, I am not missing you. But I think you may be missing me.

Ryland Connors: I don't believe you, but OK. And yes, I think you should come and hang out with me X

Gracie Jackson: I can't, sorry. I have too much to do. I will see you at school.

Rylan Connors: Your loss! See you at school.

She didn't reply to me after that, and I didn't say anything else to her after that. I got back to what I was doing, wanting to get everything sorted before dinner.

*****

I was in my bedroom, getting ready for bed. I headed over to close the blinds of one of my windows, realising I can see right into my neighbor's room from here. Why would they build houses like that? There isn't any privacy between the homes. I had the cord in my hand, about to pull them down when something caught my eye inside the window across from me. I saw a female standing in the room, her back to me, in a cute set of PJS. I found myself looking at her for a moment, something inside of me, telling me I knew the person.

I looked closer and realised who it was. It can't be, can it?

Gracie!

I couldn't see her face, but in my gut, I knew it was her, and never mind how strange that sounds. I smirked to myself. I think it is time for me to mess with her a little more. I grabbed my phone, finding her on messenger again. She is going to freak when she receives my message.

Ryland Connors: Cute PJS, sweetness � � *X*

I stepped to the side a little, making sure if she turned around, she wouldn't see me, but I could still see her. She started looking around frantically, looking out of the window, checking her closet, under her bed. Everything she could check, she did. Does she honestly think I would be in her closet or under her bed????

I couldn't help but stand there in fits of laughter as I watched. I have never seen anything as hilarious in my life. I see her grab her phone, her fingers moving quickly. I soon received a message from her.

Gracie Jackson: WTF? How do you know I am in my damn pjs? Are you some creepy assed stalker? What is wrong with you?

I think I have made her paranoid enough.

Ryland Connors: Turn around X

I moved back into full view just as Gracie turned around, looking straight at me. The shock on her face was priceless. I couldn't help but look at her smugly and wave. She turned her attention back to her phone.

Gracie Jackson: What the heck??????

Ryland Connors: Meet me outside, and I will tell you X

Gracie Jackson: Fine! Be there in two minutes!

I sat my phone aside, slipping my shoes on and heading outside. My mom was already in bed, sleeping. By the time I got there, Gracie was pacing back and forth on the small piece of grass that was between our houses. She had an oversized hoodie on.

"Fancy running into you here," I said.

"Why are you even here? Who do you know that stays in that house?" She asked, finally stopping and standing in front of me.

"I don't know anyone in that house, well except my mother," I said, "That is my house, we moved into today," I added.

"You are messing with me, right?" she prompted.

I couldn't work out if Gracie was mad or confused, maybe a mix of both? I don't understand why she would be mad though, I know she enjoys having me around whether she wants to admit it or not.

"No, I am being honest with you," I said, "I am your new neighbor, so it looks like you will not be getting rid of me that easily," I added, stepping into her personal space.

"I guess I will have to get used to having you around!" she giggled.

"Yes you will," I said, "I think you will enjoy having me around," I added, placing my hand on her hip.

She winced slightly, it had nothing to do with the way I was touching her. It was the sort of noise you make when you are in pain.

"Are you OK? Have you hurt yourself?" I asked.

Gracie quickly took a step back from me and I saw a look of panic flood over her face.

"Um, no I am fine," she said. "I should get back inside," she added, rushing away.

I was not going to allow that though. There was something wrong with her. I reached for her, grasping her hips gently and turning her back to me.

"You are lying, Gracie," I said softly, "Did someone hurt you?" I added.

"I told you, I am fine," she said firmly.

She used all her strength to pull away from me and rushed into her house and this time I didn't have a chance to stop her. I stood there, watching as she disappeared. I had a very strong gut feeling that she was lying. She was hurt, but what I don't know is if she had an accident or someone hurt her.

I sighed, heading back inside and up to my room. I looked over, seeing she had now closed the curtains. I stripped down, climbing into bed and decided to message her again. I wasn't sure if she would reply this time.

Ryland Connors: I am sorry if I was coming across as pushy outside, but I know you are lying. I know you are hurt. I also know you won't tell me what happened since we barely know each other. Just know that if you need to talk, I am here, without judgment, brown eyes X

Yes, I will be the first to admit that I am an asshole, but that doesn't mean I don't have a heart. I hate knowing anyone is hurting in silence because I know first-hand what that is like.

Gracie Jackson: Thank you, I appreciate that, but I am fine. I can just be clumsy at times. No one hurt me. I hurt myself by accident X

Somehow, I don't believe that, not with the way she worded it. To me, those are words someone says to hide what truly happened to them. It wasn't my place to push, though. If she doesn't want to tell me the truth, then I can't force her.

Ryland Connors: OK. Can I give you a ride to school tomorrow? I know you have your own car, but what is the point in taking both? X

Gracie Jackson: Yeah, that would be fine. I am going to try to sleep. See you in the morning. Goodnight X

Ryland Connors: OK. I will see you at 7:30am? Goodnight, rest well X

I left it at that, trying to get myself settled for the night. I am glad she agreed to let us ride to school together. Maybe if we spend some time together, she will begin opening up. I knew from the moment I set my eyes on her, she had secrets, but now I have a feeling they could be worse than I first thought.

I hope I was wrong.

CHAPTER FIVE

Gracie

I was dreading seeing Ryland after what happened last night. He saw right through my lies; it was written all over his face. I will just need to make sure I convince him that I hurt myself. I don't want or need him to find out anything else. I just have to find a way to distract him.

I finished off getting myself ready, pulling my baggy hoodie over my outfit. I could get away with it today because it was colder than what it had been recently. I was trying to get out as quickly as I could since my dad was still passed out, and I would rather not be here when he wakes up. I grabbed my bag and rushed out of the door. I was outside fifteen minutes before I had to be, so I sat on the front porch, playing around with my phone.

"Someone is eager to get to school,"

Ryland! I turned to face him, smiling.

"Always, I enjoy school," I laughed.

"Weirdo," he laughed.

I got to my feet, going out to the front path, Ryland soon joining me.

"Good morning, beautiful," he said happily.

"Good morning," I said.

"We have a little time, do you want to grab a coffee before

school?" he asked.

I nodded, Ryland softly placing his hand on the small of my back and led us over to his car. I was surprised when he opened the door for me. I turned to him, the look on my face clear to read. He chuckled loudly, motioning me to climb in. I didn't think he would be the opening the door type. But then again, I don't know him that well.

"Thank you," I smiled, slipping into the passenger's seat.

He closed the door behind me, ran around to the driver's seat, and got on the road. I suddenly became nervous because I was in a moving car with him, meaning it wouldn't be as easy for me to get out or away. I am not saying I am scared to be alone and locked in the car with him, it isn't that at all. I am just naturally anxious. Realizing I couldn't dwell on that, I turned to watch out of the window, sighing to myself.

"Hey, are you OK?" Ryland asked, placing his hand on my knee.

"Fine," I said, refusing to look at him.

It was strange, with his hand on my knee; I felt comfort taking over me.

"I meant what I said last night, Gracie. If you need to talk then I am here," he said.

I managed to get a strained thank you out, hoping that if I didn't say much, he would leave it at that. It worked, he left it at that, though he didn't remove his hand from my knee. Not another word was spoken as we drove. I still can't believe he is my new neighbor, out of all the people in the world, he had to be the one who moved in next door. What are the chances of that? It was all a little strange in my eyes, but I guess coincidences can happen, right?

He pulled up outside the coffee shop, the one that happens to be my favourite, Marco's; it makes the best coffee in this town.

"Nice choice," I said.

"Thanks. I saw you here one time with your friends, and decided to come somewhere that I know you may like," he smiled.

"Thank you. It is the best place in town," I said.

Ryland finally removed his hand from my knee, and it made that feeling of comfort disappear. I don't understand, why is a person I barely know making me feel at ease? Another question to add to the long list that I already have.

"Come on then," he smiled.

Rylan got out of the car, and I followed. He came around to help me, but he was too late. His hand fell on the small of my back, once again, only this time I shuddered when he did, his touch getting to me. I turned to look at him and found him watching me, a strange look in his eyes. One of which I could not work out what it meant.

"I knew you were attracted to me," he said, a smug look painted on his gorgeous face.

I went to protest, but he never gave me a chance. He laughed loudly, pulling away and heading into the coffee shop. I groaned to myself, frustration took over me. Why does he need to be this smug? And what makes him think that I am attracted to him in any way? I have not given him any reason to think this, have I? I don't blooming know anymore. I am tempted to turn, and walk the other way, the way that would take me away from him.

"I swear if you run away from me, I will come after you, throw you over my shoulder and carry you in," he said, "Is that what you want, brown eyes?" he asked.

I rolled my eyes, not responding to him with words. Why does he insist on calling me that all the time? I barged by him, heading in. Ryland followed, laughing. I swear, I will end up slapping him one day if he keeps on irking me this way! I took a place in the line, which was pretty long. It was that time in the morning when people were going to school and work. It was always busy at this time.

He came up behind me, standing at close proximity, which was not needed. I tried my hardest to ignore him but having him this close was not easy. The scent of his aftershave was strong, not in the way where he has too much on, but enough that the smell will follow behind him. And damn, he smelt amazing! I feel his warm breath brush against my neck just as his lips fell to my ear.

"Do you like me being this close to you?" he whispered.

"Hmm," was the only word that I managed to let fall from my lips.

"I will take that as a yes," he said, his hand on my hip once again.

"Are you always this annoying and arrogant?" I said, looking over my shoulder at him.

"Nope! I am delightful, ` `" he said, the cutest smile playing on his lips.

I couldn't help but giggle. I do have to admit one thing; he is a funny guy, and his sense of humour is good.

"That is better," he smiled, winking at me.

We were called forward for our orders, both ordering the same thing, Vanilla latte. I went to get my purse from my bag to pay, but Ryland stopped me, paying for them.

"Thank you," I said gently, kissing his cheek.

His smile seemed to grow when I did this, and I felt the heat rise on my cheeks. Why did I do that? Why did I not just say thank you, and left it at that? I don't know what came over me.

"You're cute when you blush," he said, trying his best not to laugh.

"Oh, be quiet," I laughed nervously, playfully pushing him, before walking away.

Ryland was quick to catch up with me, wrapping his arm around my shoulder.

"I am only messing, well, sort of anyway," he said, "You are cute though, I wasn't messing around when I said that," he added.

I let out a scoff when he said that. Me, cute? I don't think so. And if Ryland believes that, then there is something wrong with him. I watched the features on his face change instantly when I scoffed. He went to open his mouth to say something, but I wasn't going to let him.

I pulled myself away from him, walking faster than I needed over to his car. I honestly hope he does not ask me about it once we are moving and I can't get away from him. The anxious feeling had taken over me, the same one that had disappeared after being around him for a little while not so long ago. Ryland opens the car for me, letting me climb into the passenger's seat while he gets into the driver's seat.

"What was that?" he asked, turning to look at me.

"Nothing. Can we please get to school? I don't want to be late," I replied firmly and turned away from him.

He let out a frustrated groan before doing as I asked him. I watched the world drive by, sipping my coffee, neither of us saying a word. The silence must have been getting too much for him because he put music on.

I turned my attention to him, watching him for a moment,

but making sure I was not too obvious about it. He was very handsome, and I found myself taking in every detail of his face from his strong jaw, the small clutch of freckles he had on his left cheek, to the tattoo on his neck, and down to the ones on his arms. I swallowed hard as I studied him. Wow! He was beautiful.

"Enjoying the view?" he asked, not looking at me, but I could see he was smirking.

"Sorry," I said, embarrassed.

I slumped down on the seat, feeling both my face and neck heat up with embarrassment. I would love for the ground to swallow me up now, please? I guess I was more obvious than I thought. I seriously needed this car journey to come to an end so I can run away. I can't run very far since he is in most of my classes today, except one. There is no way of escaping from him.

"It is OK. I don't mind, beautiful," he chuckled, his hand falling on my knee once again.

He squeezed my knee, and that was enough to make me shiver for a moment. I turned to him, and I could see he was watching me out the corner of his eye, a smile now on his lips, not a smirk. I smiled shyly back at him. I can't work out his interest in me. I sighed, shaking my head, turning away from him again.

"What's wrong?" Ryland asked.

"Nothing, I am fine," I said softly.

"I don't think you are, but if you insist," he said, as we pulled up outside of the school.

Thank God! The moment the car came to a halt, I rushed out of it, taking a few deep breaths. Why is he doing this to me? I do not act this way when it comes to guys.

"Gracie, are you OK?" Lola said as she approached me.

"Hmm, yeah fine," I said, with a small smile as I tried pulling myself together.

Rylan got out of the car, coming around to where we were. Lola smirked, giving me a "oh I know what is wrong with you" look. I glared at her, which only made her giggle. Ryland was looking between us, seeming baffled. He was trying to work out what was going on.

"Hey, Ryland," Lola smiled.

"Hey, right back at you," he said, returning the smile, "Did Gracie tell you I am her new neighbor?" he added, smugly might I add.

"No, she never," Lola said, the same look on her face as Ryland had.

I groaned, tossing my arms in the air before walking away from them, and headed into school. I went straight to my locker, putting away everything that I didn't need until later on.

"I think you enjoy running away from me," Ryland laughed, appearing next to me, resting against the lockers.

"Whatever!" I huffed, closing my locker and turning to him, "Do you not have someone else to annoy for a bit?" I added.

"I could if I wanted to, but I don't," he said, "Come on, beautiful, let us get to class, we can't have you freaking out because you are late," he added.

I could have argued with him, but what would be the point? And I didn't want to be late. He was right about that.

I have a feeling the rest of the day is pretty much going to be the same as this morning. I don't think I am getting a break from him. To top that, I don't know how I feel about him living right next door to me. I guess I'll need to learn to deal with it given that there is nothing else I can do.

CHAPTER SIX

Ryland

"See you tonight?" Ben asked.

Ben was in some of my classes, and we got talking today. He is like me in many ways. He has a wild side and likes to get himself into trouble. We never actually got to talk in class but at the principal's office. He was there as a consequence of getting into a fight with some douche of a jock. I was there due to being cheeky to the teacher. After our little trip, we sat with each other in class, and now we were making plans for tonight.

"Hell yeah," I smirked.

"You should bring Gracie along, and her friend Lola too," he said, smirking back at me, "I have yet to see Gracie go wild, Lola is a fun girl, but Gracie seems more well behaved," he added.

I have picked up on that myself. They were opposites, Lola seemed like the type who can go wild whenever she wants to, while Gracie seems more reserved.

"I plan on changing that," I said.

"Nice! Though, I don't think it will be that easy, buddy," he said, "Gracie doesn't date or do hook-ups, I don't think I have ever seen her with a guy unless she was only hanging out in a friendly way," he added.

"Yes, but that was before she met me," I said, "By the time I finish with her, she is going to be a completely different girl, she needs to lighten up," I added.

Ben and I spoke for another few minutes before he headed off. The plans for tonight? We were going to his place for a week-day party as his parents were away. The plan? To get wasted and high, hook up and have some fun. I needed something in this stupid town to keep myself busy, or I would get into some serious trouble simply because I tend to get into more trouble when I am bored.

I headed over to my car, waiting for Gracie. I was her ride to school, therefore I will also be her ride home. We didn't have the last class together, but I had texted her to tell her to meet me at my car when she was done. I'm going to try my best to get her to come with me tonight. I hope that Lola is with her when she shows up owing to the fact that there is a better chance of Gracie coming if Lola asks her. I was getting impatient with all this waiting; she was late. I thought she didn't like being late. I checked my phone to check if she had text me, there was nothing. I soon heard a familiar laugh, knowing instantly it was Gracie.

I looked up, seeing her coming towards me with Lola. The two of them were laughing and talking.

"You are late," I said, "I thought you didn't like being late?" I said, raising my brow at her.

"It isn't her fault, one of the jocks was trying to chat her up," Lola laughed.

I felt a twinge of jealousy when Lola said that. A jock? I thought she had more sense than to go out with an idiot like that. I'd like to hope so anyway.

"And failed miserably," Gracie laughed, "When are they going to get the hint? I don't date jocks," she added, rolling her eyes. She doesn't date jocks?! By what Ben said, she doesn't date anyone. I will change that, not maybe, I will do it.

"You can do better than a dumb jock, brown eyes," I said with a smile.

"Yes she can," Lola said, agreeing with me.

Gracie rolled her eyes, her cheeks heating up. I smirked because I love the way I can make her blush. Lola came over, leaning against my car, as Gracie stood in front of us.

"Did you manage to stay out of trouble for the last hour?" Gracie asked.

"I did, yes," I said, winking at her.

"Good boy," Lola said chuckling.

Good boy? What am I? A dog? I turned to look at Lola, giving her a 'what the fuck' look. She shrugged, laughing louder. I swear, this girl was crazy, I could sense it. I shook my head, laughing with her.

"So ladies, I am going to a party at Ben's house tonight, and I think the two of you should join me," I said.

I was asking both of them but looking at Gracie. I was giving her my best pleading look and I could tell by the look on her face that she was going to turn me down.

"Yes, I like that plan," Lola said, "Please, can we go, Gracie? Pretty please, with a cherry on top??" she added, batting her lashes at her best friend.

I am hoping that with us both begging her, she will cave in and say yes.

"Fine! If it will get both of you off my back, yes!" she whined.

"Yay!" Lola said, doing a little happy dance.

Thank you, Lola! I knew if I were the only one asking Gracie, she would have said no. We arranged a time to meet before Lola said goodbye to us, heading to her car.

"Come on gorgeous, let's go," I smiled, opening the car.

Gracie smiled at me shyly before climbing in. I followed, getting us on the road home, a silence filling the car. She really was not one for talking, was she?

"Do you want to go grab some food before we go home?" I asked.

"No, I can't, sorry," she said "I need to get straight home," she added, her voice sounding fearful when she said the last part.

I don't understand why she should be fearful about going home. I don't even know who she stays with. I think she mentioned her dad, but there was no mention of her mother.

"Do you stay with both parents?" I asked.

"No, my mom passed away a few years ago," she said sadly, "What about you?" she added.

"I am sorry to hear about your mom," I said, "I stay with my mom, my dad left when I was a kid, haven't seen him since," I added, shrugging.

I never cared for my father, even when he was around. He was an asshole from what I can remember.

"Sorry about your dad," she said.

"I am not. He was an asshole," I shrugged.

The conversation ended there. It was not easy trying to have a conversation with her and I wondered if I will ever get a conversation out of her that will last longer than only two minutes. I sighed, not sure of what else to say to her. Instead, I put music on because I don't like silence. I don't do well with it; it makes me uncomfortable.

I wanted to ask her why she sounded fearful about going

home, but I had a feeling that she would not tell me. It makes me wonder if she has a bad home life. He's better not be hurting her in any way, because if I find out that he is, I will not be held responsible for my actions. I hate when the people who are meant to care and protect you, hurt you, especially when they are in a place of power.

"Are you sure you are OK driving us there tonight? What if you want a drink?" I asked as we pulled up to our street.

"I don't drink, never have," she said, "So, yes, it is fine," she added.

Has she ever even tried alcohol? I thought everyone our age would have tried it, at least once.

"Have you ever tried it?" I asked.

"It isn't for me. I don't like what it can do to people," she answered.

I was sure there was more to it than what she was telling me, but I was not going to force it out of her. If she wants to tell me more, then she will, but why would she? We have only known each other for a couple of days.

Gracie said a quick goodbye to me, telling me she would see me at seven before rushing out of the car and heading inside. I swear, she can't get away from me quick enough sometimes. I groaned, a little annoyed. I wish she would give me something, anything. I don't like the way she closes up around me; it is frustrating. I understand it, though. I don't tend to open up to anyone either. You need to trust people to open up, and I just don't trust anyone. It is better that way, reason being people can't fuck you over or destroy you.

I was making my way inside when my phone beeped. I was surprised when I saw that it was a text from Gracie.

Gracie: I am sorry I keep rushing off. It isn't anything per-

sonal, I promise. I will see you at 7pm x

It may not be personal, but sometimes it is easy to think it is with how she always disappears on me.

Ryland: It is OK! Why do you keep doing it though? X

Gracie: I can't tell you. I will see you in a few hours. I have a lot to do before then x

Ryland: OK. See you later X

She never got back to me after that, consequently I just left it. She must have her reasons, and what they are is none of my business. I will see her later, anyway. I was glad my mom wasn't home. She was at work, and I can't be dealing with her right now, primarily because she may have heard about my trip to the principal's office today, and if that's the case, it will result in another lecture that I don't need, thank you very much! I don't know why my mother bothers anyway; it isn't like it changes anything. I do what I do, no matter what she or anyone else says to me. It is who I am, and people need to deal with that. The sooner they accept me for me, the easier everyone's life will become. I decided to grab a quick shower and get myself some dinner before playing on Xbox for a bit until it's time to go meet Gracie.

I was looking forward to getting wasted. Life is always more fun when you're wasted because you don't give a damn!

CHAPTER SEVEN

Gracie

As soon as I got home, I made sure I did everything that needed to be done, including my dad's dinner. I wanted to make sure I never forgot anything, not wanting to set him off. He hadn't bothered me since I got home, thankfully. It gave me time to get on with everything before getting ready to head out. I didn't want to go tonight, not really, but it was hard to say no with them both looking at me. At least it would get me out of the house, and away from my dad for a bit.

I wasn't dressing up. I had gone with a pair of shorts, an oversized hoodie and my converse. My hair was in a high ponytail, and I had little make-up on. I grabbed my bag, heading out.

"And where the fuck do you think you are going?" my dad hissed as I came into his view.

"I am going to meet Lola," I said softly.

"What, dressed like a little slut?" he snapped, "You're better not be going to meet some boy," he added.

"What, no of course not," I said.

That was a lie. I was meeting Ryland first. I text him to tell him to meet me further down the street a bit. I see the anger on my dad's face because I answered him back, even though I never meant it cheekily. He got to his feet, coming over to me. I froze, not knowing what to expect. He grabbed me by the scruff of my hoody, looking at me with his eyes full of anger. I stayed si-

TWO BROKEN SOULS (NEW COVER)

lent because if I said anything, it would only anger him more.

"You're fucking better not be, because I swear Gracie, if you end up pregnant, you are out of here," he hissed, "I wouldn't give a single fuck about you and it being out in the street because it would be your own fault for acting like a slut," he added.

"I won't. I promise," I said, fearful.

"Good, now get the fuck out of my sight, I am sick of seeing you," he said before letting me go and storming off.

I let out a whimper when he was out of earshot and rushed out of the house. I quickly wiped the tears away from my eyes. I don't need Ryland picking up that I had been crying. I can tell he already knows something is wrong with me. I will not tell him what though. It isn't worth the trouble that will follow if my father finds out I have told someone. I headed into my car, driving down the street to wait for Ryland, he should be here soon.

Those few minutes gave me time to pull myself together. I put my best smile on, just in good timing for him getting into my car. He was looking good in his jeans and hoodie. Then again, he always looks good.

"Hey," I said brightly.

"Hello, Miss Gracie," he replied, "Are you ashamed to be seen with me? Is that why you told me to meet you down the street?" he added, laughing.

"Of course not, my dad is just a little over-protective," I said, lying through my teeth, "If he saw I was meeting you, he wouldn't like it," I added.

My dad over-protective? Yeah right, he was the complete opposite, but Ryland does not need to know that.

"Excuses, excuses," he laughed.

I giggled, sticking my tongue out at him. I wasn't going to let my dad ruin my night, in fact since I was out I was going to try and enjoy myself. I changed the subject swiftly from me around to him, asking him what he has been up to for the last couple of hours. If we were talking about him, then the attention wouldn't be on me. He happily told me as we headed to pick Lola up.

I pulled up outside her house. She only stayed about ten minutes away from me. I tooted the horn, letting her know we were here, and my way of telling her to move her ass. The girl is always running late. I was surprised when she came out soon after I tooted.

She was a little more dressed up than me. She had shorts on too, but they were way shorter than mine, and a top that showed off her stomach only covering her boobs and nothing else. I love how confident she is with her body, I wish I were like that. She is gorgeous, and when I say this I really mean beautiful enough that she could be a model if she wanted too.

"Damn!" Ryland said as soon as his eyes fell on her.

Lola gets a lot of attention from guys, she always has.

"I know, right?" I said, "She is fucking stunning," I added.

"Yes she is, but so are you," he said, turning to smile at me.

I had to stop myself from laughing when he said that. I was nowhere near as stunning as Lola was.

"Yeah, right," I said sarcastically, rolling my eyes.

Ryland went to say something, but he never had the chance due to Lola getting into the car.

"Hey bitches," she said, laughing.

"Hey, bitch," I giggled.

"Did you just call me a bitch?" Ryland chuckled, looking at her.

Lola nodded, flashing her best smile at him, and all got forgiven. That smile has helped get her out of a great deal of things and she knows how to use it.

"What is the address?" I asked Ryland.

He grabbed his phone, checking it and giving it to me. It was half an hour away. Ben stayed in the more prominent part of town. I put it into my satnav because I don't know that part of town too well. I concentrated on the road as Lola and Ryland talked. Lola was asking him if Ben was single. What silly questions, of course he was available, he isn't the relationship type. He was the bad boy of the school. It makes sense that he and Ryland hit it off; they were alike. She decided right there and then she was setting her sights on Ben for the night. I am sure Ben will have no complaints about getting some attention from Lola for the night.

We got a little lost, the stupid satnav taking us down the wrong street, but we pulled up outside, forty-five minutes later, rather than half an hour. You could hear the music from outside. I am surprised the neighbors aren't complaining. I only hope that there are not too many people here from school, because I honestly don't want to see some of them. I can also only hope that Lola and Ryland don't get too preoccupied and I end up spending most of the night alone.

"I am so ready for this," Lola said excitedly, Ryland agreeing with her.

I gave them a soft smile and nodded my head. The truth was, now that I was here, I didn't want to go in, but it was a little late now. I never had a choice; they would probably drag me in if I told them I had changed my mind. Plus, I am their ride home tonight since they will both end up wasted.

"Come on, brown eyes, let's get inside," Ryland smiled.

Lola was already out of the car making her way inside. My best friend was something else, that was for sure.

"You alright, gorgeous?" he asked, after a few minutes of me sitting there and not moving.

"I am fine, come on, let's head inside," I said, "Before my best friend gets herself into some trouble," I added, giggling.

He climbed out, waiting for me until I got out. I locked the car up, and we headed in. Ryland's hand fell around my waist. I shivered a little but felt better walking in with him close to me; it made me feel more at ease. There weren't too many people here, maybe about thirty, and thankfully not too many from school. Ryland did mention on the ride here that Ben wasn't inviting too many people. I searched around for Lola. I couldn't help but laugh when I saw that she was already talking and flirting with Ben. She works quickly, and he looked like he was enjoying it.

"She is quick," Ryland laughed.

"Yeap! That is Lola for you, she knows what she wants and goes for it," I said.

She doesn't care about what people thought of her. She was herself; there was nothing fake about her. If people can't accept that, then she tells them where to go. We headed over to them, Ben looking up, and smiling when he saw us.

"I am glad you both could make it," Ben smiled and gave Ryland a "bro" hug before coming to me and hugging me too. Once he pulled away, he went straight back to Lola's side. I think she will be getting what she wants tonight.

"Drinks?" Ben asked, looking at us.

"Yes," Ryland said, "The strongest thing you have," he added.

"Not for me. I don't drink, plus I am the designated driver for the night," I said.

He nodded, motioning us to follow him to get the other drinks. Lola took a beer, Ryland taking a couple of shots with Ben before grabbing a Scotch.

"Anyone looking to hook up tonight? Let me know. I am sure I can find the right people for you," Ben laughed.

"No, thank you," I said, holding my hands up.

Ryland shook his head, using that as his answer, and that gave my stomach some butterflies, since I was sure he would want to find someone to hook up with while he was here. Lola didn't say anything, she smirked at Ben instead, and that gave him the answer he needed.

"If you change your mind, let me know," Ryland whispered in my ear, only loud enough for me to hear.

I flung my head around to face him, glaring at him.

"Keep dreaming, because that will never happen," I said, firmly.

"Hmm, you say that now," he said smugly.

I shook my head, turning away from him and talking to Lola. Is that what he thinks? That I am going to hook up with him? That will not happen, because I don't do those things. He can try all he wants; I won't change my mind, no matter how gorgeous he is. I can't go there for more than one reason.

I think I need to find someone that will help take his attention away from me tonight. I need him to back off because I can't let him get too close. After all, if I do, then he will see the things I am trying to hide. It is strange as he can see right through me, better than what Lola can after being my best friend for years.

CHAPTER EIGHT

Gracie

I relaxed and was enjoying myself. I do know how to enjoy myself, but sometimes it is hard too with everything that has been going on. It was just a chilled, fun night with no drama. Lola had got what she wanted, Ben. He was running after her like a lost puppy; it was sort of sweet. Though I had enough of them making out, I don't need to see that. Ryland surprisingly had not left my side all night, even when he was getting hit on by other girls, he brushed them off, much to their dismay. Mostly everyone was either high or drunk, the odd few including myself were sober. Ryland fitted in perfectly with everyone. I think these people are more his crowd, rather than the other assholes we go to school with.

As much as I was happy with the company I needed to go out and get some air because if I don't, I swear I will get high on the fumes of the weed they are smoking. I decided to disappear while they seemed preoccupied. I headed out to Ben's backyard. It was huge and so beautiful. It had a pool too, well isn't he a lucky boy? I would love my own swimming pool, maybe one day.

I made my way over to the porch swing that sat by the pool. It was peaceful out here, even with all the people and noise inside, I couldn't hear it too much from where I was. I rest against the seat, closing my eyes and breathing in the fresh air, clear air, rather than the kind I was breathing in when I was inside. It isn't my thing, smoking weed, but I don't judge anyone who smokes it, after all they could be getting high on much worse stuff.

"There you are, brown eyes," I hear from behind me.

I knew who it was, Ryland was the only person that called me that.
"Here I am," I smiled.

"You OK?" he asked.

"Yes, just need some fresh air," I said, "I swear I was getting high by just sitting in there," I added, giggling.

"Sorry about that," he chuckled, "Can I join you?"

I nodded, moving over to make space for him. He smiled, taking the spot next to me and placing his hand on my thigh, just resting it there. I don't mind that, as long as it stays put. If he starts rubbing my leg, then I will not be as relaxed. A silence came between us, something that tends to happen a lot, but this one wasn't awkward, it was mellow.

"Why are you out here, anyway, not like I mind?" I asked.

"I was looking for you, duh!" he laughed, "I thought you came out here to get away from me since I haven't left you alone since we met," he added.

"I guess you aren't that bad after all," I teased.

"I don't know if I should be offended or pleased about what you said," he said.

"You shouldn't be offended," I said, "I know I ran off a lot, but I promise that has more to do with me than with you," I added.

I don't know why I found the need to tell him what I just did. I know I don't need to explain myself to him, but it was the truth. It was more about me than him.

"It is OK, you have your reasons, and they are none of my business," he said.

I gave him a grateful smile, one which he returned. He moved his hand from my thigh, wrapping it around me while I rested my head on his shoulder. I don't know why I automatically did it when his arm went around me. Ryland doesn't seem to be bothered by it. I am sure that if I did something he didn't want, he would tell you without even thinking twice about it. He started playing with the small strands of hair that had fallen. For a moment I closed my eye lids and smiled because it felt nice. It was relaxing.

This moment was all a little strange. It was like we fell into it naturally without even trying. Our serenity came to an abrupt end when people started coming out, stripping down and jumping into the swimming pool.

"What did we miss?" I laughed.

"I have no clue; everyone must have decided to go for a swim," Ryland laughed.

"You two coming in?" Lola said, standing in front of us, stripping down to her underwear.

I could see Ryland watching her out of the corner of my eye. Lola didn't seem to notice, but then again, she is used to it, and as for Ryland, well he is a teenage boy after all.

"Hell yeah," Ryland said, getting to his feet, "You coming, gorgeous?" he looked at me.

"No," I said softly.

"Aw come on, why not?" Lola huffed.

Why not? Because if I did, then everyone would see what I have been trying to hide for years, and I can't have that.

"Come on brown eyes, get half-naked and go swimming with us," Ryland said.

I would need to come up with an excuse and quickly. And the perfect excuse soon came to mind.

"Um, I can't, girl things," I said.

What better way to get a teenage boy to back off than to talk about periods? He soon held his hands up, backing off.

"Being a girl sucks sometimes," Lola pouted at me, and I nodded in agreement.

It wasn't the truth, though, but I knew it would get me out of going swimming. Ryland started stripping down in front of me, and my eyes fell on his bare chest. I gulped, oh my, he was gorgeous. The tattoo on his stomach got my attention, and it read the words *Keep fighting!*

I have never read words that hit me quite as hard. It made me wonder though, why does he need to keep fighting? I moved my eyes back up, taking him in for another moment.

"Can I go swimming now, or would you like another moment?" he said, making me pull away.

"Sorry, yes, you can go," I giggled, trying to cover my embarrassment.

He smirked, winking at me before going to join everyone that was in the pool, Lola too. I sat back, watching them all and laughing as they messed around. Everyone was having fun. I just wish I could join them. I sighed to myself; it wasn't fair. There was a part of me that wanted to head home, but if I let things get to me all the time, then I wouldn't do anything, and I don't want that.

My eyes fell on Ryland as he was carrying on with one of the girls. She was giggling and enjoying his attention. I should be thankful because if someone else is stealing his attention, it takes his attention off of me, except I didn't feel that at all though. I found myself becoming jealous. Maybe it was only because she was doing what I wish I could be doing, not having a care in the world and enjoying myself like everyone else.

He must have felt my eyes on him because he looked up at me, smiling at me; it seemed like a sympathetic smile. I gave him my best smile in return, not wanting him to work out something was wrong. After that, he got back to what he was doing.

***

"Come on, Gracie, give me a hug," Ryland laughed.

He was out of the pool, most people were still in, and he had been trying to hug me for the last five minutes, but I refused him because then he would make my clothes all wet.

"No, go away," I giggled, backing away from him.

He came back towards me, and I looked around, seeing that I had nowhere to go because the only thing behind me was a wall. Damn it! I should have checked. He looked at me, a smug look on his face, he also worked out I couldn't go any further.

"What are you going to do now?" he asked.

I looked around for an escape route, but before I could, he grabbed my hoodie, pulling me into him, and wrapping his arms firmly around me so I couldn't pull away from him.

"Oh my God, get off me," I squealed, feeling the wetness from him transfer onto me.

"Nope," he laughed, continuing to hold on to me.

I struggled in his arms, trying to pull away from him, but I was failing at doing so. I found myself beginning to giggle, the longer he held on to me. Ryland did finally pull away, letting me go.

"Asshole!" I whined, folding my arms over my chest.

"Do not pretend like you never enjoyed that, baby doll," he smirked, "You loved having my half-naked body against you, don't deny it," he added.

He was such a cocky fuck at times! It was rather annoying.

"Do you want to walk back home?" I said, glaring at him.

"Hmm, you have a point," he said, "I apologize,"

"That is what I thought," I said.

I found myself getting distracted by him again for a moment. Why does he need to be this sexy? Wow, is he sexy now? I have gone from handsome to gorgeous to sexy, what is wrong with me? I am not supposed to be thinking about any of these things when it comes to him. He was not my type; not like I had a type. I knew he was trouble, and trouble is not something that I need in my life.

"I need to find towels, you can come and search with me," he said, extending his hand to me.

I looked at him strangely for a moment and in return, he chuckled and grabbed my hand in his, leading us inside, our fingers linking as we went in search of towels in this big house. There were so many rooms, many of which were occupied with horny teenagers. We finally found what we were looking for, Ryland took us into one of the free places.

"It is a shame you couldn't come swimming," he said.

"Next time, maybe," I said, "You seemed to have fun though," I added.

I went over and sat on the bed, while Ryland got organised.

"I did. I would have had more fun if you were in there with me," he said.

I felt my cheeks heat up when he said that to me. He wrapped the towel around him, reaching under it, and slipping his boxers off. I turned away from him, letting him get changed.

"Why are you turning away? I am not naked, `" `he chuckled.

"Just in case," I laughed.

"I honestly don't mind you seeing all of me should my towel accidentally fall," he smirked.

"I do not need to see all of you, thank you," I said, shaking my head.

He shrugged, laughing loudly before getting himself dried off and his clothes back on. He came over, sitting down next to me on the bed.

"Gracie, is everything OK at home?" he asked suddenly.

Why is he asking me that? I haven't even mentioned home, and yet here he is, bringing it up.

"Yes, everything is fine," I said quickly, "We should go join everyone else," I added.

I walked away quickly before he had a chance to take it any further. By the time I got out, mostly everyone was out of the pool, so I headed over to talk to Lola and Ben, making sure I was in conversation when Ryland joined us. I could feel his eyes burning into me, but I ignored him. He came over to me, his hand falling on the small of my back.

"You and I will talk later," he whispered.

I was silently praying to myself that he would end up wasted and forget about our conversation, or he ends up hooking up with someone and doesn't need to get a ride home with me. I wish he would stop taking an interest in me. I honestly wasn't worth it! He would see that soon enough.

CHAPTER NINE

Ryland

I was helping get Lola to her front door; she was messed up. She drank a little too much, but she had fun, that was the main thing.

"Are you sure you will be alright getting in? What if your parents catch you?" I laughed.

"I will be fine," she slurred, "My parents will be sound asleep, I will be very quiet, shh," she added, giggling.

I opened the front door for her, and she staggered in, waving behind her. She left her key in the door, and it was lying wide open. I chuckled, taking the key out and locking the door, posting the keys through the letterbox. I shook my head, going back to the car where Gracie was waiting for me.

"Will she be alright?" I asked.

"She will be fine, she is a pro at this, no matter how drunk she is," Gracie laughed.

I had sobered up, not entirely, but I wasn't as bad as I was earlier.

"Do you need to go home right now?" I asked.

It was already midnight, but I don't know if she has a curfew or not. I don't, my mom tries, but she knows I will not follow it. I think she has given up trying to tell me by now.

"Not really, my dad will be sleeping," she said, "Why and what did you have in mind?" she asked.

"Nothing specific, just go for a drive for a bit, maybe find somewhere to stop," I shrugged, "You know this place better than me, anywhere we can go?" I added.

I was not ready for home, and I was not prepared to say goodnight to Gracie either. I know I told her earlier that we would be talking at some point, but I decided to let it go for tonight. Why? Because since I said that she seems to have fallen quiet and anxious. I would leave it for tonight. I don't want to pressure her.

"Yes, there is a park not too far from here. We could go there?" she suggested.

"That will do fine, but firstly is there anywhere around here to get coffee at this time?" I asked.

"Yes, there is a twenty-four-hour diner in town, we can go there," she said.

I nodded, and she got us on our way. The drive wasn't too far, Gracie waited in the car as I headed in, bringing us both some coffee. I did offer her food, but she said she wasn't hungry. I ordered some fries anyway to take with us.

"I got fries just in case," I shrugged as I got back into the car.

"They do have the best fries," she said, pinching one and giggling.

So much for her not being hungry. Gracie and I got back on the road, heading to this park she mentioned. I had no clue where it was since I don't know this town very well yet. I never realised she meant a swing park until we pulled up to it. I thought she meant just a park with benches and whatnot surrounding it. It was quiet, and away from everything else, it will do.

"I love this place at night, it is peaceful," she smiled.

I took her word for it. Gracie got out first, and I followed her. By the time I caught up with her, she was sitting on one of the swings. I sat on the one next to her, passing her the coffee. She thanked me with a smile, gently swinging back and forth. She was staring up at the sky, getting lost in her own thoughts.

I let her be, sipping my coffee. The place was tranquil, not a single sound surrounding us, only the soft whispering of the trees as they blew in the wind. I can see how she likes the place.

"Fries?" I asked, offering them to her.

"Yes please, have you tried them yet? If not, get to it," she said firmly.

The light coming from the moon was enough for me to see her face still, and I could see a cheeky little smile on her face as she basically demanded that I try the fries.

"Yes, mam," I laughed, shoving a couple into my mouth.

She was right; they were good.

"Was I right?" she asked, and I nodded, "Told you," she stated looking a little smug. I liked that she relaxed around me again. I prefer it this way rather than her closing up and keeping her distance from me.

"Yeah, yeah, whatever," I chuckled, throwing a fry at her.

"Hey! Do not waste them," she pouted, prodding my arm.

"Sorry, Miss," I said sarcastically.

Gracie rolled her eyes, sticking her tongue out at me before a comfortable silence came between us. It stayed this way until after we had finished eating and drinking. It was long enough, and now the silence needs to go.

"Would it be childish if we had a go on everything here?" I asked.

"Probably, but who cares? We are the only ones here," she pointed out, getting up from the swing, heading over to the slide, climbing up only to slide down, giggling as she did.

I went and joined her, both of us having a go of everything in the park. Both of us laughed the whole time. I enjoyed listening to her laugh; the laughs seemed real, something I have not heard until now. Any other laughs had been fake. I will mess around here for as long as she wants, as long as it keeps her laughing.

*****

Gracie and I were laying on the grass, watching the stars after playing around for half an hour.

"I am curious, how many tattoos in total do you have? And how did you get them when you are still underage?" she asked.

"In total, I have six," I said, "Fake I.D, baby girl," I added laughing.

"Oh, yeah, I never thought of that," she laughed, "What made you get the one on your stomach?" She questioned.

She was referring to the one on my stomach that read 'Keep Fighting!'

"Because sometimes that is all we can do, no matter what we are going through," I said, "Keep fighting and never give up," I added, smiling at her.

There was more to it than that, but that is a story for another day.

"I like that one, it has a lot of meaning," she smiled, "If we just gave up, we wouldn't get anywhere in life," she added.

I had a feeling she liked that one because the words spoke to her. Again, that is a story for another day. A day that I really hope will come; a day when she feels comfortable enough to open up to me. Though I don't think that day will come easy.

"Exactly," I said.

I moved my hand, that was laying between us, and took hold of hers in mine. I linked our fingers, and she let me. It was my way of telling her I was there if she needed me without saying the words. Gracie rolled onto her side, and I did the same, so we were facing each other. I smiled, reaching in and pushed the strands of hair away from her eyes; those eyes were too beautiful to hide.

"I have a question for you," she said, "Why did you decide to take an interest in my life?" she added.

"Hmm, I don't know," I said, "I saw you one day, and you sort of pulled me in, but I never expected to see you at the lake or end up at the same school," I added.

I didn't want to tell her everything because if I did, she might freak out on me once again.

"OK. I was curious," she smiled.

I was expecting her to question me more than she did. I guess I gave her enough to answer her questions. Gracie fell silent, watching me for a moment.

"You have the most beautiful eyes," she said softly.

"Thanks," I smiled.

I wanted badly to move in closer and kiss her. I don't know how she would react to that; she may end up slapping me. I sighed, running my fingers through my hair. Gracie, she is getting to me in a way I can't explain.

"I should probably go home," she said, sounding disappointed.

"Can you not stay out a little longer?" I asked.

"No, I am up early tomorrow. I have things I have to do before school," she said, "And I don't want my dad realizing I am not home either, he will not be happy if that happens," she added.

I had a bad feeling about her dad; my gut was telling me he was not a nice man. I wish I was wrong, but my gut doesn't tend to be wrong often.

"OK," I said, the disappointment evident in my voice.

"Can I give you a ride to school tomorrow?" she asked as we got up and headed back to the car.

"Sure, that would be good," I smiled.

Gracie and I got into the car and headed for home. She pulled up outside my house.

"See you in the morning?" she prompted.

"Yes, goodnight, brown eyes," I said, kissing her cheek, lingering there a few seconds longer than necessary.

"Goodnight, Ryland," she said, blushing after I kissed her cheek.

I hugged her and moved my lips to her ear.

"You know where I am if you need me, for anything," I said, pulling away and getting out of the car.

Gracie sat outside my place until I got inside. My mom would be sleeping, so I grabbed some water and headed straight to bed. I stripped down, pulling my joggers on. I went over to close the curtains, and just as I did Gracie was doing the same. She gave me a small smile and a wave before she shut her window and then the curtains. I sighed once again, doing the same.

Tomorrow was a new day. Maybe things can be different then.

CHAPTER TEN

Gracie

I was hiding in my bedroom. My dad was wasted and in a nasty mood. I was trying to stay out of his way. I had already got a slap earlier for nothing, and he was still drinking, which meant he was going to get worse. I wish I had the money to just move out and get away from him.

"**GRACIE, WHERE ARE YOU?**" I heard him call out in a snarl.

I could hear him coming up the stairs, and I decided I wasn't letting him anywhere near me tonight. He can find another way to take his anger out. I quickly dashed around my room, pulling joggers on, grabbing my phone and making my way to my bedroom window. I shimmied down the drainpipe.

"Where did you go, you little bitch?" I heard him hiss.

As I walked towards my car I realized I forgot to bring my keys. Shit! My house keys were attached too, which means I won't be able to get back in, well unless my dad is too drunk to realize the window is open, I can get back in that way. But until then, I had no clue what to do. I will need to wait a few hours until he passes out. I couldn't text Lola as she was over at Ben's place. I knew I had one last option. I grabbed my phone and texted Ryland. I had been seeing him a lot this first week, and not only at school.

Gracie: Hey, are you free? X

Ryland: Hey, for you? Always! X

I smiled when I read it. He was always that sweet with me but seemed to be an asshole with anyone else.

Gracie: Can you drive, or have you been smoking? X

Ryland: No, I haven't been smoking. So yes, I can drive x

Gracie: I am already outside X

Ryland: OK. Give me a minute to get dressed. I don't think the neighbors would appreciate me coming out naked ha-ha X

Gracie: No, probably not ha-ha. See you in a few X

I headed to his car, leaning against it and waiting for him to come out. It was already close to eleven, but it was the weekend, so no need to be home too early. I wasn't in any rush to get back home.

"Hey, sweetness," he said happily, as he made his way over to me.

"Hello," I replied with a smile.

"Where do you want to go?" he asked.

"As far away from here as I can get, please" I said, going to the passenger's side.

Ryland unlocked the car allowing me to get in, and he followed.

"Gracie, are you OK?" he asked.

"I don't want to talk about it, can we please just drive?" I said.

"Do you want to go down to the lake or further afield to the beach?" he offered.

"The beach," I said.

It was an hour drive from here to the closest one, but I did not care. All I wanted to do was get away from here, away from my father. Ryland never asked any more questions after that. I preferred it stayed that way. I don't want to talk about it, and I don't want to think about him. All I wanted to do was get away with Ryland. I can't explain why, but around Ryland, I always feel at ease and safe. I am trying to work out why, but no such luck as of yet.

It would be after midnight when we got to the beach, but at least it would be peaceful. I closed my eyes, trying to get a little sleep on the way because I didn't have a great sleep last night due to my anxiety being through the roof, and it would have been the same tonight if I stayed at home. To put it mildly, I hate going to sleep when my dad is wasted because sometimes he barges into my room, for the sole purpose of waking me up and making sure I don't get enough sleep. So I will take advantage of the time I have to sleep.

****

"Wake up, brown eyes!" Ryland says, shaking me gently.

"Hmm, we are here already?" I said, rubbing my eyes.

"Yes, you slept the whole ride," he laughed.

"Sorry, I never slept much last night," I said.

"You don't need to be sorry," he smiled, "I am sure the cold night air will soon wake you up," he added, laughing.

I agreed with him, that would wake me up no problem. I got out of the car, Ryland taking a little longer than needed to come out. I soon realized why when he had a spare hoodie in his hand, handing it to me.

"Put this on before we go anywhere, it is far too cold for you to only have a tee on," he said.

I was grateful for it because I was only in a strappy tee, the bruises on my arms now away too. I slipped it over my head, comfort taking over as I feel the soft, warm material against my skin as well as the smell of him, which was without a doubt another bonus for me, he always smelt good, never mind it being way too big for me. I was sort of small compared to him.

"I think it is a little big, but thank you," I giggled.

"Just a little, but it will keep you warm, and you look good in it," he added, winking when he spoke the last part to me.

I was glad it was dark enough for him not to see my red face after he complimented me. There was not another soul in sight, the place was quiet. All you could hear was the crashing of the waves and the wind blowing. I was hoping the tide wasn't too far in so we could go onto the sand. I went over to the wall, seeing the tide was out.

"Come on, let's go down to the sand," I smiled.

Ryland placed his hand on the small of my back, nodding and went onto the sand. I would usually take my shoes off, but since it was dark, I thought that would be a bad idea considering I can't see what is lying on the sand. I felt myself relax instantly, not only because he was close, but also the sound of the waves crashing, they were soothing me.

"Thank you for doing this," I said as we walked.

"You are welcome," he said, "I told you, I am always free for you," he added.

I found it all very sweet that he makes time for me. Though at the same time there is a part of me that is still on edge, thinking this was all part of some game or something.

"That is very sweet," I said, kissing his cheek.

The smile that painted on his lips grew when I did that. I let out a small giggle, the smile he was giving me was sort of dorky. I could only make out his features and no more with the little light that did surround us. It was a perfect night to be out, all the stars were in the sky, and the reflection from the moon was hitting the water. It was gorgeous. I would need to get some photos before we go back.

I feel him remove his hand from the small of my back, his hand moving to his side, and his fingers brushing against mine. He did little things like that all the time. I don't know why he does them. We shared small talk as we walked for about twenty minutes and at the end of it, he was holding my hand.

"Do you want to sit for a bit?" he asked.

"Yes," I said softly.

We took a seat on the sand, only then did he unlink our hands, telling me sorry before slipping his hands into his hoodie pocket.

"What happened Gracie? There must be a reason you wanted to get out of the house quickly," he asked softly.

"I don't like my dad when he is drunk, he can be nasty," I said.

"Gracie, does your dad hurt you?" he asked, looking me in the eye.

I saw worry flash across his eyes when he asked.

"With words, sometimes, yes," I said, turning away to look out to the ocean.

I wasn't going to tell him about the physical abuse. That is a secret I will keep with me; no one ever needs to know that. Ryland moved in closer to me, slipping his arm around me, my head falling automatically onto his shoulder.

"I am sorry your dad treats you that way," he said, "He is supposed to care for you, love you, not hurt you like that," he added.

"I know, but nobody's life is perfect right?" I said biting the inside of my cheek.

"I guess not, but that isn't an excuse," he said.

"No, it isn't, but I will be OK," I said, giving him my best fake smile.

"I hope so," he sighed, kissing the top of my head.

I closed my eyes, taking a deep breath. His gesture took me off guard, but I found it sweet at the same time. He claims to be some sort of bad boy, but around me he doesn't act that way. He does occasionally get into trouble at school, but nothing major.

Then again, I have only known him a week, well nearly a week. I don't know what he was like before he got here or what he gets up to when I am not around, and to be fair it is none of my business, as long as he doesn't get himself hurt.

"Are you in any rush to get home? Or can we stay here for an hour or two?" I asked.

"I am in no rush, we can stay here for as long as you need," he said, "And if you don't want to go home I can sneak you into mine, and you can stay there," he added.

I was not sure what I thought about the idea, but I may need to since I have no keys to get in.

"I may need to. I forgot my keys," I giggled.

"You are more than welcome, though you will need to hide when my mom comes in the morning before she goes to work," he said.

"I am sure I could do that," I chuckled.

I have somewhere to sleep, that is something. It will be new for me, sleeping over at a guy's house. I have never done that before but I was OK with it; it isn't like we are together, we really would only be sleeping.

"Thank you," I said, kissing his cheek again.

"You can stay with me anytime, I am only next door," he said.

Maybe having him next door will not be as bad after all.

CHAPTER ELEVEN

Ryland

"Are you sure this is OK?" Gracie asked as we sat in my car outside of my house.

"Yes, it is fine," I laughed, "My mom will be sleeping, but she will check in on me in the morning so you will need to hide then, it'll be only for a moment though," I added.

I knew she was freaking out about staying at my house, but what else was she going to do? Sleep outside? I wouldn't let that happen. And going by what she was saying about her father, I don't think he would be best pleased if she knocked and woke him up to get in. We have been sitting outside my house for ten minutes, me trying to convince her to come inside, needless to say I was losing my patience a little.

"OK, let's go before I change my mind," she sighed, getting out of my car.

I followed, locking up and getting my house keys out to let us inside. I could sense her nerves as we made our way to the door, so I took hold of her hand telling her to be quiet, I led her upstairs to my bedroom, curiously she was giggling on the way up.

"Why are you giggling?" I laughed as I closed my bedroom door.

"Sorry, I don't do things like this, it makes me feel a little naughty," she laughed.

"Hey, if you want to be naughty, stick with me, and you will be," I said, smirking.

If she wanted to start being naughty, then she has come to the right person. I can show her things she has probably never experienced. And no, I do not mean dirty things, well unless she is up for that, but I actually meant more on the fun side of things.

"No, thank you, this is more than enough for me," she giggled.

"Hmm, you say that now, just you wait," I said winking at her.

Gracie shook her head and rolled her eyes at me. I shrugged, I was only telling the truth after all. If she sticks around me long enough, I will be a bad influence on her. I tend to be that to "good girls" I don't know if that is what I can call Gracie, but it may as well be.

"I will go down and get us something to drink and some snacks, and then we can find a movie or something to watch, unless you want to go to sleep?" I said.

"No, I am not that tired. I think the fresh air woke me up," she smiled.

"OK. Help yourself to a tee or joggers or both," I said, nodding to where my clothes were.

Gracie thanked me with a smile. I made my way back downstairs, making sure to be quiet. I grabbed us some water, and some snacks before making my way back up. She had disappeared, but then I saw the light was on in my bathroom. She must be getting changed. I stripped myself down to my boxers. I sat on the bed, waiting for her to come back out.

I couldn't help but laugh when she stepped out. My tee was like a dress on her, and my joggers she had on were way too big. It was adorable.

"Stop laughing. I can't help that I am so small compared to you Mr Six feet whatever," she said, placing her hand on her hip.

"I am not quite six foot," I chuckled, "I think you look cute in my clothes," I added, giving her my best smile.

And just like all the previous times when I have complimented her, her face turned bright red. I kept the smirk off my lips, no matter how badly I wanted to smirk. I enjoy making her blush. Gracie brushed my compliment off, coming over to the bed and sitting on top of the covers.

"You can go under the covers, you know," I said, standing up, and turning to her.

I watch as her eyes dance over me and I swear I see her lick her lips as she does. The sooner she admits she is attracted to me, the better. I stood, letting her take her time. Gracie was quick to pull away, apologizing when she realized she had been caught. Her eyes darted around, looking at everything that wasn't me. I laughed loudly and went to join her on the top of the bed. I slid under the covers, Gracie debating in her head whether she should do the same or not, she decided she should and slipped under them with me. She kept a distance though, and if she moved any further away, she would fall off the bed. I let her be because I know that she isn't used to any of this, I will ease her into it.

I let her choose a movie, and thankfully it was not some sappy romance movie. I was surprised when she chose an action movie, Hobbs and Shaw. I liked this one, so it worked out well.

"Thank you for letting me stay," she said once again.

"I couldn't have you sleeping outside, could I?" I said.

"You could have, but you chose not to, that means a lot," she said, kissing my cheek once again.

What sort of asshole would do that? Make someone sleep out-side? I know I am an asshole, but I would never dream of that.

"You are welcome in my bed anytime," I said, "Sorry, that sounded dirtier than it was meant to," I added laughing.

"Yes, it did," she giggled.

"I have a dirty mind and mouth, you will come to learn that, and you should probably get used to it," I said.

"Hmm, as long as you don't corrupt my innocent ones," she said.

I cannot make any promises on that, I may rub off on her. I just smirked and shrugged, making her roll her eyes at me for what felt like the tenth time tonight. She does that a lot.

"Let's just watch the movie," she laughed, getting comfortable.

****

It was now two a.m. and Gracie and I were still wide awake. We had watched most of the movie, but right now we were talk-ing. We were both on our sides, facing each other. We had been talking about the most random things, getting to know each other, if you like.

"I want to ask you a personal question, OK? If you don't want to answer, that is OK," I said and watched Gracie become nervous, but she nods.

"I heard you don't date, is that true and if so, why do you not date?" I asked.

"Yes, it is true," she said, "I find it hard to trust people, and I don't think it would be fair of me to start something with someone when I can't be a hundred percent honest with them," she added.

I understood that, I am the same. I stick with hooking up, flirting and messing around. At least that way, I am still getting some sort of human contact without any expectations from either side. Though Gracie saying that, makes me believe even more that she has many secrets that she hides behind that gorgeous smile.

"I get that, but don't you get lonely?" I asked.

"Sometimes, yes," she said honestly, "What about you, something tells me you aren't the dating type either, more of a hook-up sort of guy," she added.

" Same reason as you," I said.

"Sorry, it isn't nice when you can't be open enough to trust people," she said sadly.

I reached over, pushing the hair away from her eyes and nodded. I wanted to ask her what her secrets were, but I knew she wouldn't tell me. I don't want to make her feel uneasy to the point that she ends up leaving. I watch as she closes her eyes as I move my fingers to her cheek, caressing it. She let out a soft whimper and moved into my touch. I wanted to kiss her so badly. I moved in closer to her, deciding to go for it. It was only a kiss, that was all I wanted. I had been craving her lips since the moment we officially met.

Gracie opened her eyes, seeing I was closer to her than what I was a moment ago. I heard her swallow hard.

"Ryland, what, what are you doing?" she breathed out, and her eyes filled with curiosity.

I licked my lips, my eyes darting to her lips and back up to look at her eyes. She pulls her lower lip between her teeth, chewing on it nervously.

"Would you pull away if I tried to kiss you?" I said, my voice strained.

I am not one for asking, if I think a girl is interested in me, I will kiss her without thinking twice about it. She shook her head, closing the small space that was between our bodies.

"Kiss me, Ryland," she whispers.

That was the green light that I needed. I slipped my fingers into her hair and closed the small gap between her lips and my own. When I felt her lips for the first time, I found a shiver take over me, and a deep moan fell from my lips. Gracie let out a soft whimper, her arms going around my neck as our lips connected. Mmm, they feel even better than what I imagined, and yes, I have pictured kissing her many times. Her lips were soft and warm, her kiss gentle. I cupped her cheek with my other hand, putting a little more pressure on her lips, but not enough to freak her out and make her pull away from me.

I felt her fingers play with the hair at the back of my neck, her lips moving in sync with mine, applying the same amount of pressure against my lips. Gracie pulled away first, much to my dismay. I opened my eyes, to see her smiling with her eyes still closed.

"I have wanted to do that since the moment we first spoke," I whispered.

She slowly opened her eyes to look at me.

"You have?" she said, "Then why didn't you, you had many opportunities," she added, giggling.

"Because I thought you would have slapped me," I laughed.

"There would be a good chance of it if you did it just after we met," she said.

"And that is why I waited until now," I said.

"OK," she smiled, pecking my lips. "I am getting tired now, so I'm going to sleep," she added.

She said a quick goodnight to me before turning to face away from me. I stayed where I was, not sure what to do. I am not used to having girls in my bed, scratch that, I have never had a girl stay over in my bed. Yes, I have spent the night in girls' beds, but I have not ever let any of them remain in mine.

"Ryland, will you, actually... never mind," she said.

"What were you going to ask?" I asked.

"Nothing. It was silly," she said, curling herself up and pulling the covers right up to her chin.

I then worked out what she was asking. I moved into her, slipping my arm over her waist. She instantly shuffled back into me, her body fitting perfectly against mine.

"Is this what you wanted?" I said softly.

"Yes, I don't sleep well at night," she whispered.

I linked my fingers with hers and kissed over her shoulders.

"Maybe you will sleep better tonight since you have someone next to you," I said.

She didn't answer as she was already sleeping. It would seem having me close and to cuddle into her had helped. I don't know if she will be here when I wake up. I have a feeling she won't be.

CHAPTER TWELVE

Gracie

I woke to the sound of an alarm. What the hell? Why do I have an alarm going off? I don't need one this morning. I went to reach for my phone to turn it off, realizing it wasn't even my phone. That made me confused until I remembered I was not at home, and I was not alone. I was at Ryland's and sharing his bed. I honestly thought I would freak when I woke up, but I wasn't freaking at all. I have not slept that great in a long time.

"Ryland, why have you got an alarm set?" I groaned, pushing him.

"Because I needed it to wake us up before my mom came in," he laughed.

"Darn! I forgot about that," I said, panicking, "Should I hide in the bathroom or the closet or something?" I added, looking around.

"No, she will only come and check on me for a second, just hide under the covers," he said.

"How do you know when she will come in?" I asked.

"Because she comes in at the same time, every morning," he said, "Which will be in a few minutes, so you should probably get under the covers right now," he added.

I can't believe I was doing this. I giggled, slipping under the covers and I could hear him laughing.

"You behave under there, Miss Gracie," he said.

I prodded at his side, making him huff and grab my hand to stop me from doing it again. I hear his bedroom door open, his mom coming in, right on time. I bit down on my lip, to stop myself from laughing or making any sort of noise.

"Are you heading to work?" Ryland asked his mom.

"Yes, what are you doing awake at this time, you are usually sound asleep," she asked.

I decided to have some fun of my own. I started prodding at his side with my other hand, running my fingers over his stomach and chest. I couldn't help myself. He was trying his best to stay still.

"I am heading back to sleep, don't know what woke me up," he said.

"Ok, well I will be back about 5pm," she said, before leaving the room.

I waited for a moment before coming out from the covers. Ryland was waiting for me, his brow raised. I flashed my best innocent smile at him.

"Oh, don't you play innocent with me," he laughed.

I batted my lashes at him, trying my best not to laugh. The look on his face was priceless.

"I never did anything," I said.

I saw a devilish look appear on his face and I knew straight away, he was up to something. He was planning something to get back at me for what I did.

"Admit it, you were naughty," he said.

I shook my head frantically, trying my best not to laugh. Next thing I knew, before I could even move, he started tickling me. Oh, God, no, I hate being tickled. I was squirming, squealing and giggling as he did it. I was about to jump off the bed, but he must have realised this because he sat on top of me, sitting on my stomach, continuing to tickle my sides.

"Ryland, stop," I laughed, "I am sorry I didn't behave," I added.

He chuckled loudly and stopped, but he didn't move off me. He kept his position on top of me.

"I honestly thought you would have left by now," he said.

I can understand why he said that, he knows what I can be like with the many times that I have run or walked away from him. I thought the same thing, but somehow, I am still here and in no hurry to get home.

"I thought I would have freaked out when I woke up, but I didn't" I said, "And to be honest, I am in no rush to get home," I added.

He smiled, reaching down and pecking my lips.

"Then don't rush off, stay here as long as you need," he said.

My dad would be at work anyway, and he usually leaves the door open, so hopefully, I can get back home. I don't know how he can keep a job with the amount he drinks, but he still manages and likes to act like a helpful, hard-working guy, when in reality, he is the opposite. He would be at work from 7 a.m. to 3 p.m., and then he would go to the pub, coming home wasted at about midnight. It kept him out of my way. I just have to make sure I hide in my room with something against the door for when he comes home.

"I am sure you have better things to do," I said.

"I don't mind," he answered.

I nodded. I may as well stick around because I didn't have anything planned anyway.

"Then sorted, you are stuck with me yet again," he said, "But right now, I think we should try to get some more sleep," he added.

"I agree, more sleep sounds good," I said.

Ryland came off me, laying down next to me. He pulled me into him. I didn't even have to ask him, like I did last night, well I sort of asked him. He worked the rest out for himself. I don't know what was going on with us, but it seems like we are drawn to each other, and I don't know why. One thing I did know, being with him made me feel safe, and that is not something I am used to feel.

****

I woke up to an empty bed, Ryland was nowhere in sight. I started to panic because I don't do well in places that I am not familiar with. It was different when he was in the same room with me. I cautiously pulled myself out of his bed and decided to go looking for him.

"Ryland?" I called out, almost fearful.

In seconds he appeared in front of me, smiling widely.

"Good afternoon, sleepyhead," he laughed.

Good afternoon? Surely, it isn't the afternoon yet, is it? I looked around, trying to find a clock and when I did, I realised it was after twelve, it was afternoon. I can't remember the last time I slept this late.

"I have not slept this late in such a long time. Why didn't you wake me up?" I asked.

"Because I have a feeling you don't get to get a peaceful sleep very often," he said, "So I decided to let you sleep in," he added.

"Thank you," I smiled, looking down.

Ryland reached for my hand, leading me through the house and into the kitchen, where he was in the middle of cooking food.

"Brunch will be ready soon," he said, "Fresh coffee in the pot, help yourself," he added.

He did this for me? That was a first. I am the one always doing everything for my dad. I have not had anyone cook for me since my mom was still alive.

"You cooked for me?" I said, the surprise clear to hear in my voice.

"Yes, we need to eat," he laughed, "I made poached eggs, bacon and hash browns," he added.

"Sounds good, can I help?" I asked.

He shook his head, telling me to sit my ass down, which I did, but not before grabbing us both a coffee first. Ryland was soon joining me, sitting a plate down in front of me, before sitting across from me. It smells and looks good. I smiled at him before digging in. I have to give it to him; he knew how to cook. It was amazing. I did not even speak. I was enjoying the food too much. And I cleared the plate, as did he.

"That was tasty," I smiled, "Thank you," I added.

"Anytime. I enjoy cooking," he smiled.

I gathered the dishes, insisting that I do the washing up. He tried to fight me on it, but I won. It was the least I could do after he did the cooking. He came over, helping me. I washed, he dried.

"What do you want to do today?" he asked as we finished up.

"I am not sure, but I will need to head home to get showered and change into clean clothes before we do anything," I said.

"Sure, then we can think of something," he said.

We went back to Ryland's room to let him get showered and changed before we went to mine. He insisted he would come along and wait for me. I can only hope he doesn't notice all the holes in the walls and doors from my dad. You see, when my dad can't get to me, he takes his anger out in the house. The holes were all over the place, it would be hard not to notice them. I used to fix the walls and the doors but it was pointless because he would eventually punch and break through them again.

I sat on his bed nervously, trying to think of a way to talk him out of coming into mine, but I couldn't think of anything. Even if I did, it wouldn't matter because I don't think he would listen anyway. He came out of the shower in only a towel.

Don't look at him, Gracie, don't do it.

I repeated these words in my head over and over again. I can't have him catch me looking at him again. I don't want him thinking I am the kind of girl that only goes for guys because of their bodies, that isn't me. My hands in my lap soon became very interesting.

"Trying to distract yourself from me being half-naked, brown eyes?" he laughed.

"Hmm," I said, not looking up at him.

"I will take that as a yes," he said, "Don't worry, I will get dressed," he added.

I knew without even looking at him that he would have that stupid smirk playing on his lips. Why do I need to be this evident around him? I didn't respond to him. I had a feeling it was going to be one of those days again. Then again, it is always one of those days when he is around.

CHAPTER THIRTEEN

Ryland

Gracie and I headed to hers, and she suddenly became nervous. It seems like she is not too keen on the idea of me going into her house. I don't know why, but I am sure I will find out once we get in. She didn't say a word as she tried her front door, luckily her dad left it open since she hadn't lifted her key.

"I am sorry if the place is a mess, my dad isn't the tidiest person and I wasn't here last night to clean his mess up," she stammered out.

He is a grown-assed man; he should be tidying his mess up, not leaving it for his teenage daughter.

"It is fine, and there is no need to apologise to me," I smiled.

She gave me a soft smile, and the two of us headed inside. The first thing that caught my eyes were all the holes on the walls around the house. Her father clearly has got a temper, as long as he doesn't take it out on her. The second thing that caught my eyes as we walked through the living room was the amount of empty bottles and cans lying all over the place.

"I will get that sorted later, come on, let's go upstairs," she said, grabbing my arm and rushing us away.

I decided not to say anything about what I have seen this far. I don't want her getting embarrassed or closing up on me since I could tell by first glance that her father is an alcoholic with a temper. I knew what that was like; my dad was a bastard with a temper. I can only hope her dad doesn't release it the same way mine did on my mother and me. I have never been happier than the day he left and didn't come back. I think if he ever showed up again, especially now, I would kill him without even thinking about it. Anyway, I don't even want to think about that piece of crap!

Gracie led us into her bedroom, the room was spotless, not a single thing out of place or any mess, only thing out of sorts was the hole in her bedroom door. It looked like someone kicked it, the others throughout the house looked like someone made them from punching, but the one on her door looked like someone had kicked it in.

"Make yourself comfortable, I won't be long," she said softly.

I nodded, going over and sitting on her bed. She grabbed a couple of towels and some clothes before disappearing to get showered. I decided to have a look around while she was showering.

My eyes landed on a photo of her and a gorgeous middle-aged woman. Given that Grace looks so much like her, I am assuming that is her mother. That was the only photo she had, and it was right next to her bed. She looked happy, like really happy, not the way she was pretending to be now. I wonder what happened to her mother. Yes, she told me she passed away, but she didn't say what happened. If she wanted to tell me, she would.

I was fearful for her in a way because all the signs are pointing to saying her dad really is not a good man. I decided to stop looking around and sit back where she left me, on her bed. I think I need to get us both away from here today. I don't know where to, but somewhere out of the way, where we can just be us, without worrying about anything else.

Gracie came through, ten minutes later, dried and dressed. That was quick; I thought girls usually take forever in the shower. Her small frame was covered with only a tee, and a pair of skinny jeans. She really was tiny compared to me. The tee she had on was a little baggy on her slim body.

"That was quick," I laughed.
"Yes, I always am," she giggled, "I have not ever understood these people who can stay in the shower for like an hour, there is no need for it," she added, shaking her head.

"I agree," I chuckled.

"I just need to do my hair then we can go," she smiled.

I nodded, and she headed over to her dressing table, sitting down to do her hair. She removed the towel from around her head. Her usual light brown straight hair, a little darker because it was wet and curly too. I watched her closely. She looks at herself, shaking her head and pulling a face, like she was disgusted with what was looking back at her. The lack of confidence she has in herself isn't right. She shouldn't hate herself; she has nothing to hate. She is breathtakingly gorgeous.

She must have felt me looking at her because she looked up at me through the mirror. I smiled at her, in return, she smiled back, but that same sadness still filled her eyes.

"There is nothing wrong with you, Gracie," I said.

"There isn't much right with me either," she said as quietly as a whisper, I don't think I was supposed to hear it. I didn't say anything, not wanting to make her feel uncomfortable. She pulled her hair up into a messy bun.

"We can go now," she said.

"Anywhere in mind? I was thinking we should just drive and see where we end up, what are your thoughts on that?" I asked.

"I am fine with that," she said.

"We may get lost," I laughed.

"I am fine with that too, my dad will not care if I don't come back," she shrugged.

"Then he is an idiot, isn't he?" I said, "Let's get on the road," I added.

I will take her away for as long as she needs to be out, especially if it keeps her away from him. I offered her my hand and Gracie hesitated for a split second before taking me up on my offer. She slipped her small hand into my large one, and I could feel it shaking a little. I linked our fingers, leading us out.

"Your car or mine?" I asked.

"Your car will be fine, I don't have much fuel left in mine," she said, "But I will give you fuel money," she added.

"My car is fine, and no you will not," I said firmly.

Gracie went to protest, but I gave her a stern look, and she sighed, looking at the ground. I opened the door for her, yes, I do have manners, sometimes. She thanked me with a shy smile. I ran around to the other side, getting in and starting the car to get us on the road to God knows where. We will see where we end up.

****

Gracie and I drove for three hours, most of which I was doing the talking. She honestly needs to start talking more. There are only so many questions you can ask someone, and only so many one-word answers a person can take. I will get her to come out of her shell.

We had arrived at some small town, one that neither of us seemed to catch the name of. It was like one of those small towns you see in romantic movies. Not like I watch romantic movies, but I know how they work.

"How about here? We can go find somewhere to eat, and then

go exploring," I said, "Book into the motel we passed if you don't want to go home," I added.

"Here is fine," she smiled.

She avoided my other question about booking into the motel. I would ask again later. If she doesn't want to go home, then why not? I have money anyway, even if she doesn't. I don't mind paying if it means I can get her all to myself again.

I found us somewhere to park before we searched for somewhere to eat. It was tea time already anyway. I had texted my mom to tell her I won't be home until later or not at all. She was not too pleased, but she knows me by now. Besides she can't complain, I always let her know if I am staying out or anything I'm up to, even if she doesn't approve of it. I could be a complete ass and make her worry all night if I wanted to.

We finally came across a diner, and that would do. A burger and fries sound good right about now. Gracie seemed happy enough with the place too. There were only a few people in, but the moment we entered, we were greeted with a friendly smile.

"Just sit wherever you like," The waitress smiled from behind the counter.

We smiled back nodding and went to sit in one of the booths by the window.

"What do you fancy? I have already decided," I laughed.

"That was quick," she laughed.

"Yes, a simple burger and fries, can't go wrong with that," I smiled.

"Hmm, that sounds good. I may have that too," she smiled, "But curly fries," she added.

"You can have whatever you like, brown eyes," I smiled.

I see her roll her eyes, she doesn't seem to like it when I call her that, but I like it, so that is what I will call her, probably more than her name. I couldn't help myself, she has gorgeous brown eyes.

She did not get a chance to complain about it though because the waitress came over.

"Hello, can I get you both a drink while you decide what you want?" She smiled sweetly at us.

"We have already decided," I laughed, "I will have a burger with fries and a coke, my date will have a burger, curly fries and I don't know what drink," I added looking at her.

I know this wasn't a date, but I couldn't help myself.

"I will have a coke too, please," Gracie smiled blushing.

The waitress took our orders and left. I could feel Gracie's eyes burning into me. I looked up at her, smirking.

"What?" I asked innocently.

"Your date? This is not a date," she laughed, "I. do. not. date," she added firmly punctuating each word to add emphasis

"Not yet, you don't," I said, smirking at her, "I can be very convincing and change people's minds easily, just you wait and see," I added confidently.

Gracie rolled her eyes at me once again, and her cheeks went bright red. I couldn't help but look sly simply because I enjoy making her blush. It is fun for me. She never responded, instead she turned to look out of the window.

I plan on making her blush many more times before this night is up, and hopefully, get another kiss from her. That kiss we shared last night, was something else.

I don't think it will be hard because I have a way of getting what I want. The rest of the night should be interesting.

CHAPTER FOURTEEN

Gracie

Ryland and I had been sitting at the diner for two hours. We had finished our meals over an hour ago, but neither of us seemed to be in a rush to leave, so we ordered milkshakes and dessert.

"Do you want to go home?" he asked.

"No, not really," I sighed.

I wanted to stay away from home for as long as I could. I was safer that way, especially with how drunk I know my dad will be.

"Do you want to stay here tonight? We can book into the motel?!" he asked.

I was not sure if I wanted to spend another night with him, but then again, last night was not bad at all.

"Yeah," I said softly, looking down trying not to blush.

"OK, we can go by and hopefully they will have a room for us," he smiled.

"Sounds good," I smiled back.

My dad wouldn't even care if I never came home, but tomorrow I know he will get mad because the house is still a mess; I will deal with that when I have to.

"Well, let's get finished up, pay and we can head over," he said.

Ryland and I finished up what we had left. I went to get money out to pay half of the bill, but he insisted he would pay for it, much to my dismay. I wasn't in the mood to argue with him about it though.

The motel was within walking distance from where we were, which was handy. Ryland quickly texted his mom on the way, telling her he was staying out tonight. He kept me close to him as we headed over. I was thankful for that because I am not the best when it comes to strange places.

"Hi, I am wondering if you have a free room? Preferably with two single beds?" he asked as we reached the reception area.

"I will check for you," The receptionist smiled, checking Ryland out as she did.

She did not look much older than us; she was pretty too and was obviously attracted to Ryland. That doesn't surprise me, I think most girls are.

"Sorry, we only have double rooms left," she said, looking up from the screen.

He turned to me, wanting to know if that was OK. I nodded, that would be the same as last night, so doing it again isn't such a big deal.

"Then we will take one of those," he said.

She got us checked in, taking the payment and just like with the food, Ryland refused to let me pay anything, it was getting rather annoying since I do have the money; he was too stubborn for his own good. We grabbed the key, heading to our room.

It wasn't too bad, and it had a bed, a TV and a shower in the bathroom. That was all we needed; it was only for one night after all.

There was only one problem, what the hell am I going to sleep in? It won't be very comfortable sleeping in all my clothes, but at the same time I can't take any of them off and just sleep in my underwear. I wouldn't feel comfortable with that around Ryland, and he would see the scars and cuts that I always hide. It looks like I will be sleeping fully clothed then, doesn't it?

"Do you want to hang out here or go for a walk around?" he asked.

It was not even 9 p.m. yet, so a little early for sleeping.

"We can go for a walk around and try to find a store or something so we can get juice and snacks," I suggested.

"Good idea, I am a growing boy, I will be hungry again in an hour or so," he laughed.

I giggled and shook my head at him. I would get hungry later too.

"Yeah, yeah, let's go," I laughed.

He flashed a dorky smile my way and placed his hand on the small of my back, and we headed out. There would be a store somewhere; we just need to find it. He moved his hand from the small of my back and slipped his hand into mine. Why does he keep doing that? I never tried pulling away. It has become a little comfort for me.

"Does it bother you when I do this?" he asked nodding to our hands.

"No," I said softly, "I don't mind," I added, chewing on my lower lip, nervously.

"OK, I just wanted to make sure," he smiled.

***

Ryland and I had got back to our motel, two bags full of snacks, way too many but that is better than not enough, right? I also managed to pick up a tee at the store, it was a horrible, cheap one, but it was enough for me to sleep in. I went for the biggest size so it would cover me up.

"Shall we see if we can find a crappy movie to watch?" he asked.

"Yeah, why not?" I replied, "I am going to go to the bathroom to get changed," I added.

I grabbed the tee, heading into the bathroom and locking the door behind me. I can't risk him walking in. I stripped myself down, pulling the tee on, and thankfully it went all the way to my knees, and I pulled my hoodie over me too. I headed back through to find Ryland sitting on the bottom of the bed, stripping himself down until he was in nothing but his boxers.

I made sure to keep my eyes away from him, heading straight for the bed and climbing under the covers. I heard him chuckle, and he never had to say anything, I knew why he was laughing, he knew I moved quickly to avoid looking at him. Soon enough he climbed in next to me.

"Ladies choice," he said, handing me the remote.

"Thank you, kind Sir," I laughed, taking it from him.

I switched it on, flicking through the channels, trying to find a movie channel. I did eventually find a movie I have never even heard of, but it would do for right now. It looked like a romance movie, which I do not mind.

"Can they not show a horror movie or something?! I hate romantic movies," Ryland groaned, rolling his eyes.

"Tuff! You will just need to watch it," I said.

"Meh! I think since you are making me watch this I deserve snuggles," he said, sternly.

He patted his chest for me to lay my head on. I hesitated for a moment before moving into him. I placed my head on his chest, and he wrapped his arm around me. I rested my hand on his stomach, the heat from his skin, heating my cold hand up. He started playing with my hair, as we put our attention to the movie.

I curled right into him, wanting to feel the same security I did last night when I was wrapped in his arms. He pressed his lips to the top of my head.

"I got you brown eyes, you are safe with me," he whispered.

He seemed to know I was going through a lot without me even telling him, it's like I was an open book to him.

"Thank you," I said, kissing his cheek.

He turned his attention to me, pushing the hair away from my eyes.

"Gracie, I don't know exactly what you are going through, but I know you are going through a lot," he said, "And I hope one day, you will learn to trust me enough to tell me," he added.

I don't know why he is so invested in me. I am sure he has better things to do than waste all his time with me.

"I don't know if I ever will, but that has nothing to do with you, that is all me," I said, "And if I did tell you, and you walked away, I wouldn't blame you," I added.

He would, everyone leaves in the end, right? Who would want to have someone like me in their life?

"Gracie, we all have our demons, our scars," he said, "We all have our secrets and our reasons for being broken, but that doesn't mean we need to go through life alone," he added, his fingertips caressing my cheek.

I felt the tears filling my eyes as he spoke those words to me. It was evident to see he has his struggles too; he was also fighting his personal demons.

"Something tells me, you haven't had an easy life either," I said.

"I am fighting my own battles, I have been for a long time," he said, "And maybe when we are both ready, we can share our battles with each other," he added.

I don't know what he was going through or what he has been through, but there was a part of me that felt relieved in not being the only one struggling.

"Maybe," I whispered.

We fell silent after that, but our eyes stayed connected. Ryland cupped my face gently and began inching closer to me. I swallowed hard, my breathing becoming louder. Was he going to kiss me again? I wanted him to, and badly. I decided then that at that moment, I was going to make a move, and hopefully, he'll accept me. I closed the space between us, brushing my lips against his, and he let out a soft moan. I pushed my fingers into his hair and pressed my lips fully onto his. I whimpered loudly, feeling his lips on mine once again. He placed his hand on my hip, holding me against him. I traced my tongue over his lips, asking for access, which he granted, letting my tongue slip into his mouth and finding his. Our tongues were soon dancing together; the kiss was slow and gentle. I have never felt a kiss like this. Then again, I have not kissed that many guys. Ryland is the second for me. I can only imagine how many girls' lips he has had against his, how many girls he has been with. I see the way females swoon over him.

I played with his hair as our lips moved in sync entirely. I was struggling to get the air into my lungs, the kiss was making me breathless. I had to pull away, I needed to breathe. I slowly opened my eyes to look at him. His eyes were still closed, his breathing heavy and a beautiful smile painted on his lips. I smiled, running my thumb over my lips; they were still tingling. Ryland opened his eyes to look at me.

"Wow!" he said.

"Yes," I giggled.

He pecked my lips once more before we settled back down for the movie. I snuggled back into him, not a word spoken between us, but it was a serene silence. I was glad I decided to stay here with him tonight. I couldn't think of a better place to be right now.

CHAPTER FIFTEEN

—

Ryland

I woke up with Gracie still sound asleep next to me, snoring slightly. She really was beautiful. I took in her soft features for a moment and for the first time I saw the little freckles that ran over the arch of her nose. Cute! I chuckled at the way she was laying. She had one leg hanging out of the bed, the covers were off her and the tee she had fallen asleep in last night had crawled up, showing her panties. I soon stopped laughing when my eyes fell on the top of her legs, and that's when I saw them. They were covered in both cuts and scars, some older and some still looked fresh. She hurts herself. I feel my heartbreak for her. I knew she had a lot going on, but I never imagined she was doing that to herself. Is that why she is always covered up? Is that why she didn't come swimming with us? She was hiding what she was doing to herself! I wondered if Lola knew. I had a feeling she doesn't though, something tells me there is a lot that Gracie is keeping even from her best friend.

I reached over, gently running my fingertips over the scars, not enough she will feel me doing. I sighed to myself, not knowing what I should do. Should I tell her that I have seen them or act like I haven't? I don't know how she will react if she knows I have seen them.

Gracie stirs, and I quickly pull my hand from her and lay back down quickly.

"Ryland," she whispers tiredly.

"Morning, brown eyes, I am right here," I said.

She turned her head to me, smiling, and I tried my best to smile back, but in reality, my heart was hurting for her. She looked down, and that was when she noticed her scars were in full view. I watch panic take over her face, and she quickly pulls her tee back, turning back to face me.

"You, you, you, saw them!?" she whimpered out, shame taking over her face and tears filling in her eyes.

"Yes, how long have you been hurting yourself, Gracie?" I asked softly, reaching for her.

"You don't know what you are talking about," she snapped, abruptly pulling away from me.

She got out of the bed, rushing to the bathroom.

"You were not meant to see them," she sobbed before shutting the bathroom door, and locking it behind her.

Damn it! This is not how I wanted this to go. Fuck! I got myself out of bed, going over and knocking on the bathroom door. I could hear her sobbing on the other side of it.

"Gracie, please open the door," I said, my tone gentle.

"It is fine Ryland, just leave right now because I know you will anyway as soon as we get back," she stammered out, "No one wants to be around someone like me, who hurts themselves," she added.

Is that what she thinks? I am just going to walk away because she hurts herself. No, I plan on doing the opposite, not going anywhere because she needs me more than I realized.

"Gracie, I am not going anywhere," I said, "I promise, baby girl," I added.
"Stop lying to me! Everyone leaves, remember? Why postpone the obvious?" she added.

I slumped down against the wall, sitting outside of the bathroom.

"Please, Gracie, open the door," I said, "I am not going anywhere, and you need to believe me when I say that," I added.

She didn't respond, but I could hear her still crying. I didn't move, I stayed where I was, trying my best to talk her into coming out of the bathroom. After about twenty minutes, I hear the door unlock. I quickly get to my feet, and the door soon opens.

Gracie appeared, her eyes were red and puffy, her cheeks damp from her tears and the sadness clear in her eyes. She was still sobbing. I reached for her, pulling her into my chest, and holding her.

"I am right here, I promise," I whispered, "You will be OK," I added, kissing the top of her head.

She buried her face in my chest, wrapping her arms around me and started crying again. I didn't say a word, just held her and stroked her hair.

"I am sorry, you shouldn't have to put up with this, not from me," she stuttered out, lifting her head to look at me.

I moved my hand to wipe the tears away from her broken eyes. She closed them again and moved into my touch.

"How long have you been hurting yourself, Gracie?" I asked softly.

She sighed, pulling away from me and made her way over to the bed. She sat down, pulling her knees to her chest and the oversized tee over them. I followed her, climbing onto the bed and kneeling in front of her.
"About four years now," she said in barely a whisper.

"Why?" I asked, taking her hand in mine.

"Because I hate myself, that is why," she said, "And I would rather hurt myself than lash out at other people," she added.

"Why do you hate yourself? There is nothing wrong with you; you are beautiful the way you are," I said.

"Have you ever just felt like you have lost control of everything in your life, and you can't do anything about it?" she asked.

"Yes, many times, why do you think I do the things I do?" I replied with a question.

"That was another reason I started hurting myself," she said, "Once my mom passed, everything became worse, and I couldn't do anything about it. I couldn't tell anyone what was going on at home because they would never believe me," she added.

I could see the tears building in her eyes. I shifted in closer to her, once again wiping the said tears away as they kept falling. I knew something wasn't right at home for her, and now with her saying that I know it is the truth.

"What is happening at home?" I asked.

"My dad, he takes his anger out on me," she whimpered out, "It is even worse if he has been drinking," she added.

"Gracie, does your dad hurt you?" I asked.

I knew the answer to my question, but I wanted her to tell me. She looked me dead in the eye, fear flashing through her eyes and she nodded.

"In what way?" I asked.

"Physically and emotionally, I don't know which one is worse," she said, "He has never been the nicest man, but after my mom took her own life things got worse, he got worse," she added.

Her mom took her own life!? Yes, Gracie mentioned briefly that her mum passed away, but she didn't say much more. What has she done to deserve such a shitty hand when it comes to life?

"She took her own life?" I asked, sadly.

"Yes, she always had her struggles since I can remember, but even with everything she was going through she was the most amazing mom," she said, "I think she never had any strength left to fight, she fought for so long, and against so much. I miss her every day," she added, the tears streaming down her cheeks.

"I am so sorry, Gracie," I said, "I didn't realize," I added.

"I was mad at her at first, but then I stopped being mad because it wasn't her fault, she just couldn't take it anymore," she said.

"Do you have those same thoughts?" I asked.

"I have had them a few times, but I could not do that," she said, "Because that means he wins. He already made my mom end her life; he isn't going to make me do the same," she added.

"If you ever get those thoughts, promise me you will come to me, OK?" I said.

"I promise," she said softly.

I moved to lay down next to her.

"Come here," I said.

Gracie lays down next to me, resting her head on my chest. I wrapped my arm around her, protectively. She snuggled into me, slipping her hand into mine and linking our fingers.

"Ryland, you can't tell anyone any of this OK? Because I will not forgive you if you do," she said, "No one knows, not even Lola," she added.

I wanted to tell someone what he was doing to her, to try to get him away from here. I wanted Gracie to get help, but I know I can't act yet because that is not what she wants. I couldn't break her trust like that no matter how badly I wanted to do something about it. I wanted to go and kill the fucking bastard for doing all of this to her, making her feel this way, but that would make me just as bad as him. I knew everything she has told me needs to stay between us.

"I promise I won't say anything," I sighed, "But you need to get help, Gracie," I added.

"I can't, not right now, I am not ready to," she said, "I don't have the strength yet to fight against it," she added.

"OK, but when you do feel ready, tell me, and I will go with you to see someone," I said, stroking her hair.

"I promise, thank you," she said, kissing my cheek.

She has told me about her struggles, her demons and I know the time will come when I need to do the same because I think she can sense I am fighting my own battles. I don't tell anyone, but she isn't just anyone. If she can trust me enough to tell me her deepest, darkest secrets, I think it is only right I tell her mine too. And I will, all in good time, and right now is not that time because she is already hurting enough.

"When do we need to check out?" she asked.

"In a couple of hours, or we can stay another night if you want?" I asked.

I wanted to keep her away from that monster for as long as I could. If I could find a way that she never had to go back, I would, but that is not an option.

"Bad idea, the longer I am away, the madder he will become when I do go back," she said, the fear evident in her voice.

"I am sorry I can't find a way to keep you away from him for good," I said, kissing the top of her head.

"I just need to get through this last year then I can get away from him, from here, from this life and start the life I want," she said.

"What is it you want in life?" I asked.

"I want to help kids that have been through what I am going through," she said, "And maybe one day have a husband and my own family, but before I can get any of that, I need to sort myself out," she added.

"I hope you get everything you dream of," I said, "And when you do find that guy make sure he accepts you for you, all of you, scars and all," I added, my voice strained.

"I don't know, I need to wait and see, that is a long time away," she said, "What about you, what do you want?" she added.

"I am still trying to work that out," I said letting a deep breath out, not being able to work out why my chest felt constricted.

"You got time," she said, smiling up at me.

I nodded, and I soon saw her beginning to drift off. I think she is mentally exhausted. I will let her sleep and pay extra if I need to get this room for a few more hours.

"I promise you, I am not going anywhere," I whispered, "I am right here for you, for as long as you need me," I added and tightened my hold on her petite frame.

And I meant every word that I was saying to her. I was going to do everything I could to protect her from it all. Well, I am going to try, but I can only hope my own darkness doesn't take over and stop me from doing that.

CHAPTER SIXTEEN

Gracie

Ryland and I were on our way home. I was dreading it; my father would be mad because I have barely been around the last couple of days, meaning I have not been there to clean the house or make his meals, I have not been there for him to take his anger out on, and I am sure he will have no problem making up for the last couple of days.

"Gracie, do you want to come to mine?" Ryland said, "I don't want you going home alone with him," he added.

"I need to, the longer I am away, the worse it will be for me," I sighed.

Ryland had not let go of my hand since we got into the car. I was still trying to come to terms with the fact that I told him everything that I did. I have not ever told anyone those things, and after only knowing him for a short period of time, I told him my entire life story. There has been something bonding me to him since day one, and after this morning I was able to see that so clearly. I have a trust in him that I have never had in anyone else, and that scares me, even though there must be a reason for these feelings.

"I know," he said, "I am right next door if you need me," he added, lifting my hand to his lips, kissing my knuckles.

"I know, thank you," I said, reaching in to kiss his cheek.

I rested my head on his shoulder as he drove. He slipped his hand out of mine, only for a moment to wrap it around my shoulder, and soon connected our hands again. I slept for a few hours after our talk, but I was still feeling exhausted. It was an emotional morning.

"Will you manage to get back out, later?" he asked.

"Yes, if he is drunk enough, he will crash out, and if not, I will climb out of my window, why?" I asked.

"Thinking we could hang out, find something to do," he said.

"Yeah, sounds good," I said.

I am all in for any reason that gets me out of the house. Maybe we can see what Lola and Ben were doing. It would keep my mind off things, and Ryland and I wouldn't need to talk about what is happening because neither of those two know, and they never will.

I love Lola, and she is my friend, but I can't tell her the truth. She is always bright, bubbly and happy. I don't want to take any of that away by telling her what is going on in my life. I knew she would be there for me, probably wanting to kill my father, but I can't do that to her. I don't need her getting sad or mad because of me. Maybe one day I will tell her, one day when I am away from this place and away from my father.

A silence fell within the car, Ryland concentrating on the road while I was lost in my head. I closed my eyes for a while, thinking of good things. I was trying to cleanse my mind of the bad stuff because I have thought about it too much over these last few days. I know my life isn't perfect, who am I kidding?! It is nowhere near perfect, but I don't want that to consume me, because that means my father is winning, and that is something I refuse to let happen.

"We should go bowling," I said randomly after a twenty minute silence.

"I have not been bowling in years, we should do that," he said.

"Yay, we could see if Lola and Ben want to come, well if we can pull them away from "doing" other things," I giggled.

"We can try, but I don't know if that will be possible," he chuckled.

"I will text her, and ask," I said.

I grabbed my phone, opening a text to her.

Gracie: Hey! Do you and Ben want to come bowling with Ryland and me later? Well, if you can keep your hands off each other for a few hours ha-ha X

I waited for a response, surprised that she responded quickly.

Lola: Hey! Yes, sounds good. You and Ryland? Are you two like dating or something now? X

Gracie: Yay! And no, we are not dating lol X

Lola: Hmm, you sure? You two seem to be spending a lot of time together. Have you at least kissed? X

I giggled as I read my best friend's text. She was too nosy for her own good at times.

Gracie: I will see you later, then we can talk. Will we get you at your house or Ben's, or shall we meet you there? X

Lola: Fine! Don't tell me ha-ha. We can meet you there, what time? X

Gracie: 7 p.m.? X

Lola: OK. See you then. Love you X

Gracie: Love you too x

I smiled, putting my phone away, and letting Ryland know that they were up for it. It would be good for us all to hang out and act like the teenagers we are.

***

We pulled up just outside Ryland's house about fifteen minutes ago and have been sitting in the car. I was in no rush to go in, and Ryland was in no hurry to let me go in.

"I should go," I sighed.

"I know," he said.

I got out of the car, Ryland followed me. I froze, not wanting to move. I should not be this fearful about going into my own house. Ryland reached for me, pulling me into him, and kissed me softly.

"Do you want me to come in with you?" he asked after our lips parted.

"No, that would only make him angrier, he doesn't want me having anything to do with boys," I said.

"Gracie, if he starts, please promise me you will get out, and come to me, OK?" his voice strained whilst caressing my cheek.

"I promise," I said, pecking his lips.

He hugged me one last time, squeezing my hand. I gave him a small smile before pulling away and heading inside. The place was quiet, and there was no sign of my father. Maybe he was out, I sure hope so.

The place was a mess. There was rubbish lying everywhere, mainly bottles; the sink was filled with dishes, the counters were a mess, and it looked like he had purposely poured liquid of some sort all over the kitchen floor. I sighed, deciding to get straight to tidying up. It never took as long as I thought. I don't see the point of cleaning up; he will just make an utter mess again when he gets home. Just as I finished up, I hear the front door open.

"Where the fuck have you been?" I hear him shout assuming he can see the place was tidy, telling him I was home.

"Out," I said in response.

He came storming into the kitchen, with anger in his eyes.

"Out? Doing what? Acting like a little whore?" he hissed, "You know the rules, you do not go anywhere until this place is clean, and you make my dinner," he added, coming towards me.

He is wasted, no surprise there. I went to move the opposite way from him, but before I could, he grabbed my wrist roughly.

" And you don't go out without my permission," he said, his grip on my wrist tightening.

I was in a lot of pain, but I was not going to show him that. He gets kicks knowing he is hurting me. Sick bastard! I didn't struggle either, because that will get him angrier.

"I am sorry," I finally whispered out.

"So you fucking should be, you little bitch," he said, slapping me hard, "Now get the hell out of my sight," he added, letting go off my wrist and pushing me away from him.

I quickly darted by him, heading straight for my room. I closed my door quickly, putting something against it and then broke down in tears. I looked at my face in the mirror. It was bright red and bruising. I needed to get out of here. I had done everything, and his dinner was in the oven, it only required heating up.

I grabbed a quick shower, putting fresh clothes on. I pulled on some jeans and an oversized hoodie, hiding the bruising that was on my wrist. I put a little make-up on, only to cover the mark on my cheek. I made sure I had everything, including my keys and climbed out of the window. I rushed over to Ryland's and knocked on his door. A middle-aged woman who I am assuming is his mom answered.

"Hey, I am Gracie. I live next door and go to school with Ryland, is he in?" I smiled.

"Nice to meet you, Gracie," she gasped like she was surprised and then immediately smiled back, "I am Melissa, Ryland's mom, and yes he is, come on in sweetie," she added, stepping aside.

I thanked her and smiled.

"Are you the one that Ryland has been spending all his time with recently?" she asked, smiling.

"Yes, we have become good friends," I smiled.

"That is good, I am glad he is making new friends," she smiled again, "He is in his room, just head up," she added.

"Yes, and thank you," I smiled, going upstairs to his room.

I don't know if I should have texted or called him first. I nervously knocked on his bedroom door.

"Mom, I am fine," I hear him sigh.

I giggled, opening the door and popping my head in.

"Not your mom," I laughed.

"Oh, sorry, come in," he smiled.

Ryland was lying on his bed, playing on his computer. He paused it when I came in. I walked over, sitting on the edge of his bed.

"Are you OK, brown eyes? I can see you have been crying," he asked.

"I will be, it wasn't as bad as I thought," I said.

Yes, he still hurt me, but I was expecting much worse to be honest. Ryland moved over, patting the spot on his bed next to him. I smiled, slipping my shoes off and laying down next to him, my head on his chest.

"What happened?" he asked, looking down at me.

I pushed the sleeves of my hoodie up, showing him my swollen and bruised wrists.

"And he slapped me, that is why I have make-up on, to hide that mark," I said sadly.

"I am so sorry, Gracie, do you want something for your wrists?" he asked, running his fingers over the marks.

I shook my head and snuggled into him. I didn't want to talk about it, not right now, Ryland picked up on that and dropped it.

"You want a go?" he asked, holding the controller to me.

"I don't know how to play these games," I said.

"I will show you," he chuckled.

I nodded, he handed me the controller and started the game. It was some sort of racing game. I just randomly started pressing the buttons and hoped for the best. It wasn't working so well. I was crashing into everything. Ryland was laughing hysterically next to me.

"I don't think I am one for playing computer games," I giggled.

"It would seem that way," he laughed, "I will try to teach you when we have more time," he added.

"Good luck with that, baby boy," I said.

"Challenge accepted," he said, "But right now I will turn it off, so we can find other ways to occupy ourselves until it is time to leave," he added.

"Hmm, OK," I said.

He reached in, pressing a gentle kiss to my lips. I responded with a deep moan, happily kissing him back in the same way. We kept kissing, but I still have no clue what is going on with us. All of it has sort of just happened.

Ryland and I lay there, kissing for the next few minutes, him pulling away first and smiling. I gave him a shy smile in return, feeling my cheeks heat. I thought I was over the whole blushing thing around him, no? He smirked and winked at me. I laughed, and shaking my head I snuggled back into him. I would be happy enough just to lay here with him like this until we need to leave. I feel safe in his arms, and that is a feeling I don't often have, so I will make the most of it whenever I can.

CHAPTER SEVENTEEN

Ryland

Gracie and I were already at the bowling alley waiting for Ben and Lola who had not arrived yet. In fact they were nearly half an hour late. We got tired of waiting for them and decided to make our way in and have a round ourselves while we waited.

"Ready to get your ass kicked, brown eyes?" I smirked, looking at Gracie as we got set up.

"I am a pro at bowling, so you should prepare to get your ass kicked by a girl, baby boy," she said, smirking back.

I stepped in closer to her, placed my hand on her hip and pulled her into me. She let out a small whimper when our bodies touched.

"Maybe we should make this more interesting," I said.

"What did you have in mind?" She giggled.

"If I win, you need to go on a date with me every night this coming week," I said, "And if you win, I will do anything you want or need me to," I added.

Gracie smirked, inching closer to me. She brushed her lips against mine, and I thought she was going to kiss me. She had other ideas; she reached into my ear and placed her hand on my chest.

"Then prepare to be my bitch for the next week," she said, a loud giggle falling from her lips once she finished that sentence.

I loved the sound of her giggle; it was the sweetest thing I have ever heard. I couldn't help but laugh loudly at her choice of words. I was not expecting them to come from her lips.

"Bring it on, baby girl," I said confidently.

I don't mind either way. If I win, basically I get to date her, and if I lose, she can ask me to do as she pleases, which means I still get to spend time with her.

"You are going to regret saying those words to me," she said.

"I don't think I will," I said, closing the small space between us, and kissing her softly.

Gracie never hesitated to kiss me back. I felt her lips growing into a smile against mine, and her arms soon took place around my neck. It was a sweet and sensual kiss. I enjoyed the feel of her lips. They were always so soft and warm. I placed my hand on her cheek, deepening the kiss.

I pulled away first, not because I wanted to, but because I had to. I had to get my breath back; that kiss had made me breathless. I opened my eyes, Gracie standing there with her eyes still closed, with the biggest smile on her lips.

I wrapped both my arms around her, hugging her to my chest. Gracie buried her face in my chest, slipping her arms around me.

"I always feel so safe with you," I heard her whisper.

I could only make the words out and no more.

"I just wish you could feel that way all the time," I said, kissing the top of her head.

"One day I will," she said, lifting her head to look up at me.

"I hope so," I said, pushing the hair away from her eyes.

I hope she gets everything that dreams of, someone who will love and protect her the way she deserves it. I hope when she gets away from this place, away from him, her life will get better.

"Me too," she said, pecking my lips, "Come on, let's get on with the game," she added, pulling away from me.

I nodded, and she went first. Just as Gracie took her first shot Ben and Lola came in.

"You started without us, how rude!" Lola pouted.

"You two were supposed to be here over half an hour ago, being late is rude!" I chuckled.

Lola flipped me off, laughing and going over to Gracie, hugging her best friend while Ben went and paid for the two of them to play on the lane next to us. Gracie and Lola were whispering and giggling, I can only imagine what those two are talking about. Ben came back over to stand next to me.

"Girls will be girls," he laughed, "So, do you want to tell me what is going on with Gracie and you? You seem to be spending a lot of time together," he added.

"Honestly, I am still trying to figure it all out," I said, looking over to where she was.

"Or you already have, you just don't know how to tell her," he said, patting my back.

Maybe that was the truth. I know, but I am apprehensive about telling her, even though I knew I wanted things to develop between Gracie and me, I need to tell her the truth about me and my past. And I will, but for the time being she has enough going on without me adding to it.

"Are you taking your turn or are you just going to stand around gossiping all night?" Gracie chuckled, looking at me.

"Yes boss," I laughed, sticking my tongue out at her.

I got too lost in my head there for a moment, I forgot it was my turn. It was time for me to try and kick her ass or let her win, but we will see how it goes.

***

"Ha, you just got your ass kicked by a girl," Gracie said, looking a little too smug.

She beat me! Scratch that, she actually destroyed me. We played three games, and she won every single one of them. It was the girl's night tonight because Lola was the same, beating Ben, though I have a feeling he let her win.

"Yeah, yeah, don't look so smug," I said, petting my lip while looking at her.

Gracie snickers loudly just as she was coming over to kiss my lips softly.

"Aww, sorry baby boy," she said, the look on her face telling me she was not sorry at all.

"Yes, you look like you mean it, not!" I snickered, shaking my head.

I am a competitive person by nature, but not with her, and the fact that she beat me was not bothering me at all.

"No, I am not sorry, not one bit," she said.

"So what do you want? Spill it, I know you have been thinking about what you can make me do since you won the first round," I said.

I don't know if I want to know what she is thinking, but I was the one who came up with the bet, no one to blame but myself.

She wrapped her arms around my neck, thinking about it.

"Anything?" she asked, and I nodded, "You can start with a date every night this coming week," she added, smirking.

"That was mine, if I had I won," I laughed.

"Well, now it is mine," she said, "But if you don't want to," she added, pulling herself away from me, attempting to walk away.

I was not going to let that happen. I swiftly took hold of her hips, pulling her back around to face me and into me.

"I want to, and badly," I said.

"Then that is a start," she said, kissing my cheek.

We got ourselves organized to head out, deciding to grab a late dinner somewhere else. We left the cars at the bowling alley, choosing to walk since it was a nice night. The girls decided we were going for pizza. They concluded that since they won, they got to choose where we eat. Ben and I knew it was better not to argue with them about it.

Gracie came to my side, linking her arm through mine.

"Thank you for making a bad day better," she said.

"Anytime, beautiful," I smiled, unlinking her arm from mine.

It was only for a moment, though. I slipped my hand into Gracie's instead, letting our fingers link together. In return, she smiled brightly at me.

"I am curious, what is going on here?" Lola asked, pointing between Gracie and me.

I wish people would stop asking me that because I can't give them an answer yet. I feel Gracie's grip tighten on my hand at the very moment her friend questioned us.

"When we work it out, we will let you know," I said, laughing.

I was trying to laugh it off in hopes that Lola would drop the subject since it was making Gracie feel uneasy. I could sense it from her. Lola nodded, letting it go. I think she too realized that neither of us were ready to discuss it. I felt Gracie's hand relax in mine soon after Lola dropped the conversation.

"Sorry," I said.

"No, it is OK," she said, giving me a small smile.

I knew it wasn't, but I nodded my head anyway. I stole a quick kiss from her just as we came to the pizza place, the four of us heading in. We decided to get two pizzas and share them between the four of us. I slid my hand under the table, gently caressing Gracie's wrist where the bruising was. She turned to me, smiling softly at me.

"Can I stay with you tonight?" she whispered, "If not, it is OK..." she trailed off.

"You can stay with me anytime you want," I whispered back.

"Thank you. I don't want to stay at home, but I will need to show my face," she said, "I will just go straight to my room, block the door, and get what I need for school, then sneak back out of the window, and then go back home early," she added.

"Anything you need," I said, kissing her.

At least if she is with me, then I know she is safe. I would sneak her back in. If I could, I would sneak her into my house every night, and keep her away from home during the day, but I know that isn't possible or practical.

"You are incredible," she said, resting her head on my shoulder.

I don't think she would be saying that if she knew everything about me. She was afraid that I would run when she told me the truth. Well, I am terrified about what she will do when she learns the truth about me. I sighed, kissing the top of her head and wrapping one of my arms around her.

I know telling her the truth will have to be done sooner rather than later before either of us get in too deep. And to be honest, I was finding myself already getting in too deep with her. I am smitten, I can't deny that. But for tonight, I just want everyone to relax and enjoy the rest of the night without any worries or issues. My past can be dealt with another day.

CHAPTER EIGHTEEN

Gracie

The four of us were down at the lake, neither of us ready to head home yet, especially me. The guys were messing around with a football, while Lola and I sat by and watched.

"Gracie, are you OK? Something seems off recently," Lola asked.

"I am OK, just some things going on at home," I said.

"Anything I can help with?" she offered.

"Thank you, but no, it will be OK in no time," I smiled.

I hated lying to her, but it was for the best. She smiled and nodded, understanding that I don't want to talk about it.

"How are things with you and Ben?" I asked, wanting to change the subject.

"Good, I know he acts like some tough bad boy, but in reality, he is a sweetheart, and he is good to me, in many ways," she said, "I know it hasn't been long, but I am sort of smitten, and I think he might be too," she added.

"Yay! I am happy for you," I smiled hugging her.

I have never seen her this way with a guy; it was sweet to watch.

"Thank you," she said, "I am going to ask a question, and I don't want you to freak at me OK?" She added.

I had a feeling I knew what this question was involving the one and only Ryland.

"Do you like Ryland? I have not ever seen you interested in a guy, ever really, but around him, you are completely different," she said.

She was right. I have never bothered with guys, but Ryland wasn't just any other guy.

"I do, a lot," I said honestly, "But, I have no clue what is going on with us, and I don't want to rush it, you know?" I added.

"I thought so, he seems to like you too," she smiled.

"Honestly, he is my safe place right now," I said honestly, looking over to where he was, and smiled.

"Nothing better than feeling that way," she said.

I was glad she didn't ask why. We didn't get a chance to say anything else because the guys came back to join us. Ryland sat down next to me, wrapping his arm around me, pressing a soft kiss to my forehead. I closed my eyes, savouring the short moment. He pulled me over to him, sitting me between his legs, my back to his front. I rested back against his chest just as he draped his arms around me while nuzzling my neck with his cold nose.

"Let me know when you are ready to go back," he whispered.

"I am in no rush," I said, looking up at him.

He gave me a sympathetic look, nodding his head. He moved in, planting a soft kiss to my lips. I let out a soft whimper, not expecting it. Ryland chuckled, pulling away. He was looking at me, with a hint of a smirk on his lips. He knows what he does to me each and every time that he kisses me.

I giggled, shaking my head and slapping his chest playfully. He let out a loud laugh, and what a beautiful laugh it was. It made Lola and Ben look at him curiously. Ryland just laughed again, then shrugged.

"Do you need to be picked up for school tomorrow? Ben is coming to get me anyway..." Lola asked.

"No, I will bring her to school," Ryland said, "Since she is staying with me tonight anyway," he added.

"You are?" Lola asked, a shocked look on her face when she looked at me.

"Yes," I said, "No need to look as shocked," I added giggling.

"Sorry, you just don't stay out much, and certainly not at a guys house," she said laughing.

She did have a point. I don't tend to stay out often, not even at her house because of my dad, but I was at the stage where I will stay away from home and from him as much as I can. If I could afford it, I would get my own apartment, but I can't.

"I know, but my home isn't the best place for me to be right now," I said softly.

"Gracie, I know you don't want to talk about whatever is going on at home but I hope you know that if you need to get away, you can always come and stay with me, anytime!" she said softly.

"Thank you, and I will keep that in mind," I smiled.

I know I can't always just invite myself to stay with Ryland, especially since his mom has no clue I am staying there, so knowing that I can stay with Lola too gives me another option. I know I can't stay away from home every night, but I will whenever I can.

"I don't know about you two, but I am ready to head back," Ben said.

"We are going to stick around for a little while longer," Ryland said.

We said our goodbyes to Ben and Lola, the two of them heading off. I know we would need to be on our way soon given that I still need to get everything I wanted for tomorrow. If I have everything with me, then I only need to go tomorrow morning quickly, do a quick clean up and make his breakfast ready for him to just heat up when he gets up.

We decided to go for a short walk around before heading back.

"I know you said it isn't a good idea, but are you sure I can't come in with you?" he asked.

"You shouldn't, it would only make things worse," I said, "I won't be long anyway," I added.

He let out a frustrated sigh, running his fingers through his dark hair, and nodded his head. I don't want Ryland getting any more involved than what he already is. I don't want to put him right in front of my father's firing line.

"OK, then I will wait around the side of your house for you, and if you aren't out in ten minutes, I am coming in," he said, sounding very serious.

It was my turn to sigh, but I did nod my head. I knew even if I said no, he shouldn't do that, he still would. He gave me a small smile, kissing me softly, and we made our way back to his car.

****

We had arrived home. I did not want to go inside, but I had to. I took a deep breath, getting out of the car, Ryland following me.

"I will be waiting right there," he assured me, nodding to the side of the house.

"OK," I said, pecking his lips, proceeding inside.

As soon as I opened the front door, I heard my father slur at me.

"Where the fuck have you been?" he hissed.

I was hoping he would be passed out by now, no such luck though. I heard him making his way from the living room to the hall where I was. He was banging into things, and he soon appeared. He had the all familiar evil look in his eyes. I knew he was looking for me to take his anger out, but not this time. He came at me, yet I managed to move out of his way, honestly he was so drunk he could barely stand up.

"Get back here, you little bitch," he shouted.

"NO!" I said firmly.

I darted towards the stairs and straight to my room. I closed the door over, putting a chair against it. I could hear him staggering upstairs. I gathered everything that I needed, shoving it into my bag. I made sure I had my keys and phone, and ran straight for the window. Ryland was waiting right where he said he would. I tossed my bag to him, which he caught, and I made my way down the drainpipe. Ryland helped me by holding me at the bottom.

"Are you OK?" he asked.

"Yes, he's wasted, so I managed to get away from him," I said.

"Let's get into mine," he said, "My mom will still be awake, so I will go in and distract her, and you sneak up to my room, OK?" he said.

"OK," I said giggling.

This should be interesting. I hope she doesn't catch me, or I am screwed and will be sleeping in my car because I wouldn't show up at Lola's at this time.

He wrapped his arms around me, and we moved towards his

house. We could hear my dad shouting and trashing things from outside and the sound of it all was putting the fear into me. I can only imagine what he would have done to me if he got his hands on me.

"I got you, baby girl," he said, sensing something was wrong.

"I know," I said, resting my head on his shoulder.

When we reached his house, Ryland let us in, and just before closing the door he told me to wait for a moment. We heard his mother saying hello from the living room. He went through, standing at the doorway of the living room, talking to his mother. I watch him closely, and he signals me with his hand to go upstairs. I move as quietly as I can, making my way up to his room. I quickly closed his curtains over, in case my dad gets into my room and sees me over here.

I sat on his bed, nervously waiting for him to join me. Five minutes later, he walks in through the door, smiling at me.

"We are safe, I told my mother I was going to do some home-work and then get an early night," he said, "Which means she will not come in and disturb me!"

He closed the door, coming over to where I was, standing in front of me.

"Do you want to go to sleep or find something else to do?" he asked.

"I am not tired, we can find something else to do," I said, "Actually, I think it is time I know more about you Ryland," I added, looking up at him.

I see fear flash across his eyes, but he nods. He knew all my secrets, and I think I need to know his.

"Just promise me you won't run," he said softly.

"I promise," I said, "I would never, especially after how you have been here for me, even after knowing everything," I added, not breaking eye contact.

"I hope that is true because I don't want to lose you before we have even had a chance to start," he said, making my heart skip a few beats.

I took his hand in mine, looking him straight in the eye.

"I am not going anywhere, I promise," I said.

"OK," He said.

He still didn't look convinced that I would stick around after he told me the truth about him. He has been my rock, my safety net, and I plan on being the same for him. I believe with the way he is acting; his secrets are as deep and as dark as mine are.

CHAPTER NINETEEN

Ryland

I had been mentally preparing myself to tell Gracie the truth about me. I had also been preparing myself for her to run as soon as she knew the truth. And I honestly wouldn't blame her if she did.

"Did you bring something to sleep in?" I asked.

I thought it was best we get comfortable before I start talking because this could be a long night.

"No, I brought everything else except that," she laughed, "But you will give me something to sleep in, won't you?" she added, batting her lashes at me.

"Do not bat your lashes at me, Miss Gracie," I chuckled, "Because it will work every time."

She smiled brightly when I said that. I think she already knew that though; it doesn't take much convincing for me to give her what she wants. I laughed, pecking her lips before going to find something for her to wear. I grabbed a tee and a pair of boxers, passing them to her.

"Thank you, now turn away until I get changed," she said, waggling her fingers at me.

"Yes mam," I said, turning my back to her.

I will not lie, there was a part of me that wanted to take a peek, but that would be wrong and disrespectful of me, so I behaved.

"You can turn back around now," she laughed.
I turned to face her, swallowing hard seeing her dressed in my clothes once again; they looked so good on her. She gave me a soft smile before climbing into my bed. I stripped myself down to my boxers while Gracie covered her eyes and giggled. It isn't like she has not seen this much before.

I soon joined her in bed. She lay down on her side, motioning me to do the same. I knew it was time to start sharing my secrets with her. I don't even know where to start.

Gracie moved to stroke my cheek.

"Take your time," she said softly.

"Promise you won't leave?" I stammered out.

She kissed me softly, taking my hand in hers.

"I promise," she said.

I nodded, taking a few deep breaths. It was now or never, right.

"I don't if you remember me mentioning my dad, and how he left when I was young?" I said, and she nodded, "Well, my dad was like your dad. He was abusive, and I mean terribly abusive to both my mother and me," I added.

"I am sorry that you and your mom had to go through that," she said.

"He wasn't only physically abusive, well to me he was, but to my mother, it was worse than that," I said, feeling anger soar through me from simply talking about him and remember what he did to her, "He, he used to rape her," I added, feeling the tears brim in my eyes.

My mother doesn't know that I know this. I never told her, but given my room was only down the hall, I could hear her crying and begging for him to stop. It broke my mother's heart to know that I was having to witness the physical abuse and suffered through it too. I think if she knew that I knew the rest, it would kill her.

"My mom doesn't know that I know that. I could never tell her," I whimpered out, "And I just lay there, listening while it happened, letting my dad hurt her. Who does that? Who does nothing to help their mother when they are being hurt in that way?" I added, my voice angry.

I was angry at myself, angry at him. I hated myself for not stopping him.

"Ryland, you were only a child," Gracie said softly.

"Maybe, but I wasn't stupid. I could have called the police, or gone through and told him to stop, but no, instead I laid there like a coward, not doing anything and just listening," I said, "I should have somehow tried to protect her, the way she always protected me," I added.

I have not ever forgiven myself for it. I still have nightmares about it, even now and that was over ten years ago, though I don't think you can get over something like that, no matter how many years it has been.

"I am so sorry Ryland, that both you and your mother had to go through that," Gracie said, the tears running down her cheeks, "No one should have to go through that," she added.

"That is why I refuse to let myself get close to anyone. If I couldn't protect my own mother, how am I going to protect the people closest to me? How am I going to protect the person I am meant to love most in the world from all the bad when I couldn't protect my mom from my father," I said, shaking my head.

"You were a kid back then Ryland, you aren't anymore," she

said, "You would protect them, just in the same way you have been looking out for me since we met. You can't let that monster ruin you, ruin your chance to love someone, to let yourself be loved," she added.

"A little too late Gracie, he has already ruined me," I said, "What if I am like him? What if I get into a relationship with someone and end up going the way he did? He wasn't like that when my mom first met him, well, that is what he made her believe and look how that turned out. I don't exactly treat people great as it is," I added.

It was something that put fear in me every single day, the thought of me being anything like him, even in the slightest. Look at the way I treat girls? I use them, what if that is how it all starts? I don't respect them. I don't care if I hurt them, as long as I get what I need. Well, every girl I have known, except Gracie. You would think after everything I saw my mother go through that I would treat females better because I saw first-hand how cruel my dad was.

"Ryland, you are nothing like him, he was a monster," Gracie said, "You act the way you do because you are scared, not because you are like him," she added.

"You don't know that, Gracie," I said, going to pull away from her.

She didn't let me though, she held onto my hand tightly and made me turn back to her.

"Yes, I do know that, Ryland," she said, "You are not a monster, you have been my saving grace recently, would a monster do that for someone he just met? No, he wouldn't," she added.

I had expected her to have walked away once she found out how much of a coward I was, and after she found out that I was scared about being like him. But no, here she was, looking at me the way she always has—no judgement in her eyes, no disgust nor disappointment.

"You don't think I am a coward and a waste of space?" I asked, surprised.

"No. I think you are strong, a fighter and you are worth more than you realize," she said, "You have been through hell, yet you are still here," she added, pressing her lips to mine softly.

Once we pulled apart, I pulled her close to me, hugging her against my chest, and holding her in my arms.

"Thank you for not running," I said.

"I promised you I wouldn't, and I meant it," she said, nuzzling my neck.

I kissed the top of her head, just holding her in my arms, as a silence filled the room. Gracie lifted her head to look up at me.

"What happened to him?" she asked.

"He left. My mom found the courage to tell him to leave after she came home one day from work, he had beaten me so badly that my head was split open and I had a broken wrist. She had to take me to the hospital, and that was the last straw for her," I said, "And after she stood up and threatened to get him arrested he realized he was slowly losing that power and control over her and chose to leave," I added.

That was over ten years ago, and we haven't seen or heard from him again. I honestly wouldn't care if he was dead. He was a worthless piece of shit that never deserved to be on this earth.

"Your mom is so strong," Gracie said, "How is she doing now?" She added.

"She is doing pretty good," I said, "After my dad left, she tried being with other guys, but they all turned out to be assholes. She was lonely, but in time she realised she was better on her own, happier. She is always saying all she needs is me," I added.

I know I don't make her life easy, but that doesn't mean I don't love her. I would do anything for my mom, no matter how much of a pain in the ass she can be at times. I know she still gets lonely sometimes, and I do hope one day she will find the right guy. A guy that will treat her well and love her even with everything she has been through. A man that she can trust and love without fear.

"Do you think she will ever let herself fall in love again?" Gracie asked.

"I hope so, but only when she is ready and finds a good man to look after her," I said.

"I hope she finds that," she smiled, "And I hope you do one day too, find someone to love whole-heartedly, someone that will love you back in the same way," she added.

I don't know if that will ever be something I will find, but I just nodded and smiled. I knew if I told Gracie I don't think I ever will, she would argue with me on it.

"Thank you for trusting me enough to open up to me, Ryland," she said.

"You did it for me," I said, "And as strange as it is, and since we haven't known each other for long, you are one of the very few people I trust in this world," I added.

I have never trusted anyone as quickly as I have trusted Gracie. I have never been as drawn and open to anyone as I have with her. It was all a little curious that we have developed such a strong bond in such a short time. She was unique, and I know that. She meant so much to me already. I don't think I could imagine my life without her now.

"Do you think, because we have been through so much, that is what drew us to each other? Do you think that is why we developed this strange yet special bond so quickly? Like, we sensed we needed each other?" she said, "Or am I being silly?" she added quickly.

I smiled, stroking her hair.

"No, that is not silly at all, it is very accurate," I said, "I believe you, and I think we were meant to meet," I added.

"Me too," she said, smiling back at me.

I pressed my lips to hers in a gentle kiss, Gracie not hesitating for a moment before kissing me back. I slipped my fingers into her hair, keeping the kiss slow and sensual, pulling away only when I needed a moment to breathe.

"I like your kisses," she giggled, her eyes meeting mine.

"Good, because I like giving you them," I said, winking at her.

She giggled once again and blushed whilst I laughed, pulling her back into my chest. It was getting late, so I knew we would need to try and get some sleep soon, but for the moment I just wanted to hold her close to me, and she doesn't seem to mind.

It felt better now that she knew the truth and was still here. I think we may both need each other more than we realize.

CHAPTER TWENTY

Gracie

"Gracie, it is time to wake up," I hear Ryland's soft voice whispering, and his warm lips pressing against mine.

I moaned softly, opening my eyes. I smiled when I was met with him looking at me, that beautiful smile painted on his lips. I reached up, running my fingers through his messy hair.

"Morning," I said, "I don't want to move. What time is it?" I added, rubbing my eyes.

"Six-thirty," he said, "We don't need to move, we can just stay here and skip school," he added.

"And how are we going to do that with your mom in the house? And without the school letting our parents know that we have not shown up?" I asked.

"Simple, my mom will go to work soon, and we can call into the school, pretending to be our parents," he said, "They will never know the difference," he added smiling brightly at me.

I have never skipped school before, not even once. But the idea was very tempting right now. It had been an emotional few days for both of us. One day won't make a difference. The idea of just hiding away here for the day with him was overly appealing to me. I thought about it for a moment.

"Yes, screw it, why not?" I said, "But I need to go home first before he wakes up, and do what I need to," I added.

I watched the emotions on his face change when I said that. I knew he was worried in case my dad was awake. I kissed him softly, hoping that would help relax him.

"I will be fine," I said, "I will be in and out as quickly as I can," I added.

"OK, but if you aren't, I am coming to make sure you are OK," he said.

"I know you will, but I will be fine," I said.

He was hesitant about it, but I reassured him. I got myself out of his bed, getting changed, and he helped me sneak out while his mom was in the kitchen getting her breakfast before she had to go to work. Ryland said he would text me when she was gone.

 I rushed home, no sign or sound of my dad. I quickly got the house cleaned up and prepared breakfast for him. He would be up soon, and I was feeling myself getting anxious because Ryland hadn't texted me yet. I decided it would be best that I wait outside because that way I will be out of the way. I grabbed my phone to text Lola, telling her I wouldn't be at school today because I knew she would be looking for me.

Gracie: Hey, I am not coming to school today. Ryland and I are going to ditch, but we can hang out after school if you don't have plans with Ben X

Lola: Hey babe, check you out, ditching school and staying over at a guys house ;) Is it wrong that I am proud of you right now? Ha-ha. And yes, that sounds good. Girl's night? Movies, ice creams and talking about boys lol X

I let out a giggle as I read the text. Trust my best friends to be proud of me for breaking the rules.

Gracie: Maybe a little ha-ha. Yes, a girl's night sounds good.

Can I stay over? X

Lola: Of course, you can! I better make a move and get ready for school. Try and not break too many rules without me in one day, OK? I will see you later. Love you X

Gracie: I will try and behave myself ha-ha. See you later, love you too X

I saw as Ryland's mom left the house, getting in her car and heading to work. I thought about everything that Ryland told me last night. She was such a strong woman; it must take a lot of strength to get through what she did. I hope she finally finds a good man to love her, she deserves it after what she has been through. I got pulled out of my thoughts when my phone started ringing. I checked my phone, seeing it was Ryland, I quickly answered it.

"Hey, beautiful, you can come back over now," he said.

"OK, I will be there in two minutes," I said before hanging up.

I headed back over to his place, and he was already waiting for me at the front door. I noticed a wave of relief take over his face when he saw that I was OK. He reached for me, pulling me in and hugging me tight, not saying a word, just holding me. I let him, happily hugging him back. He did pull away after a few minutes before leading us into the house.

"Do you want to go back to bed for a bit?" he asked, "It is still early," he added.

"Yes, I could do with some more sleep, but we will need to stay awake for a little while so that we can call the school," I said.

"I am sure we can find a way to keep ourselves awake for half an hour," he said.

He took my hand in his, leading us back upstairs. I stole a tee and a pair of his boxers again, him stripping down to his boxers before we got back into bed, laying on top of the covers in case we get too comfortable and end up falling asleep.

"I think you are a bad influence on me Mr, I have not ever ditched school," I giggled.

"Gotta break the rules sometimes, baby girl," he said.

"I have a feeling that with you I will be for sure doing that, but I don't mind," I said, smiling at him.

"Yes, probably," he laughed.

I watch his eyes fall on my legs, a sad look taking over his face. I looked at him confused, moving my eyes to where his were, and I soon worked out what the look was for. The boxers had crawled up, my scars and cuts were on show. I quickly pulled them down, covering them up again.

"Gracie, you don't need to hide them for me," he said softly, "They are part of you," he added.

"I don't like having them on show," I sighed.

His next move took me by surprise. He grabbed my legs, pulling them over his lap, and pushed the boxers back up. He gently traced his fingertips over my scars. I whimpered, closing my eyes and trying to stop myself from crying.

"I hope one day you will be able to stop hurting yourself," he whispered.

"I hope so too," I said.

He reached down, his lips falling on my thigh, his lips softly kissing over my scars. I felt the tears escape from my eyes.

"You are still beautiful to me, every part of you," he said.

My scars were something I was ashamed of. I hated them and hated myself for doing it to myself, but the way he was with me at this moment made me hate myself a little less. I don't know how to explain it, but him being so gentle with me, and not judging me, made me feel less shame.

He looked up at me, and the look in his eyes made me feel like I meant something, it made me believe I may not be as worthless as I think. I didn't know it was possible to feel that way with just a look.

"I am sorry, I didn't want to make you cry or upset you," he said with panic in his voice.

"No, you didn't upset me," I said, "You doing what you just did made me feel... how can I put it? It made me like I was not completely worthless," I added, my voice shaky and my cheeks heating up.

Ryland wiped the tears away and pulled me over to him, so I was on his lap. He took my face in his hands, looking me straight in the eye.

"That is because you aren't worthless Gracie," he said, "You are beautiful inside and out. You are special and unique, and one day I hope you will realize that," he added.

I felt the tears well in my eyes again. Ryland pressed his lips to mine, the kiss sweet and sensual. I was soon smiling into his lips, my fingers falling in his hair as I kissed him back. He took hold of my hips, his lips not breaking away from mine once.

I let out a small whimper with the closeness between us. He gently ran his finger tips up and down my back, as our lips continued working together. He pulled away first, and when I opened my eyes I saw Ryland still had his eyes closed while a smile was playing on his lips. He ran his thumb along his lips, his smile growing.

"Um, Ryland, are you OK?" I giggled.

He finally opened his eyes to look at me.

"Yes, sorry, my lips were tingling," he chuckled.

He pushed the hair away from my eyes, pressing a soft kiss on my forehead. It was my turn to close my eyes and smile.

"Gracie?" he said, nervousness to his voice.

"Hmm, yeah?" I asked, opening my eyes to look at him.

I watch him take a deep breath, and then another one. I had no clue what he was going to say, but by the way he is acting, it seems important. I started fidgeting on his lap, worry taking over me.

"I want to be with you," he said softly, "I don't know if I will be any good at the whole boyfriend thing, but I want to try, with you. If you want me, that is!?" he added.

He wants us to be together, as in a couple? I knew something was going on between us, but I wasn't expecting him to ask me that.

"I want to be with you too," I said, "And I don't know if I will be any good at it either since I have never had a boyfriend. I haven't done much as you have, you know," I added.

I did want to be with him, but knowing he had already been with girls, sexually I mean, worries me because I can't give him that, not right now. I am not ready for that.

"We can learn together?" he asked, his eyes filling with hope, "But I need to ask you to be patient with me, brown eyes. I may mess up, but I don't mean too. I just don't know how to be with someone," he added.

It would seem I am not the only one worrying about things. I rubbed my thumb against his cheek.

"I can do that, but you will need to be patient with me too, Ryland, in other ways," I said, "I am not ready for other aspects of a relationship," I blushed.

I didn't want to say the exact words, but I was hoping he would pick up on what I was trying to say.

"Gracie, I would never pressure you into something like that," he said, "I don't want to be with you for that, I want to be with you because I like and care for you," he added.

"Then we can learn, try and mess up together," I said.

"Yes, and hopefully we can work out how to do it right as we go," he said.

I nodded, kissing him softly, snuggling into his chest, and letting his arms wrap around me once again, realizing I have a boyfriend, my first boyfriend. I honestly didn't think I would be ready for that until college, but that was before I met Ryland. I knew he was different from the moment he said hello to me.

"Thank you for giving me a chance and not giving up on me," he said, stroking my hair.

"You too," I said, placing a feather-like kiss on his neck.

We need each other, we both know that, but I think we need each other in more ways than one. I don't think either of us realizes how much we could impact each other's lives, and hopefully for the best.

CHAPTER TWENTY-ONE

Gracie

I was over at Lola's place for our sleepover, something we have not had the chance to do much because I believed I had to stay at home to keep my dad happy. Now, if I am not there he can't get me, right?

"I am glad we are finally doing this," Lola smiled.

"Me too! Sorry, it took so long," I said.

"It is OK," she said, "Maybe one day you will tell me the reason," she added.

"I promise I will, one day, but when I am ready and we are away from this damn town," I said.

Lola and I were planning on applying to the same Colleges, and getting a place together once we have graduated. When we do that, then I will tell her everything.

"I know you will," she said, giving me a one-arm hug.

She is such an amazing best friend. She knows that even though I don't tell what is going on, it doesn't mean I don't trust her, in fact I trust the girl with my life.

"Now let's get into our PJS and watch 'Never been kissed', " I said, smiling brightly at her.

"Yes, good idea," she said.

I grabbed my bag, heading through to her bathroom to get

changed—my nightwear consisting of joggers and one of Ryland's tees that I stole from him earlier today. I told him since he was my boyfriend now, I can take what I please, and he was alright with that. I was still trying to get my head around it, having a boyfriend.

"Cute tee," Lola giggled as I came out.

I haven't told her yet about Ryland and me, but I will.

"Thank you," I giggled, feeling my cheeks heat up.

We put the duvet and pillows on the floor, sitting there and putting the movie on. We would probably not see much of it if we got to chat.

"So...how was your sleepover last night?" Lola asked, turning to look at me.

I was wondering how long it would take for her to ask me that very question. I could only tell her so much though, I would never tell anyone the things Ryland told me last night.

"It was good, we spent a lot of it talking," I said.

"Just talking?" she smirked.

"And a little kissing," I said, turning away from her.

I knew my face would be bright red by now.

"Aww, you are blushing, how cute," she laughed.

"Stop," I said, pushing her arm gently.

"Sorry, I just haven't ever seen you like this," she said.

"That is because I have never met anyone like Ryland," I said, "It is strange, we have a strong connection and bond, something I had never felt with anyone else before," I added.

"Yes, it seems to have been that way since the first time you both met," she smiled.

I didn't realise other people noticed it. Yes, the outside world can see we have become close, but Lola can see the connection we share too.

"He asked me to be his girlfriend," I whispered out.

"Yay! This is so exciting, about time for you two," she said, smiling widely at me.

"It is still all a little strange," I said, "But I'm sure I will get used to it with time," I added while I blushed and winked at Lola.

The conversation flowed after that; us talking about her and Ben, and Ryland and me. I was enjoying our girl time. I need to do this more often. It felt good to be acting just like an average teenager, without worrying about anything. We did turn our attention to the movie but not until it was halfway through. I loved this movie; it was so sweet and romantic.

Suddenly, we heard a noise, and it sounded like a rock against the window. Lola and I looked at each other, the same 'what the heck' look on our faces.

"What the hell is that?" I asked.

"I don't know," she said, just as the same sound happened again.

Lola and I nervously got up, and went over to the window, peeking between the curtains, soon finding out what the noise was.

"What are they doing here?" I giggled.

It was none other than Ben and Ryland outside of her bedroom window. There was enough light outside for us to see the two of them looking smug. We looked at each other, laughing and rolling our eyes. I don't know why they are throwing rocks at the window; it isn't exactly late. It was only ten p.m. Lola opened the curtains, and then opened the window.

"What the heck are you two doing here?" she laughed.

"We missed our girls," Ben said, smirking.

"Oh, hush," Lola laughed, blushing for a change.

"Hey brown eyes, did you miss me?" Ryland smirked.

Well aren't these two just charmers, and maybe slightly arrogant.

"You wish, baby boy," I said, smirking back at him.

He pouted up at me, holding his hand to his heart and giving me a sad look. His way of saying I just broke his heart. I rolled my eyes, shaking my head at him. Ryland was laughing in return.

"Sneak out," Ben said.

"We can't, my parents are still up," Lola said.

"You two come down, or we are coming up, the choice is your baby," Ben said.

Lola and I looked at each other, both wondering what to do.

"I think they would be better coming up, at least that way they can hide if we hear my parents, and then we can go out when my parents are in bed," she suggested.

I am not sure if this was such a good idea, but she was right, it would be far easier to hide them both than us sneaking out. I think it would be obvious what we have done if her parents come to the room and we aren't here.

"Come up, but you will need to climb up the drainpipe because I can't exactly let you in the front door," she laughed.

The guys were OK with that. I am sure they both have done it before, probably more than once. Lola opened the window all the way, and we stepped back. It didn't take long for them both to be up and in through the window. Lola was mid sentence telling them to be quiet when Ben pulled her in and kissed her, effectively and quickly shutting her up. I swear they better not start making out or something, or I will be climbing out of the window that Ryland and Ben just climbed in.

Ryland reached for me, bringing me into him, kissing me softly. A small moan fell from my lips at the feel of his kisses. It was only for a moment before he pulled away.

"You missed me, baby girl, admit," he said.

"Hmm, maybe a little," I said.

"I missed you too, gorgeous," he said, "So am I going to get this back or have you claimed it?" he added, laughing and pulling at his tee that I had on.

"I have claimed it, sorry," I beamed.

"That's alright, you look good in my clothes," he said.

Ben and Lola finally pulled apart, and we made sure the guys knew that since they hijacked our girls' night, they would be watching the girly movies with us. Neither of them were thrilled with the idea, but knew they didn't really have a choice. We put the film back to the start, not wanting the guys to miss anything.

Lola and Ben made themselves comfortable on her bed. Ryland and I were doing the same on the floor. I was laying between his legs as he sat with his back against the bed.

"You doing, OK?" he whispered.

"Yeah, I am fine," I said, looking at him, "You?" I added.

"Better now," he smiled, kissing me.

I feel myself become all giddy when he says things like that, simply because what he means is that he is better now as he was with me. How sweet! I took my position back against him, his arms wrapping around me. I closed my eyes, that feeling of protection taking over me because I was in his arms.

****

The movie was nearly coming to an end, but we paused it quickly due to Lola's parents. We could hear them coming upstairs.

"Both of you, closet, now!" Lola said quietly pointing at the guys and then at the closet, "Hurry up," she added, shooing them along.

I could see they were trying their best not to laugh, and doing as they were told. This would be interesting; Lola's closet isn't very big. I bit on my lip to stop myself from laughing too. The moment the closet door closed, there was a knock on the bedroom door. Lola and I quickly got onto the bed, telling them to come in.

"Hey sweetie, we are going to bed," Lola's mom smiled, "You know not to be staying up too late, you both have school in the morning," she added.

"We will head to bed soon, mom," Lola smiled.

Her mom smiled, saying her goodnight to us, and telling Lola she loved her before leaving us to it. That was a close call; it was lucky that we heard them approaching. We waited to make sure the coast was clear before telling the guys to come out. We could hear them falling about, groaning and complaining as they tried to get out. Lola and I looked at each other and busted out laughing.

"Not funny, I do not need to be that close to a dude ever again," Ben said pouting.

His annoyance just made us laugh more, the guys soon glaring at us. It never helped; it made us worse.

"Sorry," I said through my laughter.

"Yes, sure you are," Ryland said, "You two are mean," he added, huffing.

What did they expect, they were being overdramatic. They can't blame us for laughing at them. I made my way to him, grabbing his tee and pulling him to me.

"Will you forgive?" I said, batting my lashes at him.

"Nope," he said, shaking his head.

I could see he was trying to fight back a smile. I pressed myself against him and kissed him.

"What about now?" I said, resting my hand on his chest.

"Almost," he smirked.

I kissed him again, and he soon slipped his arm around me and kissed me back, smiling into my lips. I would say he has forgiven me now. I pulled away and smiled proudly because I knew I won.

"Hmm, I don't know what I think about this! How easy it was for you to get me to forgive you," he laughed.

"What can I say? You have a soft spot for me," I said.

"I would call it more than that," he said.

"You would, and what would that be?" I smirked.

He brought me back into him and reached into my ear.

"I like that you are turning me into a weak-assed man," he whispered.

I shuddered, feeling his warm breath fanning the skin of my neck. All I could do was nod. I hear Lola clear her throat, making us pull apart. Ryland shot a smirk my way before we turned to the others.

"Come on. We are heading out for a bit," Lola said.

It would seem we are sneaking out tonight after all. I don't mind, as long as we don't get caught or Lola gets into trouble for it.

"Where are we going?" Ryland asked.

"We can work that outside," Ben said.

It wouldn't be for long, we had school tomorrow, and I can't miss another day after not going today. I am sure we can find something to do for a bit to keep us occupied. This was becoming a habit for me, sneaking out and climbing out of windows. It was new, but I am OK with it because it isn't like we are getting into trouble, we are only enjoying being teenagers.

CHAPTER TWENTY-TWO

Ryland

I had just pulled up outside my house getting back from my time with Ben and the girls. I stepped out of my car, and as I did, I saw Gracie's "father" staggering up the pathway. He looked like a pathetic excuse of a human being. My anger was building just at the sight of him. My fists were clenched by my side, and my breathing was getting heavier. I have not felt this angry in a long time, and being this mad is not a good thing for me. I was using all the control I had in me to stop going over to him and knocking him cleanout. Who would know it was me? Except I knew I couldn't do that; Gracie wouldn't want that. So, I decided to head inside before I did something I shouldn't. He was not worth it. His time will come, Karma will come back around to bite him. I just wish I could take Gracie away from that house, and from him for good.

I was glad Gracie was safe and away from him for tonight. I headed inside, trying to keep quiet because I didn't want to wake my mom up. I grabbed some water and headed to my room, but not before I checked in on my mom. This is something I do a lot, just to make sure she is OK. She was sound asleep, so I headed to my room, stripped down and got into bed. A distinctive feeling took over me when my back hit the mattress, and I knew exactly what it was. Gracie wasn't here and that simply doesn't feel right. It was a feeling of loneliness that took over me. I had never felt this way before at all. It was like a part of me needed her, and I had never needed anyone before. Well, it was more like I have refused to let myself need anyone. And needing her was terrifying for me.

Gracie Jackson, what are you doing to me?

I don't know exactly what she is doing to me, but she is sure doing something. I was still getting my head around that I had a girlfriend, that Gracie was my girlfriend, and I felt a smile growing on my lips when I thought about it. I got pulled out of my thoughts when my phone went off telling me a text came through. I grabbed it, my smile growing bigger when I saw it was Gracie.

Gracie: Hey, baby boy, did you get home, OK? X

Ryland: Hey brown eyes! Yes, I am home safe. What are you doing? X

Gracie: Good! I am trying to sleep, but no luck �� it doesn't help that Lola is snoring and talking in her sleep ha-ha. What are you doing? X

Ryland: Aww, I am sorry that you can't sleep, baby girl! You could always leave her a note and come to stay with me? ����. I'm just lying in my abnormally big and cold bed, it feels like something missing from my bed X

I have a feeling she will know that I mean her.

Gracie: I can't do that ha-ha. I think you have seen enough of me recently. And I wonder what is missing from your bed? �� X

I can safely assume with the wink at the end, she knows I am talking about her, but is acting coy about it, well trying to anyway. I chuckled to myself before texting back.

Ryland: Yes, you can ha-ha. You know exactly what, or who is missing from my bed. Are you sure I can't talk you into coming to stay with me instead? X

Gracie: Aww, how sweet. I miss you too. No, don't be greedy lol X

Ryland: I am allowed to be greedy because you are now my girlfriend X

Gracie: Oh, is that how it works now? X
Ryland: Yep! That is just how it is now, you should get used to it, beautiful X

Gracie: Hmm, I don't know what to think about that lol X

Ryland: Come on now, gorgeous, don't even try and deny that you love spending all your free time with me X

Gracie: Maybe a little � � X

Gracie and I texted back and forth for the next hour until we decided it would be best that we both got some sleep. Plus, the quicker I get to sleep, the quicker morning will come, which is when I get to see her again. Who knew I was the needy type? I couldn't help myself with her. To put it plainly, around Gracie I was at my happiest and I could be myself, with no secrets or acting like someone I am not. I was excited to see her in the morning.

***

I suddenly woke up, a familiar giggle filling my room. It sounded like Gracie, but I must be dreaming because she isn't here. I hear it again, and this time a pair of lips is pressing against my neck.

"Ryland, wake up," I hear her soft voice say.

I turned around to where the voice came from, and right enough, she was here. I think.

"Gracie?" I said tiredly.

"Hey, baby boy, you should really close your window at night," she laughed.

At night? What time was it? It was still dark, so it couldn't be morning. I searched for my phone in the dark and checked the time, my phone telling me it was four a.m.

"Are you really here or am I dreaming?" I asked, rubbing my eyes.

"I am here," she said, "I couldn't sleep at all, so I woke Lola to tell her and she suggested I come here because dear God, she does not like being woken up," she added, laughing.

"Her loss is my gain," I smiled.

"You don't mind me showing up at this time?" she asked.

"Of course not, you can show up here anytime you want," I smiled.

Gracie found my lips in the dark, pressing a soft kiss to them.

"Good, because I wanted snuggles," she said.

She moved in closer to me, snuggling in close and resting her head on my chest. I slipped my arm around her and kissed the top of her head.

"Snuggles are welcome at any time," I said.

She slipped her fingers into mine and linked our hands together.

"Good, because I can be very needy," she laughed.

"That is quite alright, sweetness," I chuckled, "You can be as needy as you like with me," I added.

I was happy that she showed up, even at this time. I only fell asleep about two hours ago because I couldn't sleep at first, no matter how hard I tried. It would seem I was not the only one.

My bed was not feeling as empty now. I played with her hair with my free hand, Gracie nuzzling into my neck as I did. She trailed a line of soft kisses along my neck, and a small moan fell from my lips.

"Sorry," She said softly, pulling away.

"Hmm, I don't mind," I said.

Her next move caught me off guard. She reached up and crashed her lips to mine. The kiss was different; it was more.. eager. I growled into her lips and kissed her back in the same way. Gracie slipped her fingers into my hair, and my hand fell on her hip. I rolled onto my side, pulling her against me, deepening the kiss, causing her to whimper. I don't know what has gotten into her, but I don't mind, yet at the same time I don't want to push her limits, except with the way she was kissing me, it was hard not to.

Gracie rolled onto her back, pulling me with her so that I was on top of her, wrapping her legs around me. Damn! Where was this confidence coming from? She ran her fingers down the skin of my back. I could feel my excitement build, and I know that was probably the best cue to pull away. I pulled my lips from hers and sat up on her stomach. She opened her eyes, looking up at me. The small light that was coming through the window was enough for me to see her. She looked both sad and confused.

"Why did you stop?" she asked softly.

"Because it was the right thing to do," I said, "No matter how good that felt, I don't want us pushing ourselves too far," I added honestly.

"Yes, you are probably right," she said, "Do you promise that is the only reason?" she asked.

"I promise, what other reason would it be?" I asked, stroking her face.

"Nothing, it doesn't matter," she said, "I am just being self-conscious, that's all," she added.

Wait, does she think I stopped because I don't want her?

"You don't need to be, not with me, Gracie," I said, "I like you, just the way you are," I added, kissing her softly.

I felt her smile into the kiss, I responded by doing the same. I don't ever want her feeling that way around me. So I lay down next to her again, and pull her to snuggle back into my chest.

"We should probably get some sleep," she said, yawning.

"Good idea," I said.

I gave her a goodnight kiss, and we got settled down. I slipped my hand under the back of the tee she had on, gently stroking her lower back, something that seems to help her sleep. It only took a few moments, and I heard her breathing becoming shallow. She was sound asleep already.

"Rest well, my love, you are safe here with me," I whispered, kissing the top of her head.

I closed my eyes again, and soon felt myself drifting off to sleep. I know having her next to me was the main reason I was drifting off. I was looking forward to waking up with her next to me.

CHAPTER TWENTY-THREE

Gracie

I was nervous as I walked into school with Ryland, his hand holding mine. I was quite a private person, this was all new to me. And not only that, I was also scared that somehow it would get back to my dad. I don't know how no-one at this school or their parents have anything to do with my father. I am sure most of them do not even know who he is, but that doesn't stop me from getting paranoid.

"Hey, brown eyes, are you OK?" Ryland asked, turning to look at me.

"Yes, just nervous, I guess," I said.

"You don't need to be nervous," he said, kissing me softly.

I could feel people staring, just as I tried my best to ignore them. I could imagine what some of them were thinking, especially the other girls. They are all wondering why I was the one to get Ryland when a few of them have tried and failed. The rest will be thinking 'what the hell?! I thought Gracie never dated.' And that last thought was true, a few guys have asked, but I have always told them no. I always thought it was for the best, to stay completely single because that way there would be no questions and I wouldn't need to lie. I stuck with it until Ryland showed up.

"Sorry, I can't help it," I said.

"I got you, baby girl," he said, wrapping his arm around my

shoulder and pulling me close to him.

I found myself relaxing after that. We had the first two classes together, so at least he would be there, and no one could say anything to me.

"Hey, bitches, wait up," we hear Lola call out from behind us. "Why does your best friend insist on calling me a bitch?" Ryland laughed.

"It means she likes you," I laughed.

"You girls are strange; do you know that?" he chuckled, shaking his head.

"Would you have me any other way?" I said, batting my lashes at him and flashing him my best smile.

He placed his hand on my hip, pulling me into him.

"No, I would not, beautiful," he said, prodding my nose.

"Good," I said, giggling and stealing a quick kiss before Lola and Ben joined us.

Lola gave Ryland and I a hug. Ryland was a little taken back with it, but he did hug her back. We headed to our lockers, putting everything that we didn't need until later away before the four of us headed to our first class. Our first-class was English, something I enjoyed. It was a good start to the day. We took the seats up the back of the classroom.

"You can sit here if you want?" Ryland smirked, patting his lap.

I rolled my eyes at him, taking the seat next to him instead.

"Fine then," he pouted.

"Don't pout at me Mr," I said, kissing his pouty lips, and he was soon smiling.

We pulled apart just in time for the teacher to come in. Ryland rested his hand on my thigh, keeping it placed there throughout the entire lesson. It was a nice comfort for me.

"So, can I steal you away after school?" Ryland asked as we headed to second class, "Well, after you go home first because I know you will need to," he added, sighing.

"Yes, of course, you can," I said, "I only need to go home for an hour or two, get the house cleaned and make his dinner, then I will leave," I added.

"OK," he said, "And I think you should come and stay with me again," he added.

"I will see what I can do, make sure to leave the window open for me," I said, winking at him.

"Always," he said, wrapping his arm around me, and kissed the top of my head.

Knowing that he will always leave the window open for me made me feel better because it gave me somewhere to go when I needed to escape.

"Thank you," I said, kissing his cheek.

"No need to thank me, babe, I would do anything for you," he smiled.

Those words coming from his lips cause that all familiar feeling of protection soars through me, the way I always felt around him. I rested my head on his shoulder, pulling away when we arrived at the second class. Geography, meh! Hate it. I am sure I can get through it.

***

I was waiting by my locker, waiting for Ryland, Ben and Lola to go for lunch. My last class was not with any of them, but we had arranged to meet here. Our class got out a little early because the teacher had to go and deal with something. I was messing with my phone to occupy myself.

"Gracie," I heard a voice and it made me look up.

Matty, the Captain of the football team, was coming towards me. I had to stop myself from rolling my eyes. He was so vain, rude and annoying. I made sure to smile at him because I can't be bothered getting into anything with him. I am pleasant to everyone, but it doesn't mean I like them.

"Hey, Matty, what's up?" I asked.

He came over to me, standing in front of me, closer than he needed to be, placing one hand on the lockers behind me. What does he want?

"I thought you didn't date?" he asked.

"I don't, well I never did," I said.

It was none of his business what I do or do not, now or ever.

"Until he showed up? What are you doing with someone like him? You should be with someone like me," he said.

Matty has asked me out a few times, but I always told him no. Even if I did do the dating thing back then, I would still have told him no because I know how he treats girls.

"What does that mean, someone like him?" I said, annoyed.

"He isn't exactly in the same class as you," he said, "He is an imbecile, and will bring nothing but trouble for you," he added, reaching in and pushing the hair away from my eyes.

I was quick to swat his hand away.

"Don't touch me," I snapped, "You don't even know Ryland," I added, pushing myself away from the lockers.

I was standing my ground. I am not backing down to him, especially when he is bad mouthing Ryland. I will not allow that.

"I know enough, Gracie," he said annoyed, "He will be moving onto the next flavor soon enough, and you will have no one else to blame but yourself," Matty added.

Seriously, who the hell does he think he is?

"You know fuck all so how about you keep your damn mouth shut, Matty?" I hissed.

"Who the hell do you think you are fucking talking to?" he growled.

He had a temper, he always has, but I wasn't going to let him scare me. I deal with a much bigger monster in my home.

"You, now back the hell up and leave me alone," I said firmly.

I pushed by him, going to walk away, but he grabbed my wrist, pulling me back around to him.

"This is not the end," he said, "I always get what I want, and I want you!" he added, smugly.

I swear he was delusional. He will never get me.

"You have two seconds to get your hand off my girlfriend, Matty," I hear behind me.

I could hear the anger in Ryland's voice. Matty was quick to let go, with a smirk on his lips as he turned to face Ryland that soon disappeared when he realized Ryland was not alone.

"Your girlfriend? Yeah right, for how long?" Matty said, "You will get bored of her and move on soon enough, and I will be waiting right there to pick up the pieces," he added slyly.

I could see Ryland's fists clench at his side, his entire body tensing and the anger in his eyes clear to see. I was not going to let him get into trouble because of me.

"Ryland, ignore him, he isn't worth it," I said softly, making my way over to him.

"Stay the fuck away from her Matty, if I see you anywhere near her again, I will not contain myself, you are warned!" Ryland hissed.

Matty let out a loud chuckle. I could see Ryland was going to dive at him, but I took place between them and looked up to Ryland.

"Don't, please, baby boy," I whispered, "He is not worth you getting into trouble," I added, taking his hand in mine.

I watch Ryland relax after that. I kissed him softly, taking his attention away from Matty. While I did that, Ben and Lola made sure Matty walked away. You do not want to mess with Lola. She is tiny, but she has some right hook, and I wouldn't want to get on the wrong side of her.

"Are you OK?" Ryland asked.

"Yeah fine, he is nothing but an idiot," I said, "I have dealt with worse," I added.

"Why was he bothering you anyway?" he asked.

"He is jealous because I am with you," I said, "He asked me out before, more than once actually and I told him no. He doesn't like that word because he is a spoiled brat that gets everything that he wants from mommy and daddy," I added, rolling my eyes.

"I would be jealous of me too if I were him," Ryland said, winking.

I giggled, rolling my eyes at him again, and kissed him.

"Always such a charmer," I smiled.

"Hell yeah, especially when it comes to you, beautiful," he said.

He was such a sweetheart at times, especially when it comes

to me. I was a lucky girl. It was like everything that happened only moments ago with Matty disappeared. I had a feeling that would not be the end of it, but right now I am not letting that idiot get to me, Matty wasn't worth it.

We walked away, Ryland's arm snaking around my shoulder and the four of us headed to grab some lunch. As soon as we walked in, Matty's eyes were on us, along with a couple of his friends. Lola, being Lola, turned to them and flipped them off. I couldn't help but giggle at the look on Matty's face when she did it, and he soon turned away.

We grabbed some food, finding a table away from everyone else —the four of us in our own little corner with no one bothering us.

"I think we should all do something tonight," Lola said.

"Like what?" I asked.

"Maybe go to the drive-in movie theatre and then grab a pizza or something after?" she suggested.

"Sounds good," Ryland smiled, "I am up for that if you all are!" he added, looking at me.

Ben and I nodded, meaning we all approved the plan. And it would keep me away from the house for a few hours.

"It will need to be after six though," I said.

Everyone was OK with that. That gives me time to get home, do what I need to and then maybe see if Ryland will let me do some homework at his place before we head out. I am sure he would be fine with that.

I was enjoying that the four of us could go out together now, no third wheel or anyone left out. Plus, it gave me things to do to take my mind off home and act the way a teenager should be acting.

"Are you staying home tonight, or do you want to come and stay with me?" Lola asked, "Maybe for the full night this time," she added giggling.

"I am going to try and sneak out and stay with Ryland," I said.

"That's fine, as long as you have somewhere to go if you don't want to stay at home," she smiled.

I nodded and smiled back at her. With our plans made for the night, we all got back to eating our lunch. I was looking forward to spend my night with them all. I guess we should take two cars since I do not want or need to watch my best friend and Ben make-out from the back seat when I am trying to watch the movie.

I don't know what was on, but that was alright. I knew the four of us would have a good night no matter what anyway.

CHAPTER TWENTY-FOUR

Ryland

I was outside, leaning against my car whilst I waited for Gracie to come out. She had texted me only ten minutes ago to tell me to hang around outside. And then in a flash, she came bolting out of the door. I have not ever seen someone run so fast in my life, and I soon realized why she was sprinting; her dad came out after her. He was shouting things at her, but I couldn't make out what they were, as they were slurred. He was definitely drunk, though he was moving pretty quickly.

"Get the fuck back in here, you little slut," he said, grabbing her arm.

No, he is not fucking touching her or talking to her like that. I made a quick dash, getting to them.

"Get your fucking hands off of her, right now, or I swear I will knock you out," I hissed, getting in between them and pushing him away from her.

"Who the fuck are you?" he asked, coming at me.

"I will be your worst nightmare if you don't back off," I said, standing my ground.

I could hear Gracie behind me, she was crying, and she was gripping onto the back of my tee.

"This is none of your business, little boy," he said, trying to get around me, "She is my daughter, I can do as I please," he added laughing.

I pushed his chest, making sure to put a distance between Gracie and him.

"Not while I am around, you can't," I said.

I could see his fists clenching at his sides; he was desperate to hit me. I wanted him to try, it would have given me an excuse to punch him in the mouth.

"You won't always be around," he laughed, "You are welcome to the little bitch, she is worthless anyway," he added.

I could feel the anger take over me again.

"No, you are the one who is a worthless piece of shit," I said, "You are nothing but a coward who thinks it is alright to take his anger out on your daughter. You ever lay a hand on her again, it will be the last thing you do, I swear that I will make sure of that," I added.

I watch as he slowly backs away. He was not so tough after all.

"Good luck with that, she can't fucking do anything right, you are welcome to her," he said, however the confidence in his voice had broken, "Don't coming running home when you end up pregnant when we all know that is what is going to happen," he added.

I dived for him. I had lost any patience, complete anger and rage had taken over. I was about to lift my fist to punch him, but before I could....

"Ryland, don't, he isn't worth it," Gracie whimpers from behind, "Can we please just go?" she asked, tugging at my arm.

I could hear the fear in her voice, and I knew the way I was acting was part of what was causing that fear. I backed off at the sound of her voice.

"Stay away from her," I said firmly, "You will never be alone with her again, because I will always be close by, remember that," I threatened.

He glared at Gracie once more, and then back at me.

"This isn't over," he warned, before heading into the house.

I turned to Gracie, wrapping my arms around her and pulling her close to me, holding her tightly to me. I stroked her hair, and she completely broke down in my arms. I wanted to go in there and kill the bastard. I don't know how I am going to keep her safe from him, but I will find a way.

"I got you, baby girl," I said, kissing the top of her head.

She lifted her head to look up at me. She looked so sad, and that broke my heart. Once again I wiped all her tears away.

"I am sorry you got brought into this," she whimpered out.

"You have nothing to be sorry about," I said, "I will protect you from that monster in any and every way I can," I added.

"Thank you, you are an incredible human being, Ryland," she said, kissing me softly, "But I don't think it is going to be that simple because I will need to go back at some point," she added.

I wish I had somewhere to keep her safe, keep her away from him. I can't exactly move her in with me. I don't think my mom would agree to it. Well, maybe if she knew the truth, but I knew Gracie wouldn't want anyone else knowing what is happening.

"We will work something out, beautiful, even if I need to be around all the time. I will do that if it means he stays away from you," I said.

"Thank you," she whispers, cuddling into me again, "We should probably go before Lola starts blowing up my phone," she added.

"Are you still up for it? If not, we can just hang out at mine or something," I suggested.

"I want to go; it will take my mind off of things," she said.

"OK, come on then," I said, stealing one last kiss.

I slipped my hand into hers and led us towards my car. I let her climb in first before running around and getting into the driver's seat. Gracie had pulled her legs up to her chest, hugging her knees and was staring out of the window towards her house. I got myself settled and started the car before reaching over and placing my hand on her knee.

She turned to face me, giving me a soft smile. I got us on the road, and then she reached for my hand, linking our fingers. It was then I spotted the marks on her wrist, her "father's" fingerprints imprinted on the skin, the bruising coming up already. I sighed, lifting her hand to my lips and kissing her wrists softly.

"I am sorry, he hurt you like that," I said.

"It is OK. I have had worse," Gracie said, resting her head on my shoulder.

I slipped my arm around, and the rest of the ride was silent. I was hoping the night would make her feel better, and then she can come and stay with me tonight. As for the rest, I will work that out tomorrow. We pulled into the drive-in, looking around for Ben and Lola, spotting them at a space close to the front. Ben was leaning against the car, whilst Lola was standing in the middle of the free space.

"I think Lola is making sure no one steals our spot," Gracie giggled.

"It would seem that way," I laughed.

We made our way over, Lola only moving when the car was

close. The movie never started for another half an hour. We parked up, getting out of the vehicle.

"Finally! Come on, let's go get some snacks," Lola said, looking at Gracie.

"You couldn't have gotten them without me?" Gracie laughed.

"No, because Ben wouldn't come with me," she pouted.

The girls headed off to grab us some snacks.

"Everything OK?" Ben asked.

"Yeah, fine," I smiled.

"So how do you think the girls are going to handle a horror movie?" he laughed.

"Oh, I am sure they will pretend to be scared, just to get cuddles," I laughed.

"Yes, probably," he said, "I won't mind though," he added, smirking.

"I am sure you won't," I laughed, shaking my head.

"What about you two? Have you moved to the next level yet?" he asked.

"No, she isn't ready for all that, and I am OK with it," I smiled.

"You really like her, uh?" he asked.

"I do, very much," I said softly, looking towards where they had disappeared to.

I saw the girls coming back over, so we ended the conversation there. Ben and I looked at each other, shaking our heads when we noticed the number of snacks they came back with.

"You two are never going to eat that much," Ben said.

"I wouldn't be so sure about that, baby," Lola giggled, kissing him.

The four of us stood outside the cars talking and messing around until we had to get settled down for the movie.

***

Gracie had a grip on my arm, her face hiding. We were nearly at the end of the movie; it would seem she isn't a big fan of horror. She has spent most of it hiding and squealing.

"Aww, don't worry brown eyes, I got you," I chuckled.

"Stop making fun of me, jerk," she pouted, slapping my chest.

I couldn't help myself, and it was both funny and cute watching her freak out. It wasn't that scary, well not to me, but everyone is different alright.

"I am sorry, my love," I chuckled, wrapping my arm around her, "I could distract you from it if you like?" I added.

"And how would you do that?" she asked with one of her brow raised and looking at me suspiciously.

That just made me laugh harder. I don't know what was going on in her head, but I am sure it isn't the same as what was going on in mine.

"Kissing, what did you think I meant?" I chuckled.

"I don't know what goes on in a male teenager's head," she giggled.

"Just kissing," I laughed.

"Hmm, that I can do, not to mention that will be a good distraction," she said, inching closer to me.

I closed the small gap between us, letting my lips to claim hers, in a soft kiss. Gracie whimpered into the kiss, her arms going around my neck. The movie ends in ten minutes anyway. I am sure I can distract her with my lips for that long. I think just being here had been a good distraction for her, after everything that happened in the afternoon.

The soft kissing that never lasted long was soon becoming very heated. Gracie slipped her fingers into my hair, pulling it between her fingers as we kissed. A deep moan fell from my lips, something I was trying my best to hold back, and failed miserably. I was trying to keep my damn teenage hormones in check because I never wanted to push, though Gracie was not making it easy for me.

"We should stop," I mumbled into her lips, and then pulled away, "I don't want to push you, and my hormones are getting the better of me," I said, through my heavy breathing.

I swear I saw her roll her eyes when I said that.

"Yeah, probably best because my hormones are going a little mental right now, too," she sighed, pulling away and resting back against the seat.

It would seem I am not the only one that is struggling to keep control. I turned to the screen, and the end titles were rolling.

"At least I distracted you long enough for the movie to end," I chuckled, trying to lighten the mood.

"Yes," Gracie snickered.

She reached over, pecking my lips before getting out of the car. I followed her, so we could see what the plans were from here.

"Where are we going now?" Lola asked.

"We can grab a pizza and head back to mine, hang out there for a bit, my parents won't mind," Ben said.

We decided that was the plan. It would save us hanging around outside or in the cars. I was in no rush to get home, my mom knew by now I would come back when I came back, and Gracie was staying with me, so we could stay out until whenever, only I wouldn't keep her out too late though.

CHAPTER TWENTY-FIVE

Gracie

It had been a few days since the run in between Ryland and my dad. I had been avoiding home as much as I could, needless to say that every time I was home, Ryland was there too. My dad has stayed out of my way. Sadly I know that won't last and despite that fact I was going to take full advantage of it while I can. But today I had other things to think about.

I was meeting Ryland's mom! Well, meeting her again, though now officially as Ryland's girlfriend!

I was a nervous wreck. I was surprised when he asked me to join them for dinner so she could get to know me properly. I didn't think he was the type, but then again, I am learning new things about him every day. It was part of the enjoyment of a new relationship, getting to know the other person.

I was trying to work out what to wear. What do you wear to meet your boyfriend's mother? Our first meeting was brief, this one was way more important, and more personal. I had never been in this situation before. My room was a mess! Luckily my father wasn't home, so I didn't have to worry about him.

"Gracie, where are you?" I hear Ryland's voice call out from downstairs.

I wasn't expecting him for another hour. I was prancing around in only my underwear.

"Bedroom," I called back.

I couldn't even find my hoodie to cover myself up a little. I was scurrying around trying to find something to put on, but even with all my clothes laying around, I couldn't find something quick and easy to pull over.

"Hey, baby girl," I hear from my bedroom door.

It would seem it was too late to cover up now. I slowly turned to face him.

"Um, hey baby boy," I said nervously.

I could see he was trying his best to look me in the eye. I giggled and made my way over to Ryland and slipped my arms around his neck and kissed him.

"What has happened here?" he chuckled once we pulled away.

"I am trying to find an outfit for dinner," I said.

"Babe, you don't need to dress up," he said, pushing the hair away from my eyes, "Wear whatever you like and what you feel comfortable in," he added.

"I don't want to look like I haven't made an effort," I pouted.

"You will look great in anything," he said, "My mom isn't going to mind what you wear," he added, laughing.

"Are you sure?" I asked.

"Yes, now please put some clothes on because I am getting very... distracted with you being half-naked around me," he said.

I thought for a moment and decided to mess with him a little. I smirked and closed the small space between our bodies and placed my hand on his chest. I reached into his ear.

"What is wrong, Ryland, can you not handle me like this?" I purred, running my fingers down his chest.

I heard him swallow hard, and he nodded his head. He gripped onto my hips, holding me against him. I pressed my lips roughly to his, his grip tightening onto me. I swear, the more we share kisses, the more I am struggling to keep control of myself. It was getting harder every day, but I still did not want to rush into anything.

"Mmm, you are a little tease, brown eyes," he mumbled into my lips.

"Sorry, I will stop," I giggled, pulling away.

I turned, to head back to my bed to find clothes and Ryland swatted my ass.

"Naughty," I said, looking over my shoulder at him.

"Sorry, I couldn't help myself," he said, winking at me.

I rolled my eyes playfully at him, making him laugh. I looked through my clothes again and finally decided what to wear. I chose a white summer dress that stopped at my knees. It hid my cuts and scars, which is what I wanted. I would wear my flats to go with it.

"Is this OK?" I asked, holding it up to him.

"Yes, it is fine, baby girl," he smiled, "You will look beautiful in it," he added.

Ryland helped me put all my clothes away and then I got ready. I was still very nervous. I hope that she will like me. I know how protective mothers can be of their sons. I hope she thinks I am good enough for her son.

"What if she doesn't like me?" I asked nervously.

"How can she not? You are incredible, with a huge heart," he smiled, "Please stop worrying," he added, kissing me softly.

We pulled apart, and I nodded. I made sure my hair was fine

and kept my make-up light. Ryland offered me his hand, which I happily took, and he led us outside. The closer I got to his house the worse my nerves became. He stopped us outside of the house, turned me to him and kissed me softly.

"Relax, sweetness," he said, "You are going to do great," he added.

He kept a hold of my hand, and we headed into the house. Ryland called out to his mother letting her know we were here. She soon came rushing through, wearing the biggest smile on her face.

"Gracie, it is great to meet you, properly that is! Ryland has told me all about you," she gushed, "And please, call me Melissa," she added.

"Hello, it is great to meet you properly too, Melissa," I replied, smiling.

And then she hugged me, which took me off guard a little, still and all I hugged her back. Melissa pulled away and then told us to follow her through for a cold drink because dinner was still in the oven. I instantly relaxed after meeting her. She seemed lovely. Hopefully, I will not do or say something to mess things up. We are off to a good start, and I can only wish it ends that way too.

***

Dinner was going well; Melissa and I seemed to be hitting it off great. Ryland was getting embarrassed with his mom telling me stories and showing me photos. I liked knowing that even with the terrible childhood he had, he still had some good memories.
"What about you, sweetie, what family do you have? Is it just you and your dad?" Melissa asked with a smile that didn't seem natural.

I started shifting in the chair never minding Melissa's subtle change, I hated talking about my family simply because I don't exactly have a family. Ryland reached under the table, placing his hand on my knee and squeezing it.

"Yes?" my answer came out more like a question, and I quickly assumed Ryland may have given her the heads up, so I continued, "My mom passed away when I was younger," I whispered, "I stay with my dad,"

"I am sorry to hear," she said with what sounded like too much emotion, "Do you get on with your dad?" she asked, her voice was strained.

I fell silent. I was not sure how to answer that. I looked at Ryland with a 'please help me' look as I never wanted to be rude and ignore the question, or lie about it.

"Gracie's relationship with her father isn't good, so can we please not talk about it?" Ryland asked, giving his mom a pleading look.

"Again, I am sorry to hear that, Gracie, it must be hard," my mom said, "You are always welcome here anytime you need to get away," she added.

"Thank you," I said softly, "That means a lot," I added.

I was grateful when she left it there and never pushed for more.

"How about dessert and then we can watch a movie unless you kids have other plans?" Melissa asked.

"No, no plans, that sounds good," I smiled.

"I will find a movie," Ryland said, kissing me softly before heading to the living room.

I gave Melissa a hand with the dishes into the kitchen. I helped her clean up, cause I would feel bad if she had to do it herself, Melissa washed the dishes, and I dried.

"I want to thank you, Gracie," she said softly, "I have never seen my boy as happy and as well behaved as he has been since he met you," she added.

"I know he has his problems, but he has a heart of gold," I smiled, "He has done so much for me," I added.

I didn't want to go into too much detail about it because that would mean explaining things and I was not ready for that just yet.

"Can I ask you a personal question?" she asked, softly and I nodded, "Your dad... I have heard a lot of shouting, does he hurt you, Gracie?" she added.

I didn't answer her, instead, I turned my attention to drying the dishes and refused to look at her. She placed her hand gently on my arm. I slowly turned to face her and at the same time I felt the tears running down my cheeks. I could lie, but I didn't want to, not to her.

"Yes," I whimpered.

Melissa pulled me into her, hugging me and gently stroked my hair.

"I am sorry, Gracie," she said, "I know what it can be like living with a violent man, have you not reported him? Told anyone?" she asked.

"The only person that knows is Ryland," I sobbed, "And no, I haven't reported him, it would be no use. He is good at seeming like a nice guy and lying his way through life. It wouldn't do any good," I added.

"Sweetheart, you can stay here with us for a little while to get away from him, to be safe," she said, "There is a spare bedroom," she added.

"Thank you, but I can't do that," I said, "I don't want to cause a problem for Ryland or you," I added.

I think that is the nicest offer someone has ever given me.

"You wouldn't cause a problem, Gracie," she said, "At least you would be away from him and with Ryland knowing everything that is going on I think he would want you here too," she added.

"I do," we heard from behind us, "If it keeps you safe," he added, looking so intensely into my eyes that I blushed.

Ryland came over, wrapping his arms around me, and hugging me tightly.

"Please, stay here with us?" he pleaded, stroking my hair.

I clung to him and let myself cry. I don't know why I was crying. Maybe because it all got brought up or perhaps it was just with the caring nature, they were both showing. I don't know, but I must have cried for the next few minutes, Ryland soothing me the best he could.

"Sorry," I said, pulling away.

I wiped my tears, feeling embarrassed with all my crying.

"You have nothing to be sorry about, baby girl," Ryland said, wiping my tears away, "Please, come and stay with us?" he asked once more.

"It would be no bother, I can set the spare room up for you," she said.
I was torn on what to do. I did not want to be a problem for anyone or cause them any hassle, but at the same time, I knew they were right. I would be safer here.

"Can I think about it?" I asked softly.

"Take all the time that you need, even stay the night and then you can think on," Melissa said.

"Thank you, I will do that," I said.

"And no sneaking into each other's room when I am sleeping," she said, pointing between Ryland and me, giggling.

"We won't," Ryland and I said in sync.

She looked at us, with a raised brow. I don't think she believed us. Then again, I had done it before, sneaked in, something I think we should keep to ourselves.

"Right, dessert and movie," Ryland said, changing the subject.

"Yes," I giggled.

Melissa laughed and shook her head. I am glad the night is going well. And the offer, no matter what I decided, will be something I will always be grateful for.

CHAPTER TWENTY-SIX

Ryland

Gracie and I were on one sofa, she snuggled into my side, and my arm wrapped around her. My mother sat on the other sofa, with a glass of wine. Tonight has gone better than I ever imagined. The two of them have hit it off well. I could feel my mom watching me. I turned to her, and she smiled brightly at me, winking. I know that is my mother's way of saying 'you have a good one there, don't mess it up'. I smiled back and nodded.

My mom turned back to the movie, and I reached down, kissing the top of Gracie's head. She looked up at me, flashing her beautiful smile at me, and that was enough to make my heart soar. I was in deep. I pecked her lips quickly, she giggled, and we turned back to the movie.

Gracie had not mentioned anything else about staying here, and we haven't brought it up again. I don't want her to feel pressured with it, but I was hoping she would say yes.

"I am going to go to bed, and read, I think," my mom said, "I think I have stolen enough of your night," she added, laughing.

"We don't mind," Gracie said, sitting up.

"Thank you, sweetie, but I am sure you both have better things to do," my mom said, "I will make the spare bedroom just in case," she added.

"Thank you," Gracie said.

We said goodnight to my mom, and she went upstairs. I turned to Gracie, tucking the hair behind her ear, and kissed her softly.

"Have you made up your mind?" I asked softly.

"Are you sure I will not be a bother if I say yes?" she asked, worried.

"I promise, you will be no bother at all, Gracie," I said, "We would both rather have you here with us, than next door with him," I added.

Gracie sighed and fell silent for a moment. She was thinking about what she should do. I was hoping she would say yes. I hate when she is in that house alone with that bastard!

"OK, I will come and stay," she whispered.

"Thank you," I said, kissing her, "You are better off here than there," I added.

"I know, but I will wait and get my things tomorrow. I don't want to go in there tonight, he was drunk and ready for me," she said.

"We can go tomorrow, there is no rush," I said, "I can give you something to sleep in tonight, and clothes for the morning," I added.

"Thank you, babe," she said, hugging me.

Having her stay here means I can protect her from him. I still want to kill him after everything he has put her through, but I am not stooping down to his level. Gracie has had enough violence in her life, never mind me adding to it. Not anymore, he isn't getting anywhere near her, ever again!

"Do you want to watch the rest in my room?" I asked.

"Will your mom be OK with that?" she asked nervously.

"Yes, she just doesn't want us staying in the same bed," I said, "Oh, if only she knew we have already done that lots of times," I added laughing.

I was surprised that we never got caught.

"Yes, let's not tell your mother that," Gracie laughed.

I jumped to my feet and offered her my hand, which she took happily. I helped her up, pulling her into my chest and kissing her. She whimpered, wrapping her arms around me, and pressing herself tightly to my body.

I pulled away first because I needed to let the air get back into my lungs. Gracie opened her eyes, looking at me and her breathing was heavy. She smiled and then took my hand, and we headed to my bedroom. I passed her one of my tees and a pair of boxers. She turned her back to me, stripping down to her underwear.

I watched her from the spot where I was sitting on my bed. I couldn't help myself. I licked my lips, my eyes falling on the perfect curves of her hips, she was so beautiful. I stood from the bed, making my way over to her. I just wanted to touch her. I stepped into her, my front to her back, and the moment I did, her breathing caught in her throat, and she rested back against me.

"You are so beautiful," I whispered, kissing over her shoulders.

Gracie moaned softly, reaching her arm up and wrapping it around my neck. I let my fingers trace over the skin of her hips and back. I was getting a little carried away, I had to quickly pull away.

"Sorry," I said.

I didn't want her to feel like I was pushing her for anything. Gracie slowly turned to me, and my breath hitched in my throat as my eyes fell on her half-naked body. She stepped into me.

"Sorry for what?" she asked softly.

"Pushing, going too far," I said.

Gracie slipped her arms around my neck and pressed herself to me.

"You didn't push. I like when you touch me," she breathed out.

"You do, uh?" I said, grasping her hips.

"Yes," she whispered, pressing her lips to mine.

I groaned, my grip on her tightening. She reached over, closing my bedroom door. I had no clue where Gracie was going with this, but I would go along with it.

"Just kissing and touching," she mumbled into my lips, "For now," she added.

I went to respond, but before I could, she grabbed the bottom of my tee, and pulled it over my head, and walked us back towards the bed. She pushed me down, giggling as she did. I smirked, resting my hands behind my head, and waited for her next move.

She crawled up the bed to me, towering over me. I moaned instantly at the feel of her skin against mine. She covered my lips, roughly with hers. I groaned, letting my hands run down her back, over her ass and thighs. Gracie was whimpering into my lips.

"I am finding it hard to fight my desire for you, every single damn day," she said, moving her lips to my neck.

I growled at her words because she doesn't often say things like that, and her lips felt good on my neck.

"I know, I am the same, but we will take this at your pace," I said.

Gracie moved, and sat up on my chest, looking down at me.

"There must be a part of you that is fed up with all this waiting," she said, softly, "I know before me you were having sex, and probably a lot of it. And now, you are with me; you are getting nothing," she added.

Yes, at first, it was hard for me because I was used to getting my needs sorted as and when I wanted them, but not now. I would rather be with Gracie and do what we are doing, without the sex, than be having sex with someone else.

"Not at all," I smiled, "All of that doesn't matter, not right now. All I need is you," I added, playing with her hair.

"Are you sure?" she sighed.

"Yes, I promise," I said.

"OK, I promise I won't make you wait too long," she said.

I don't like her thinking like that. I don't want her thinking we need to take it to the next level, and soon. I kept my grip on her as she flipped us over, putting her below me.

"Gracie, stop please, darling. I will wait as long as needed until you are ready for all that. I don't want it soon, unless you are one hundred percent sure that is what you want," I said in one breath.

"You promise?" she asked.

"I promise," I smiled.

"OK, then shut up and kiss me," she giggled.

"Yes, ma'am, that I can do," I chuckled.

I let our lips meet again, the moment they touched I got that all familiar feeling running through me, the one that makes my heart speed up, and my pulse race. It happened every single time that she kissed me, touched me, or was close to me. Gracie did something to me that I have never felt. And there may be a good chance that I was falling in love with her—falling in love for the first time in my life.

Gracie wrapped her legs around my body, letting her hands wander as our lips moved perfectly together. She rolled her hips up against me, and the moment she did, I am sure she felt my growing excitement. We got into a heated make-out session, one that was sending bolts of pleasure through me.

She pulled away from my lips, and her lips fell at my ear.

"I need you to touch me, Ryland," she panted in my ear.

I ran my hand up over her bare thigh, over her hips and her stomach and she moaned, her body responding to my touch as it arched up from the bed. She slipped her hand around my wrist and slid my hand between our bodies making her final statement, she rested my hand on her panties.

"I need you to touch me here," she breathed out.

"Are you sure?" I asked.

"Yes," she whispered.

I didn't want to push too much at once. I gently brushed my fingers over her underwear, watching as her eyes closed, and she moaned softly. I ran my fingers over her stomach, sitting them just above her panties.

"Can I?" I asked once again, to be sure.

She opened her eyes to look at me and nodded. I was nervous, why? I don't know. I have done this plenty of times, but then again, none of them has been Gracie. I slowly slid my hand in, resting my fingers on her clit. I decided that was as far as I was going tonight. I can give her what she is craving by using only that.

"Are you sure?" I asked again, and she nodded, "OK, I am not going down, just here, to ease you into it," I added.

"OK," she breathed out.

I gently circle my fingers on the small bud, slowly to start with. She closed her eyes again and moaned softly. I could feel that she was excited. I pressed my lips to hers, kissing her and began working my fingers a little quicker against her clit. She breathed deeply into my lips. Gracie gripped onto my arms. I pulled my lips from hers.

"Mmm, yes, that feels good," she panted out.

My lips fell on her neck, kissing and sucking on the skin. I slid my fingers down her folds, making her gasp, and her head fell back. I ran them back up, more swiftly this time, and she gasped again. I placed my fingers back against her clit, rubbing, and tugging on it. I used my free hand to touch the rest of her body.

"Ryland, oh, yes, I think I am close," she said, between soft groans.

I moved quicker, eager to give her the release she needed. It only took another moment, and Gracie's back arches up from the bed and her lips part. I covered her lips with mine because I didn't want my mom to hear her call out. I felt her shake, rolling her hips up against my hand, as her climax hit, and she whimpered roughly into my lips. Her body relaxed below me after a moment.

"Did you like that?" I asked.

"Yes, it felt seriously good and was just what I needed," she said, smiling up at me, "Next time, will you please touch me lower?" she added, a blush creeping onto her cheeks.

"Yes, ma'am, one step at a time," I chuckled, pecking her lips.

I slowly took my hand out of her panties, wiping my fingers with the wipes next to my bed. I was trying my best to ignore my excitement, there was no way to hide that doing that for her, turned me on.

"What about you?" she asked, nodding at my evident hard-on.

"Don't you worry about that, nothing a cold shower won't fix," I said.

"A cold shower?" Gracie giggled, "I am sorry," she added, pouting.

"Don't worry about it, love, I have done it lots of times," I chuckled, "I am a teenage boy, I am constantly horny, so I am used to cold showers," I added.

Gracie laughed loudly and shook her head.

"Um, can I get in first and clean myself up before I get changed?" she asked.

"Sure thing, on you go," I smiled.

She got up from the bed, steadying herself and making her way to the bathroom to clean herself up, taking my clothes with her to change.

"All done, you can go for your cold shower now," Gracie chuckled, coming back into my room.

"Thanks," I laughed, shaking my head.

I pulled her in for a kiss before going to get myself showered and sorted. It was only a quick shower, and I got myself dried and pulled some joggers on while I was in there. By the time I came back through, Gracie was curled up in my bed, waiting for me. She looked up at me, her eyes trailing over my naked chest, licking her lips. I couldn't help but smirk.

"Better?" she asked.

"Yes, but now I'm blooming freezing," I laughed.

"Well get in here then, it is nice and warm," she snickered, lifting the covers.

I rushed over, climbing in next to her. Gracie pulled the covers over us and snuggled into me. I slipped my arms around her and kissed her softly. She placed her head on my chest, and her hand on my stomach.

"These are my favourite times with you," I smiled.

"Mine too," she said, snuggling in as close as she could.
We put the rest of the movie on. I wouldn't change our time like this for the world. It was perfect. She was perfect.

CHAPTER TWENTY-SEVEN

Gracie

I was sitting at the breakfast table with Ryland and his mom. I was playing with the food on my plate. I was too nervous to eat because I was dreading facing my dad. I was hoping he wouldn't be home.

"Gracie, are you OK?" Ryland asked, placing his hand over mine.

"I don't want to go home and get my things, but I know I need to," I sighed.

"I promise you will be fine. I will be there with you," he smiled.

"I know," I said, smiling back.

My dad will not care that I am moving out. He will only care because I will not be there to clean up after his ass, make his meals and be his personal punch back.

"Sweetie, do you want me to come with you both?" Melissa asked, looking a little nervous.

"No, it is OK, thank you though," I smiled.

I wouldn't put her in that position, especially since I know what she has been through personally at the hands of a man. I don't need her meeting another monster. I tried to push it to the back of my mind and eat my breakfast. Melissa had taken her time to make it, and I don't want to waste it.

"I need to get to work, but please let me know how you get on, OK?" she said, adding "And I mean it Gracie, stay here as long as you need,"

"Thank you, I honestly appreciate it," I smiled back.

Melissa headed off to get ready. Ryland and I headed upstairs to get ready and get my things before heading to school. Ryland gave me clothes to wear until I grabbed my things.

"Are you ready for this?" Ryland asked.

"As ready as I'll ever be," I sighed.

The sooner I get this over with, the better. He slipped his hand into mine, and we headed out. My hands were shaking, the closer we got to my house. When I arrived at the door I was hesitant to open it .

"I am right here, babe," Ryland said, kissing me.

We walked in, and the moment we did....

"Where the fuck have you been?" my dad demanded, arriving in front of us.

He looked between Ryland and me before a look of disgust took over his face.

"Don't answer that, you have obviously been out acting like a little whore," he snapped.

I felt Ryland tense next to me, and his fists clenched at his side. He was trying to contain his temper. I know all he wanted to do was knock my dad out. I would probably let him if I knew it wouldn't get Ryland into trouble, but unfortunately my dad would be the kind to make sure problems happen.

"Go and get your things, Gracie," Ryland said softly.

"And where do you think she is going?" my dad hissed.

"Away from you, and somewhere she is safe," Ryland spat back.

I wanted to go and get my things, but it was like I had frozen on the spot. I couldn't move.

"You aren't taking her anywhere," my dad said, stepping in closer.

Ryland stopped in front of me, putting a block between my father and me.

"Yes, I am, watch me! And if you do not let her go, I will make your life hell," Ryland said, "I will make sure you are reported to both social service and the police. I will make sure you get charged for every little thing you ever did to her," he added.

I watch my dad slowly back off, fear taking over his face. He has always known I wouldn't do that, report him. He doesn't know Ryland, and he can't be sure whether Ryland is telling the truth or bluffing.

"You know what, take her!" my dad said, pure venom in his voice, "But don't send her back to me when you realize, she is nothing but a worthless piece of crap," he added, laughing.

I saw Ryland getting ready to dive at him, but I wasn't going to let that happen. I grabbed Ryland and pulled him away with me to go up and get my things.

"Let's just get what I need and get out of here," I said.

I was trying my best not to cry. I don't want to shed any more tears because of that horrible man. He has taken enough from me already, and I just wanted to get away from him. Yes, it was only next door, but at least I won't need to stay in the same house as him. Also, my dad won't try to start anything at Ryland's because he knows if he does, the neighbors will see him for who he really is, and that is the last thing he wants.

I gathered as much as I could, essential things, everything else can wait.

"I will take what I need for the moment, the rest can wait," I said.

Ryland grabbed a couple of bags, while I grabbed the others and we headed back downstairs. My dad was standing in the very spot we left him.

"Once you walk out that front door, don't ever step back through it," he said, "You will not be welcome here, ever again," he added.

If I didn't know any better, that was his way of giving me a choice. I didn't need to think about it. I had not left before because no one knew the truth and I had nowhere to go. That was all different now.

"Why would you think that I wanted to stay? You made my life hell dad. You use me as your slave. You hurt me, just because you can," I said, "I wish it was mom here, and not you. You don't deserve to be here, she did," I added, shaking my head.

My dad didn't flinch. He didn't show any emotion. I don't know what I expected. He doesn't have a heart or a caring bone in his body.

"I hope you find a way to get better dad, and maybe one day find a way to get rid of the monster you have inside of you," I said, feeling the tears brim in my eyes, "Goodbye," I added.

I turned, walked away and didn't look back. I was done with him. I have my college fund, which my mom made sure was there for me, and no one is allowed to touch it, but me. I have some money saved too. I need to find work and get my own place. I can't stay with Ryland and Melissa until after I graduate since I will be going away for College, six hours away to be exact. I would only need a short term lease.

"You OK, Gracie?" Ryland asked, appearing at my side.

"I will be," I said, giving him a small smile.

I know being away from home, from my dad, it would take time to get used to, but it was the right thing to do. It was the safest thing for me too.

"Are you up for going to school? Maybe a sick day would be best.." he said softly, "I will take it too, my mom will understand," he added.

I wasn't in the mood for school. Taking a sick day sounds good. I am not one for sick days so that it wouldn't get me into trouble.

"I think I might, but you don't need to," I said, "I don't want you getting into trouble, Ryland," I added.

"I won't. It will be OK. I don't want you to be alone today," he said.

I would usually argue with him on it, but today I didn't have the energy. I nodded, giving in. We called the school, I pretended to be Ryland's mom, and he pretended to be my dad. Ryland's mom understood when he told her we weren't going in today.

"Come on, beautiful, let's put your things away, and we can go back to bed for a few hours," he said.

Sleep sounds good. I was exhausted. I didn't sleep much last night because I was worried about today. I wanted to sneak in and stay in Ryland's room, but I didn't. I didn't want to disrespect Melissa like that after everything she has done for me.

Ryland and I got my things up to the room, putting everything away. I kept the tee he gave me on, taking everything else off, before slipping under the covers. Ryland did the same, pulling me close to him.

I rested my head on his chest, and he wrapped me tightly in his arms. I snuggled into him as close as I could. He gently stroked my hair.

"I got you, baby girl," he said, kissing the top of my head, "Always," he added in a whisper.

I didn't think it would ever be possible to feel this safe. I lifted my head to smile at him. He was looking down at me, a look in his eyes that was new.

"Ryland, why are you looking at me like that?" I asked softly.

He tucked the hair behind my ear. I hear him take a deep breath. He opens his mouth and then closes it again. I knew he wanted to say something, something that made him feel scared.

"Is everything OK? You can tell me anything, Ryland," I said.

"I know, I just don't want to freak you out," he said, nervously.

I don't think I have seen him this nervous before. I kissed him, hoping that would help relax him. I had no clue what he wanted to say, so I pulled away from his lips.

"Gracie," he called me and then paused, "I, I, I love you," he whispered.

Wow! That was not what I was expecting at all. I just stared at him, not saying anything at first, and I could see him beginning to panic.

"You do?" I asked.

"Yes, and I am sorry if that isn't what you wanted to hear right now, but I, I had to tell you," he stammered out.

I pressed my lips to his, kissing him.

"I love you too," I said, pulling away.

"Really?" he asked, surprised.

"Yes," I said, "Do not look so surprised," I added, giggling.

"Sorry, I wasn't expecting you to say it back," he said, "I thought you would have freaked out, thinking I was a crazy person," he added, laughing.

I know it hasn't been long since we got together, but neither of us can deny that there has been something there since the get-go. Since the start, we have shared a bond, even if to start with, it was an unspoken bond.

"Not at all," I said, "I think we both have known there has been something here since day one, even if you were an ass when I first met you," I added, smirking.

"Yes, that is very true," he smiled, "I am sorry I was an asshole," he added, pouted.

"I forgive you," I said, letting our lips meet and dance again.

And we lay there kissing for the next couple of minutes. He pulled me in against his chest once we pulled apart.

"We should get some rest, and then when we wake up, we can have a day of fun, just you and me," he said.

"Sounds perfect," I said.

He stole one last kiss, then we told each other I love you once more before getting settled. I couldn't stop smiling, as I let myself drift off. Ryland loves me. ME! No one had ever loved me; well, not like this.

And laying there with Ryland made me realise something; I was going to be OK. Yes, I still have a lot to overcome, but I will be OK somewhere down the line. I am away from my father, and that is a start.

I feel a strength in me, a strength I never thought I would have.

CHAPTER TWENTY-EIGHT

Ryland

Gracie and I were sitting at the table having breakfast, well trying to, but we were too distracted with each other's lips.

"That is enough of that, especially at the breakfast table," we heard my mom laugh from behind us.

Gracie quickly pulled away, her entire face heating up, and she whispered a sorry to my mom. I, however, just smiled brightly at my mom.

"Ryland," Gracie giggled, slapping my arm.

"What?" I smirked, "I am not embarrassed," I added, shrugging.

My mom and Gracie looked at each other, rolling their eyes and laughing. I think they both know what I am like by now.

"Also, you two aren't very good at sneaking around," Mom said, looking between us, "I know you have been sneaking into each other's rooms," she added with her index finger moving between the two of us.

"I swear, nothing is happening," Gracie said while panicking. "I just don't sleep well if I am on my own," she added.

I could tell Gracie was freaking out. I took her hand in mine under the table, trying to get her to relax.

"She is telling the truth, mom; nothing is happening between us. We just sleep, I promise," I said.

I know my mom wanted us in separate rooms, but Gracie feels at ease when I am next to her. Even though I was expecting my mom to be mad, I was so glad when she wasn't.

"I understand that, but I wish you would have come to me and asked, rather than sneak around," my mom said, "And if, or I should say when, something does end up happening, please be safe," she instructed.

"Promise, now can we drop it, please?" I asked softly as I could see Gracie was getting embarrassed with it all.

"Yes," mom said.

I guess things could have gotten worse. My mom could have gotten mad, but I am glad she didn't.

"Thank you," I smiled.

"I need to get to work," mother said, "I am going out tonight with some friends from work, will you two be OK? And do you want me to make you dinner?" she enquired.

"No, it is alright, I can cook us something," I said, "You go out and enjoy yourself. You deserve it,"

My mom smiled, hugging us both before heading out. Gracie and I finished up with breakfast before heading upstairs to get ready for school.

"How about a date night tonight?" I asked, "I can make dinner, and then we can watch a couple of movies?" I added.

"Yes, that sounds good, babe," Gracie smiled, kissing me softly.

I wanted to take care of her tonight, spoil her because with everything she has been through, she deserves it. Gracie had been staying with us for a few days now, and she was settling in, but I could tell she was still a little anxious, and it was understandable. Yes, she was away from that house, but her father was still next door. I don't think she will ever completely relax until she is far away from him.

"Then it is a date," I said brightly.

Gracie giggled and smiled back at me in the same way. I pulled her in for another kiss before we headed to our designated separate rooms to get ready as Gracie's things were in the room that she was supposed to be staying in.

I headed to my room, stripping down to get changed. I would get a shower later. I got distracted, though, watching stupid videos on my phone. Blame Ben; he sent them to me.

"Why are you not ready?" Gracie laughed, coming into my room.

I looked up and smiled when I saw her. She looked beautiful. Her hair was down but not straightened how it usually is. She had her natural wavy curls.

"Blame Ben and his stupid videos," I laughed.

Gracie rolled her eyes, coming over to where I was. I pulled her onto my lap, resting my hand on the small of her back.

"You look beautiful," I said, playing with a strand of her hair.

"Thank you," she blushed.

"But to me, you are always beautiful," I said, "I love you, Gracie," I added.
"I love you too, baby boy," she said, kissing me softly.

I moaned into her lips as her arms slipped around my neck. Gracie pressed her lips to mine a little harder. I didn't have any complaints about that. The kiss was soon becoming heated, and as much as I would love to stay like this and kiss all day, I knew we needed to go.

"Mmm, easy, sweetness, we need to get to school, and if you keep kissing me like this, we are going to be late," I mumbled.

"In a minute," she moaned into my lips.

Who am I not to give *my* girl what *she* wants? I smirked into her lips, my fingers tracing up and down her back, resting them on her ass. I could kiss her lips for hours. Gracie sighed and hesitantly pulled away from my lips.

"We probably should go," Gracie pouted.

"Yes, but later, my lips are all yours," I winked.

"I look forward to it," she said, winking back at me, "Can I borrow one of your hoodies, please?" she added, batting her lashes at me.

"Of course, help yourself, my love," I smiled.

Gracie pulled herself from my lap, told me to move my backside and get the rest of my clothing on. I did as she told me, and she took one of my hoodies, pulling it over her and we headed out to go to school.

"Your car or mine?" I asked, slipping my arm around her.

"We can take yours," she smiled.

We headed into my car and got on our way to school. I reached over, placing my hand on her knee. I watch as the smile grows on her lips when she feels my touch. A comfortable silence came between us on the ride to school. I didn't hate school as much as I used to. It is Gracie's influence on me. All too soon we reached our destination, got out, and I slipped my hand into her as we walked in.

We didn't have first-class together this morning, but we had all our other classes together. I walk Gracie to her locker, making sure she gets everything she needs. The moment she turns back around, I pressed my lips to her, Gracie responding with a loud whimper. I don't think she was expecting it.

"I love you, and I will see you in the next class, beautiful," I said.

"I love you too, see you then," she said, "And try to stay out of trouble," she added with one of her brows raised.

"I am a good boy now, thank you very much," I said proudly.

Gracie shook her head, laughing.

"One more kiss, then I will go," I suggested.

"One, and then you go, so I am not late," she said.

I stole one last kiss before heading off to my first class. I stopped outside of it, turning to look where Gracie was.

"LOVE YOU, GRACIE," I called out.

It was that loud. I am sure most of the other students in the school heard me. I heard a couple of the girls cooing when I said it. Gracie however, was looking slightly embarrassed. I let out a small laugh, blowing her a kiss before heading into class. I am sure she will kill me later for it. That was alright, though. I don't mind the entire school, knowing that I was in love with her.

"You are so fucking whipped," Ben said as I sat down next to him.

"I know, and for the record, I am not ashamed of it," I said confidently, "And you are one to talk," I added, laughing.

"I don't shout 'I love you, Lola' in the halls," he laughed.

"Well, maybe you should start," I said.

Ben shook his head at me, looking a little disgusted. It was bullshit, everyone knew he was utterly smitten too, we all know how he acts around Lola. We stopped talking because the teacher came in. Yes, I was trying my best to stay out of trouble and do my schoolwork. I didn't think I would ever see the day, and this is one of the many things I have Gracie to thank for. Gracie is always thanking me for helping her, but she has helped me too. We make a good team.

I have a feeling today is going to be a good day.

***

It was the end of the school day and Gracie and I were leaning against my car, kissing.

"I will be back for about five probably," she said once we pulled apart.

Gracie and Lola were going to grab a coffee and go into town because Lola needed a few things.

"OK, gorgeous," I said, "I will see you then, and we can start our date night," I added.

That gave me time to go and get what I needed for dinner. I also planned on getting a surprise for her, so a stop to the jewellery store was on the cards for the way home. I knew what I was looking for. It was my way of showing her what she meant to me and to let her know I wasn't going anywhere. I wasn't going to leave like she believes everyone does.

"I better go. Lola is getting impatient," Gracie snickered.

"Yes," I chuckle.

Gracie kissed my cheek, hugging me quickly before heading off. I gave her ass a quick swat as she walked away. She looked at me over her shoulder, flashing a sexy little smile at me before going over to Lola.

I waited until they drove off before getting into my car and getting on my way. I was looking forward to our date night. We don't often get any time alone at my house. It would be nice to just snuggle up, make-out a little and watch movies.

I enjoyed cooking too, so hopefully, the meal will be OK. I wasn't sure what I was going to make yet. I will decide when I get to the store, but I know what Gracie likes, so it shouldn't be hard to find something. I know I had some prepping to do, but I was fine with that.

I needed tonight to be perfect! Gracie deserves nothing more than perfection! I want her to feel looked after, and for a change not have to do any cooking or look after someone who wouldn't appreciate her efforts, and I was going to do whatever I needed to make that happen.

CHAPTER TWENTY-NINE

—

Gracie

I was sitting with Lola at the café, having a coffee. There was a reason I suggested coffee, the reason being I needed some girl talk.

"Lola, can I ask you something?" I asked.

"Sure you can. What is on your mind?" she smiled.

"How did you know when you were ready to have sex for the first time?" I whispered as I didn't want the people in the café hearing what we were talking about.

"Honestly, Gracie, I don't think I was ready for my first time," she said, her voice somewhat sad, "I thought I was, but looking back, I wasn't. I wish Ben would have been my first," she said in a low voice.

Lola was fifteen when she lost her virginity. She was dating some douche bag, and she honestly thought he loved her. It turned out he didn't. In return, he got a punch in the face from her.

"Do you regret having sex, or do you just mean having it with the wrong person?" I asked.

"I mean having it with the wrong person. I enjoy it very much," she smirked, "But with Ben, it is different, in the best way possible. Why do you ask?" she added.

"I-I think I-I am ready to take that step with Ryland," I replied nervously.

"You are? Are you sure?" Lola asked.

"Yes, I have been thinking about it recently, and tonight would be a great opportunity for it since we will have the house to ourselves," I said.

I hadn't told Lola, or Ben that I was staying with Ryland and his mom officially because again, that would raise too many questions. Yes, they know I sneak in and stay with him some nights, and that is all I need them to know for the time being.

"Does Ryland know?" she asked.

"No. I want it to be a surprise in a way, I guess," I smiled, "He is always doing and saying things first, and tonight I want to be one doing something first," I added.

There is something else that has been crossing my mind a lot recently. Every time Ryland touches or kisses me, I lose a little more control, but I kept that to myself...

"Gracie, are you one hundred percent sure?" she asked softly.

"Yes. I love him, Lola, and he loves me," I smiled, "I don't need to tell you that he has been nothing but incredible to me, and patient too," I added.

"Follow not only your heart, Gracie, but your head too," she said.

"I know. And every part of me is ready," I said.

"Then go for it," she smirked.

My best friend has a unique way with words. However, her words did make me giggle.

Yes, I was ready, but at the same time I was nervous and also worried. Although I know Ryland had been with plenty of other girls, I don't think I want to know exactly how many. Even though I have always known that Ryland had a past, which never bothered me before, it goes without saying that I am scared I won't match up to those other girls. I have no experience. What if I am no good? What if I don't do it for him?

"Lola, what if I don't compare to all those other girls?" I sighed, running my fingers through my hair.

"You won't compare to them, Gracie, there is a big difference between them and you; Ryland loves you, those others girl meant nothing to him," she said looking into my eyes, wanting to ensure I understood what she was saying, "You mean so much more to him than what any of them ever did, scratch that, I think you mean more to him than anyone else in the entire world," she added, smiling.

I know she has a point, there was a difference; he loves me.

"I know, but still, what if I am no good? What if I don't, um, turn him on," I said.

"Are you kidding? You turn that boy on just by kissing him," Lola giggled.

"I think there is a difference between kissing and having sex," I laughed.

"Gracie, you don't need to worry about not turning him on," she said, "He is crazy about you, and he practically drools any time you are close to him," she added.

I let out a loud laugh, shaking my head. Lola smirked and shrugged. I think him drooling is an exaggeration.

"I just hope my non existing experience doesn't get in the way," I said.

"I am sure Ryland will keep you right," she said.

Lola and I chatted about it for the next half-an-hour, Lola was giving me the best advice she could and a few tips too. I did feel a little better after talking to her. I was over-thinking it, and that would make my nerves worse. Lola told me to relax and go for it when Ryland least expects it. Live in the moment of sorts, rather than planning it in my head. And I decided that is what I was going to do.

"Are you on birth control?" Lola asked.

"No, because it isn't something I have had to think about or needed before," I said.

"OK, then we need to get you condoms," she said, "But, you should make an appointment to get birth control, and I will come with you if you don't want to go alone," she added.

"Yes, I definitely need to get protection," I said, "And I will make an appointment too," I added.

"We can go and pick some up from the store right now," she smiled.

"Thank you for today," I said, trying my best to look her in the eyes whilst looking like a ripe tomato, "I would be lost without you," I added.

"What are best friends for!?" She said brightly.

We finished our coffees and headed out, going to the store to get condoms. And then I was all set. Once I got what I needed, Lola dropped me off at Ryland's, about five-thirty.

"Have fun," Lola winked, "And remember, don't over-think it," she added.

"I will try not to," I said.

"I want details tomorrow," she said.

"Why doesn't that surprise me?" I giggled.

I gave her a quick hug and went inside. Melissa was still at home, and would be heading out soon. I need to say a quick hello to them both and run upstairs to hide the condoms. I don't want Melissa or Ryland seeing them.

As I entered the house, I heard Ryland and his mom chatting. I paused when I heard my name being mentioned.

"Mom, Gracie is going to be alright, isn't she?" Ryland asked.

"I am sure she will be, son. She is strong," Melissa said.

"I know she is. I just wish I could find a way to get that monster away from her," he sighed.
"Gracie will be safe as long as she is here with us," Melissa said, "She really does mean a lot to you, doesn't she?" she asked.

"Yes, she has become my entire world, and I love her so very much," Ryland said.

I smiled, feeling the tears well in my eyes.

"You two are good for each other," Melissa said.

I still have doubts from time to time about why anyone would love someone like me, but when Ryland says things like that, all my doubts and worries disappear.

"Hello," I called out, acting as I had just arrived.

"Living room, sweetheart," Ryland called out,

I popped my head in, saying hello and smiling.

"I am just going to put my things in the room. I will be back soon," I smiled.

I headed upstairs, dumping my things, and hiding the condoms in one of the drawers until later. I would get a shower and change in a bit. I headed back down to join Ryland and Melissa, Melissa handing me a coffee. I chuckle, thanking her. She knows me so well already.

"How was your girly time?" Ryland asked as I sat down next to him.

"Good," I smiled, pecking his lips.

Ryland slipped his arm around my shoulder, and I snuggled into him.

"Are you looking forward to going out?" I asked Melissa.

"Yes. It has been a while, and I am ready for it," Melissa laughed, "But I need to find something to wear first," she added.

"I am sure you will find something," I laughed.

"You girls are so picky when it comes to clothing," Ryland

laughed, shaking his head.

"Says you, you take longer to get ready than what I sometimes do," I teased.

Ryland tries to deny it, but Melissa and I continued to tease him about it until he's gone all pouty at us, which only made us laugh harder. Melissa left us to go and get dressed.

The moment she was out of sight, I grabbed Ryland's tee, pulling him closer and pressing my lips to his. A loud grunt fell from his lips. He was not expecting it. I smirked into the kiss. I think Lola is right. I will not have any issues turning him on if this is what my kiss can do to him. He was quick to grip onto me and kissed me in the same hungry way.

I abruptly pulled away, the kiss leaving us both breathless.

"I am going to go get showered and dressed," I smirked, turning to walk away from him.

"Gracie, that was mean," Ryland called after me.

I stopped just before leaving the living room and turned to face him.

"I don't know what you mean, babe," I said innocently.

I didn't give him a chance to say anything. Instead, I winked at him and headed upstairs. I could hear him groan from the living room. I giggled to myself as I ran upstairs. I will call it revenge for what he did to me at school this morning.

I went to my room to get towels and clothes to take to

the bathroom with me. Two seconds after entering it, Ryland followed behind me.

"Can I help you?" I asked.

I placed my hand on my hip, and tilted my head to the side, and plastered my sweetest smile on my lips.

"Don't play Little Miss Innocent with me," he laughed.

"I am not playing. I am innocent," I said, batting my lashes at him.

Ryland shook his head, chuckling and pulled me into him. I slipped my arms around his neck.

"One more kiss, and then I will let you be and get started on dinner," he said.

"Hmm, I am sure I can do that," I said, playfully rolling my eyes at him.

He didn't give me a chance to speak after that, he silenced me with his lips. Mmm, I love his kisses. The kiss was sweet, unlike the way I kissed him, but that was OK. I like his sweet kisses. Ryland pulled away first this time.

"I will see you downstairs, sweetness," he said, patting my ass before pulling away.

"Yes, I won't be long," I smiled.

Ryland pecked my lips once more before heading out, but not before telling me he loves me one more time, and I happily returned those same words to him. I don't think I will ever get tired of hearing that from him. Only one other person who has ever told me that was my mom, well and Lola too. These aren't words I am used to hearing.

I smiled, grabbed my things and finally headed for my shower. I was a little anxious about tonight, but I was excited at the same time. I know he is not expecting it, and I think that will make it more fun and exciting, rather than any plans. I know Ryland will go at the pace I need. I also know he will be gentle with me. I trusted him with every part of me, and that is why I know I am ready for this. I couldn't even imagine my first time being with anyone that wasn't Ryland.

I will have no regrets after tonight, and I know that for a fact. I don't think I could ever regret anything with Ryland. There I go again, getting lost in my head. I need to stop that, for the moment anyway.

Everything was going to be OK! It was going to be perfect. I got this!

CHAPTER THIRTY

Ryland

I was getting the dishes done after Gracie, and I had finished with dinner. Lola has called Gracie for something, so she was on the phone. I didn't mind, though. I did say I would look after her tonight. I had made way too much food. There was enough for dinner tomorrow as well, better too much than not enough. I was lost in my world as I washed the dishes and only got pulled out of it when I felt a pair of arms snake around my waist and soft lips on my neck.

"Sorry I couldn't help with the dishes, babe," Gracie says.

"It is alright, my love, I got them," I said, smiling over my shoulder at her.

"But you cooked, so I should have been doing the dishes," she pouted.

I laughed as she pouted at me and turned around to face her immediately placing my hands on the curves of her hips, and pulled her close.

"Tonight I am looking after you, gorgeous," I said, kissing her softly.

"Aww, thanks, love," she cooed, slipping her arms around my neck, "Thank you for dinner. It was great," she added.

"You are welcome, sweetness," I said, bringing her lips back to mine.

Gracie happily kissed me back, but there was an eagerness to her kiss. She pressed herself against me. I groaned, my grip around her tightening. Mmm, this kiss was different. She pulled away first, much to my dismay.

"You should probably finish those dishes," she smirked, stepping back from me.

"Tease," I laughed.

"I know," she replied confidently, biting her lip.

"Oh you do, do you?" I smirked, going to pull her back.

Gracie shook her head, stepping further away from me.

"Yes," she said, slowly running her tongue over her lower lip.

What was she up to? I looked at her with a raised brow.

"What are you up to?" I asked.

"Nothing, my love, nothing at all," she said sweetly.

Gracie didn't give me a chance to say anything. Instead, she gave me a sexy little look and walked away confidently, a little extra sway to her hips. I watched after, groaning and feeling an excitement stir in me. Yes, Gracie likes to tease, but this was different. I liked it, though. It was showing her confidence and that she was relaxed.

I finished up with the dishes and went through to join Gracie, who was laying on the sofa, watching God only knows what. I went over, lifting her legs and sitting down, placing her legs on my lap. Gracie smiled brightly at me before turning back to the TV. I ran my fingers up and down her legs slowly, Gracie letting out a soft sigh of content.

"I love you, Gracie," I said.

"I love you too, Ryland," she smiled.

You probably think I say that way too many times to her in a day, but I don't care. I like letting her know that she is loved, I believe she needs that reassurance after all the shit she went through. Gracie motioned me to her with her finger, with that same smirk from the kitchen playing on her lips. I removed her legs from my lap and moved to tower over her. She was quick to pull my body down on top of her and cover my lips with hers. She slipped her fingers into my hair, pulling at it, as she kissed me harder. I moaned deeply into her lips, and this seemed to encourage her.

Gracie bit gently on my lower lip, pulling it. I groaned, my lips parting, and she took the opportunity to slip her tongue into my mouth. I happily gave her the access she wanted, and our tongues were soon dancing together. Everything about this kiss felt different.

The kiss was becoming very heated very fast and she wrapped her legs around my waist, rolling her hips up against me. Fuck! That feels good. I took hold of her thigh, doing just the same, in order to return the favor. Gracie moaned, her back arching up from the sofa. Her next move took me by surprise, as she pushed me to sit up and swiftly climbed into my lap. My hands were instantly falling at her hips, and she crashed her lips back to mine.

Things were getting more heated than what they usually do. My hormones were in overdrive, and I could feel the excitement rise in my jeans. Gracie was wearing a nice dress and due to the position we were in, the only barrier between us were my jeans and her lacy panties. She ground herself against me, brushing right against my excitement. A loud grunt escaped from my lips. As much as I was enjoying it, I pulled away. I was panting, and my pulse was racing. I was turned on.

Gracie's breathing was the same. She slowly opened her eyes to look at me.

"Why did you pull away?" she breathed out.

"Because I need to catch my breath, sweetness, and I am getting very turned on," I said honestly.

A sexy little smile raised on her lips, and she reached into my ear, placing her hand on my chest.

"Did you ever think that maybe this was my plan?" she whispered.

A shudder ran through me at the feel of her warm breath on my neck and the words coming from her lips. She pressed her lips to my neck, trailing kisses along the skin and gently biting on it.

"Gracie, fuck baby girl, yo-you are driving me crazy right now," I stammered out.

"Good, that is what I was going for!" she purred, sucking on my neck.

Gracie let her eyes meet mine, but the look they held was different. They were darker than usual, and her cheeks flushed. She was as turned on as I was. She took the bottom of my tee in her hands, tugging at it.

"This needs to come off," she said, pulling it up.

I lifted my arms, letting her take it off, and dropping it to the floor. She ran her finger tips over my chest. I gulped, closing my eyes shut, feeling her warm lips soon mapping over the skin of my chest.

"Gracie, what, what are you doing?" I panted.

"Do you want me to stop?" she asked.

"No, not really.. unless you want too," I said.

"Do you not think if I wanted to stop, I would have by now?"

she giggled.

I went to respond, but she didn't give me a chance to, her lips falling on mine again. The kiss was rough and passionate, just as all of the previous ones were. I ran my hands down her back, resting them on her briefly then grabbing and pulling her closer. She whimpered into my lips before pulling away. I opened my eyes, curious about her next move. She grabbed the bottom of her dress, pulled it off, and let it join mine on the floor, leaving her in only a sexy red lacy bra and panties matching set. I groaned, licking my lips at sight in front of me.

"I need you to touch me, Ryland," she said.

She didn't need to ask me twice. I let my hands run over her almost-naked body, pressing my lips to her, exploring the skin. Gracie let out a loud moan, her head falling back.

"Beautiful," I whisper, "Perfect," I added.

"Ryland, I need you," she said, her eyes connecting with mine again.

"You need me?" I questioned.

I had a feeling I knew what she meant, but I didn't want to jump to conclusions just in case I was reading the signs wrong. She nodded, pecking my lips before getting off my lap and up. She offered me her hand to take.

"I want all of you, Ryland," she said softly, "And I want to give all of me to you," she added, looking so innocent and sexy at the same time.

"Gracie, are you sure, my love?" I asked, maintaining eye contact.

I wanted to make sure she was a hundred percent sure. Yes, I wanted her badly, all of her, but not before I knew she was ready and won't regret it after. I didn't want her regretting anything when it comes to her and me, and this.

"Yes. I don't want to wait anymore," she said, "I have been thinking about us and all of this a lot recently," she added, waving her hand between us.

I took her hand, and she pulled me to my feet. I let go of her hand so that I could bring her close to me.

"And you are one hundred percent sure?" I asked searching her eyes for confirmation

"Yes," she said, "I have the condoms to prove it," she added, snickering.

"Mmm, OK then," I smirked.

I pressed my lips to hers, kissing her once more. I was nervous, I won't lie, It was because it was Gracie. I have not had sex with anyone I loved before. Any sex I have had was meaningless and only to fulfil my own needs. But this, this was different. Not only because it was Gracie, but also because I would be her first. I need it to be perfect. If I am this nervous, I can only imagine how nervous she is, even if she isn't showing it.

Gracie removed her lips from mine and took my hand in hers once again. She intertwined our fingers and led us towards the stairs, and then to her room, closing the door behind her. She let go of my hand, grabbing the belt of my jeans and pulled me close.

"I have never wanted something so much in my life, I want you so badly right now, Ryland," Gracie said seductively.

"Well, in that case, I better give *my girl* what she wants then, uh?" I smirked.

"Yes, you should," she said confidently, except her body language every so often betrayed her by blushing, or not being able to keep eye contact.

I walked her back towards the bed, laying her down on it, and crawled up to join her, then I lay on top of her.

"I love you, Gracie, so much," I say, stroking her hair.

"I love you too, and I couldn't imagine my first time being with someone else," she replied, the most beautiful smile on her lips.

"I am happy you trust me to be your first, baby girl," I smiled, "We take this at your pace, OK? And if you change your mind at any time, tell me," I added.

"I am not going to change my mind, Ryland," she said, "Now, shut up and kiss me," she added.

"Mmm, OK then," I said, doing as she asked.

I was ready for this with her. I just hope I can live up to the expectations of what her first time should be like. I need to stop overthinking and concentrate on what I am supposed to be doing.

CHAPTER THIRTY-ONE

Gracie

I was eager and anxious whilst Ryland and I stripped each other of the rest of the clothing between us. I suddenly felt self-conscious, being completely naked in front of him for the first time, in front of anyone for the first time. I was fighting against the will to cover myself up.

"Don't even think about it, baby girl," Ryland said softly, "You are perfect the way you are, every inch of you," he added.

Ryland started kissing over my neck, moving down to over my throat, and proceeding to the valley between my breasts. I whimpered, arching into his lips. He placed wet kisses on my breasts, and that was enough to make me cry out and make my head drop back. I tangled my fingers in his hair, tugging at it as he continued to kiss his way down my body. I closed my eyes, savouring every second of it, feeling a heat rise through my entire body.

"Ryland," I breathed out.

I felt his warm breath fan between my thighs, his lips gently brushing over my clit. I moan, gripping onto the sheets below me. Oh my, that felt good. It was a brand new sensation. He ran his lips briefly over my folds, and my hips lifted from the bed. My breathing was already heavy. He was turning me on badly.

Ryland's hands ran over my thighs, and his lips soon replaced where they were. As his lips traced where his hands had just been I cried out again. He kissed his way back up my body until he was resting over me.

"You OK, sweetness?" he asked with a smirk.

He was getting a little smug plainly because he knows what he can do to my body.

"Oh, don't look so smug, "I giggled.

"I can't help it. I like what I can do to your body," he said honestly, pressing his naked body to mine, causing no end of pleasure to flow through me, especially since I can feel just how excited he is with his hardened length pressed right between my thighs.

"Well, someone is ready," I groaned, slipping my hand between our bodies, stroking his impressive length.

"Fuck! Yes, I am," he breaths out.

It was my turn to smirk. I love what I can do to his body too. I pulled away after a moment.

"And I am too," I said, taking hold of his wrist and guiding his hand to between my thighs.

I was as aroused as he was. Ryland let out a deep moan, once he ensured I was ready too.

"Damn, gorgeous," he panted out.

"Yes, now please, Ryland, I can't wait anymore," I whined.

I was ready, and more than willing, and I didn't want to wait any longer.

"Where are the condoms?" he asked.

I nodded to the drawer, and he grabbed the box, taking one out. He rested back on his knees, only long enough for him to suit himself up. He took his position on top of me once more, and I slipped my legs around his body. He brushed his length over my folds, teasing me further.

"Ryland, please, baby," I begged, rolling against him.

"This is probably going to hurt, gorgeous," he sighed.

"I know, and I also know it will be worth it," I said, smiling.

Ryland pressed a soft kiss to my lips, holding onto both my thighs. He asked me if I was ready once more, and I nodded. I closed my eyes, preparing myself. Ryland pushed his hips forward slowly and firmly into me, growling as he filled me up. I gasped, gripping tightly onto him as he broke the barrier, and it did hurt. I kept my eyes closed tightly, taking a few deep breaths in attempt to help ease the pain.

"Gracie, I am sorry. Are you OK?" he asked, keeping still inside of me.

"Yes, I just need a minute," I whisper.

I needed a moment to let the discomfort ease off, while adjusting to him, and adapting to the new sensation.

"Take all the time that you need," he said, kissing my forehead, and staying perfectly still.

After not very long, the pain was no more, and I told him he could move. He started slowly, his strokes deep and slow. I soon forgot all about the initial pain as it began to feel really good.

"Mmm, Ryland, that feels good," I cry out, "You can go faster," I added.

Ryland picked up his speed, groaning as he did.

"You feel good wrapped around me, baby girl," he panted out.

He buried his face on my neck, and I ran my nails down his back. I went with instinct and began moving my hips with his, Ryland gripped my hips tightly as I did so. We soon fell into the perfect rhythm, our bodies seeming to fit perfectly in every way. It felt so damn good.

"Harder, Ryland," I begged.

He did as I asked, thrusting harder into me. I called out, his name falling from my lips. I used his hair to bring his lips to mine, kissing him roughly as he continued to move inside me. I have a familiar feeling starting to take over me, which I only ever felt twice before, a feeling only Ryland has ever given me.

I felt my body beginning to shake, my walls clenching around him.

"Fuck, Gracie, that feels good," he grunted, "Perfect," he added, kissing all over my check.

"I am close, Ryland, so close," I squealed out, arching up from the bed.

It only took him a few more thrusts before I called out his name, and I released around him. I clung tightly to him as my entire body shook with pleasure. Ryland pinned my hips to the bed, thrusting quickly and deeply into me. He was panting and cursing, and he followed only moments after me.

I held him against me as his climax hit. His face fell on my neck again, our bodies close and tight as we rode out our highs, Ryland stilling inside of me, falling motionless on top of me. The room filling with our heavy breathing.

"I love you, Gracie," he says, nuzzling my neck.

"I love you too, Ryland," I said, stroking his back.

We took a few moments to catch our breaths before he lifted his head to look down at me, pushing my damp hair away from my face.

"You OK, beautiful?" he asked sweetly.

"Perfect," I smiled, "That was incredible, Ryland," I added.

"Yes, I have not felt anything like this before," he said, kissing my forehead.

"Really? But you had done that many times before," I said, caressing his cheek.

"Yes, but none of them were with you, Gracie," he said, "I didn't love any of them. You are special, sweetness. You will always be special to me," he added.

"And you will always be special to me too, my love," I smile.

He smiled brightly at me, kissing me over and over again. He gently removed himself from inside of me, and I winced, as it stung a little. He gave me a sympathetic look.

"Sorry, sweetheart," he said softly.

"Don't be. It was worth it," I smirk, "And if you give me a little time, we can do it again," I added, winking at him.

"I am yours anytime, anyplace, baby girl," he said, winking back at me.

"Is that a promise?" I asked.

"Yes," he said, stealing another kiss before moving to dispose of the condom.

He came back to bed, laying down and pulling me close to him. I rested my head on his chest, the sound of his heartbeat relaxing me. Comfortable silence filled the room as we snuggled up for a bit. This is perfect. Ryland is perfect. I moved, groaning a little, as my body was still sensitive.

"I will run you a warm bath, that should help ease the soreness a bit, beautiful," he smiled.

"Thanks, love. Will you join me?" I asked, batting my lashes at him.

"I am sure I can manage that. No need to bat your lashes at me," he laughed.

I shrugged, he chuckled and shook his head at me before going to the bathroom to get our bath started. I slowly got out of the bed, grabbing one of his tees and pulled it over my naked body. I looked at the bed, and saw a little blood, I instantly became a bit embarrassed with it.

"Don't worry about it, gorgeous. It will wash," Ryland said, coming up behind me.

"Sorry," I said, looking at him from over my shoulder.

"Nothing to be sorry about," he said, kissing my shoulders.

I sighed, resting back against him, and he wrapped his arms tightly around me.

"I hope it was everything you wanted, Gracie," Ryland whispered.

I turned to face him, slipping my arms around his neck, and kissed him softly.

"It was," I smiled, "And no matter how it happened, it would have been everything that I wanted simply because it was with you," I added.

"No regrets?" he asked, a nervousness to his tone.

"None at all," I said, "I could never regret anything with you," I added.

"Good, because I would do anything for you," he replied, stroking the small of my back.

"I know you would, and I would do the same for you," I said.

I always told myself I wasn't going to have sex until at least college. I told myself I shouldn't do a lot of things until I got to college, but that all changed the moment Ryland appeared in my life. He pecked my lips before pulling away with the intention to strip and change the bed. I offered to help, but he told me it was alright.

"Come on, lovely, let's go get that bath," he smiled, offering me his hand.

I happily took it, and he led us to the bathroom, adding a bit of cold water into the bath before we climbed in. He sat behind me, letting me rest my back to his front. The warm water felt good around my body. I relax back against him.

"Are you still sore?" he asked, stroking my arm.

"A little, but this is helping," I said.

He placed his hand on my chin, tilting my head back to steal a kiss from my lips. I grinned against his lips. Once we pulled apart, we got ourselves washed before climbing out of the bath, Ryland wrapped a towel around me before wrapping one around himself. He placed his hand on my waist as we made our way back to his bedroom this time.

"Are you stealing my clothes tonight?" he chuckled.

"Always," I giggled.

"Then help yourself," he said.

We got ourselves dried off and changed, climbing into his bed. I was exhausted. I needed a little time to rest, and then I wanted to do that again while we had the place to ourselves. Maybe this time I can try being on top.

"What are you thinking about? You have your thinking face on," Ryland said, wrapping me in his arms again.

"It is a secret, but if you give me a little time, I can show you what I am thinking," I said.

"Hmm, well, I shall look forward to that," he said.

I don't think I could have asked for a better guy to give everything to. I know he loves me, and I love him. I wouldn't change a thing about tonight.

CHAPTER THIRTY-TWO

Ryland

Gracie was sound asleep next to me. I smiled as I watched her. She was beautiful and I was a lucky guy. I gently removed my arms from around her, not wanting to wake her up because I would only be away for a minute. I headed downstairs to grab the present I had bought her. I didn't get a chance to give it to her after dinner since Gracie had other ideas. I didn't mind, though, not one single bit. I grabbed the clothes we had tossed on the floor in the living room, not wanting my mom to see them as I am sure if she sees it all together, she would work out what we were up to.

I made my way back up, Gracie still sleeping when I got back. I crawled up the bed, resting over her and pressed my lips to hers softly. She groaned but kept her eyes closed, so I did again, only this time a little harder. Gracie whimpered and slipped her arms around my neck, kissing me back.

"Mmm, hi," she mumbled into my lips.

I pulled my lips from hers, sitting up on her stomach. Gracie pouted at me, not happy about the kissing being stopped. I chuckled, pecking her lips before moving to sit next to her, and she sat up.

"How long was I out?" she asked, running her fingers through her messy hair.

"Not even an hour," I said.

"That isn't too bad, I guess," she said.

"I have something for you," I said.

Gracie looked at me, cocking her brow slightly and wondering what I was up too. I took a deep breath, handing her the gift bag.

"You didn't have to get me anything, baby boy," she said.

"I know, but I wanted to," I said, "I hope you like it,"

I think she will, and if not, I can change it for something else. I sat nervously next to her as she opened the gift bag and took the box out. I swear she was doing it slower than needed to get to me.

"Gracie," I whined.

Gracie giggled, opening the box.

"Oh my God, they are beautiful," she gushed.

I had bought a set of promise rings, one for Gracie and one for me. I didn't even know such things existed until I went into the jewellery store. I was going to get Gracie a promise ring anyway, but then I saw them. They were rose gold with silver writing around the bands. The words read; I love you. The guy's one had a little black through it. They came with chains, too, so they could be worn on the hand or around the neck.

"You like them?" I asked.

"I love them, Ryland. They are perfect," she cooed, kissing me, "Thank you," she added.

"I am glad. It is my way of promising you that I love you, and I am not going anywhere," I smiled.

"I honestly do love them," she said.

"You can wear it on your fingers or around your neck," I said.

"I didn't even know you could get matching promise rings," she said.

"Me neither, beautiful," I said, kissing her cheek.

Gracie took her one out and slipped it onto her finger. It fitted perfectly because I managed to get the size from one of her other rings when she took it off to shower. I took mine out, putting it on the chain to wear it around my neck. I don't want to lose it, and I think it will be safer around my neck.

"I love you so much, Ryland," Gracie whispered.

"I love you too, gorgeous," I said, "And I promise you, Gracie, I am not going anywhere. I am going to be right here with you, no matter what, for as long as you want me," I added.

Gracie looked at me with the most beautiful smile on her lips and tears in her eyes. I knew they were happy tears. She climbed into my lap, resting her face on my cheek.

"If I say for-forever, would that scare you?" she stammered out.

"Not at all," I said, stroking her cheek.

"Good," she smiled and covered my lips with hers.

I guess if it was anybody else asking me that I would have freaked. I would have walked away and messed up, but Gracie isn't just anyone. Gracie is unique. She is my Gracie.

I groaned loudly, wrapping my arms tightly around her and happily kissed her back. We parted lips moments later, but she kept her place in my lap. She rested her forehead on mine.

"I promise you all those things too, Ryland, the things you promised me," she said, playing with the chain around my neck.

"I don't want to wear it on my finger in case I lose it," I say.

"I don't mind where you wear it, babe," she smiled, kissing me.

I pulled Gracie into my chest, holding her against me. She snuggled her face into my neck, slipping her arms around me.

"Tonight has been perfect," I said, kissing the top of her head.

"Yes, it has been more than perfect," she said, her cheeks going a lovely shade of pink.

I felt her warm lips press to the skin of my neck. The kisses were feather-like but enough to send a shiver through my spine. The light kisses turned into small bites, Gracie giggling into my neck as she did.

"Mmm, easy kitten, you are going to get me going again," I breathed out.

"When do you think your mom will get home?" she asked, running her hand down my chest.

"I don't know," I said.

"Do you think we can risk it?" she asked.

"Risk what, babe?" I said, smirking to myself.

I know what she meant. Gracie refused to answer me because she knew that I knew what she meant. She reached over into the drawer and pulled a condom out. She had brought some through with her earlier.

"Lift," she said.

I lifted my hips, and she pulled my joggers off and dropped them on the floor. Gracie pushed my tee that she had on up by her hips before leaning in to kiss me again, a little rougher this time, rolling against me. I moaned, feeling her against me again, and I was soon getting excited. I took the condom from her and moved only enough to let me slip it on.

Gracie lifted her hips, hovering over my length that was ready for her. I took hold of her hips to help guide myself inside of her. Both of us, groaning in sync as we connected again. She held onto me and began moving her hips against me.

"Does that feel OK?" she breathed out.

"Yes, it feels incredible," I grunt out.

Gracie smiled proudly when I said that. God, I was so in love with this girl, every single part of her. She picked up her speed, gripping onto the headboard as she moved back and forth.

"Mmm, Ryland, this feels good," she cried out, her head falling back.

"Fuck, yes, yes it does," I was panting out.

We got into a rhythm, one that seems to make our bodies work perfectly together. For her first time doing this, she was doing amazingly, she was a natural. The way she was working me was driving me wild.

"Ryland, ahh, I am close, baby," she called out after a little while.

I used my grip on her to flip us, so she was below me. I pushed back into her, thrusting deeply. It only took another few moments before my name fell loudly from her lips, and her climax hit, her body shaking as she released around me. Feeling her was enough to end me, and I followed only seconds later, the both of us holding onto each other as we came to our ends.

I pulled out of her, rolling onto my back, but took Gracie with me, so she was laying on top of me. I just wanted her close to me. I gently caressed her back as our bodies calmed down.

"I think you have got me addicted," Gracie chuckled in my ear.

"I am sure I can keep up," I laughed.

I kept Gracie on my chest for the next ten minutes until we had to move to get cleaned up and covered up, too, in case my mom got home. We got ourselves settled back down in my bed.

Gracie had her head rested on my chest, and our fingers linked. Not long after we settled, we heard my mom coming in.

"I will be back in a minute, just going to check on my mom," I said, kissing Gracie's forehead.

She nodded and smiled. I got out of bed and headed downstairs to check on my mom. When I got there, she was trying to sneak around, giggling to herself as she did. I think she may be a little drunk.

"Did you have a good night?" I laughed.

"The best," she said brightly, "How about you two, did you have a good night? Did you give Gracie her pressie?" she added.

"I am glad, mom, you deserve it," I smiled, "We had a good night too, and she loved it," I added.

"Thanks, sweetie," she smiled, "I knew she would. Ryland, I know I don't tell you enough, but I am proud of you and the way you look after Gracie," she added.

"Thank you, mom," I smiled, "And I would do anything for Gracie," I added.

"I know you would, but remember I am too young to be a grandmother," she laughed.

"You don't need to worry about that right now," I chuckle.

"Just making sure," she smiled, "I think I need to go to bed," she added.

I agreed and told her to go up to her room, and I would bring her some water up. She hugged and kissed me, telling me she loved me before making her way upstairs. I grabbed three bottles of water and headed back up. I made sure my mom was safe in bed, saying goodnight to her before going back to my room.

"Did your mom have a good night?" Gracie asked.

"Yes, she is drunk," I laughed, "But, as long as she had a good night, that is all that matters," I added.

"Yes, she deserves it," Gracie smiled.

"That she does," I said, getting back into bed.

"I think sleep sounds good right now. I am exhausted, again," she smiled.

Gracie and I got snuggled up again, switching the light off.

"Goodnight, my love, I love you," I said, kissing her goodnight.

"Goodnight, baby boy," Gracie said, "I love you more," she added.

That wasn't possible, but I wasn't going to argue with her about it because she always wins. Gracie curled into my body, where she fits perfectly. It didn't take her long to fall asleep. I smiled, stroking her hair.

"I got you, beautiful, always and forever," I whisper, "I promise no-one is ever going to hurt you again," I added.

I let myself drift off. My arms wrapped protectively around her. I was looking forward to waking up next to her tomorrow morning.

CHAPTER THIRTY-THREE

Gracie

I got woken up with a pair of warm lips tracing over my shoulders and neck. I moaned softly.

"Behave, your mother is still home," I giggled.

Melissa didn't start until later today. That is why I knew she would still be home.

"I am not doing anything, just waking you up," Ryland chuckled.

"Yeah, yeah, if you say so," I said, turning around to face him.

"I do. Good morning my love," he said, going to kiss me.

I quickly pulled the covers over my face.

"No kisses, morning breath," I laughed.

Ryland laughed loudly, pulling the covers away from my face.

"I don't care," he said, pressing his lips to mine.

I tried pulling away, giggling the whole time, but Ryland wrapped his arms around me tightly, effectively holding me in place for a split second until he decided to roll me onto my back, pinning me to the bed and planting kisses all over my face while tickling me too.

"Ryland, stop," I squealed.

"Nope!" he laughed, continuing with his attack.

"I will push you off this damn bed if you don't stop," I said, squirming below him.

My stomach was hurting from all the laughing, though.

"You wouldn't," he pouted.

"I will, if you don't stop," I said.

"Fine!" he said, "You are no fun,"

"I am plenty of fun," I said.

"Oh, yes you are," he smirked.

"I didn't mean like that, perv," I laughed, slapping him play-fully.

It has been a few days since our 'first' night together, and now we are struggling to keep our hands off each other. It goes without saying that we take every opportunity we can. I just can't help myself.

"You love it really, gorgeous," he winked, pecking my lips just as he removed himself from me, offering me his hand. "Come on, let's go get breakfast," he smiled.

"Can I at least put a little more clothing on first?" I asked, raising a brow.

"Yes, probably a good idea," he said, "I will meet you downstairs, love bug," he added.

"Love bug? What the heck?" I snigger.

"I thought I would try something different," he chuckles.

He stole one last kiss, pulling his joggers on and heading downstairs. I looked around for something to cover myself up with until after breakfast, and then I will get back here in order to get dressed and showered. I made my way down, joining Melissa and Ryland in the kitchen.

"Good morning, sweetie," Melissa smiled.

"Morning," I replied, grabbing myself a coffee.

"Help yourself to breakfast, Gracie," she smiled, "We have pancakes, eggs, and bacon," she added.

"Sounds delicious, thank you," I said, grateful.

She was such an amazing woman and mother. She reminded me of my own mother in a way. Melissa still has so much strength, despite everything life has thrown her way. Watching her just now made me miss my mom, though. I could feel tears build in my eyes as I helped myself to breakfast, quickly wiping the tears away I joined them at the table.

"Gracie, if you need to get more things from the house, we can find room for them," Melissa offered.

"I have a few things that mean something to me, but the rest are just things," I said, "Thank you," I added.

"Just get what you need, I want you to feel at home here," she said with a warm smile.

"And you do, both of you do," I smiled back.

I haven't felt at home like this since my mother was around. Even with everything that happened between my dad and my mom, she always made me feel safe. She always made sure we had fun. It was mostly just her and me, and I hated that bastard for taking her permanently away from me, effectively turning me into an orphan. I can safely say that If it weren't for him, she would still be here.

"Gracie, are you OK, my love?" Ryland asked, concerned.

"Yes, why?" I asked, confused.

I then realized I was crying. This time I didn't manage to fight back the tears because they were now running down my cheeks. I quickly wiped them.

"Sorry, I was thinking about my mom," I said.

"Tell me about her," Melissa smiled.

My mom isn't someone who I talk about much. The only one I mention her to is Ryland, but even with that, it isn't much. My dad made sure I didn't talk about her, anytime I tried to bring her up, he would slap me. I think that is why I don't talk about her. Well, that, and because it still hurts.

"Are you sure? I am sure you have better things to do," I said.

"Yes. Gracie, I know you miss her, and it hurts badly to talk about her, but maybe talking about her can help," Melissa smiled, squeezing my hand over the table.

I smiled and nodded. Ryland wrapped his arm around me, and I rested my head on his shoulder and started telling them about my mom. I told them everything I could remember. I was crying, yes, but I was smiling too because it was nice to talk about all my memories with her.

"She was so beautiful too," I gush, grabbing my phone.

I looked through some photos on my phone, showing Melissa one of them.

"Yes, she was," she smiled, "You look so much like her," she added.

"Yes, everyone says that" that always makes me smile. Thank God I look more like her and nothing like my father. I don't understand what she ever saw in him. My mother was too good for him.

"Thank you, this was very soothing. My father never allows me to talk about her," I said sadly.

"Well, in this house, you can talk about our Katelyn as much as you want, Gracie," Melissa smiled, "And if you need anything, you know where I am," she added.

I gave her a gracious smile before Ryland, and I had to go get ready for school. I felt better after talking with them about my past and my mother.

"Your mom is amazing, Ryland! She makes me feel like I belong, as if she had always known me" I said as we headed upstairs,

"She is and does indeed," he smiled, kissing the top of my head.

We got ourselves ready and headed out. As we get to the car, I see my dad coming out of the house. I froze, but only for a moment. I am not letting him get to me anymore.

"Gracie, you better get your crap out of my house by the end of the day, or I will sell or burn every damn thing, including your photos," he snarled loudly.

"I will," I hissed at him, I swear if he burns my photos, I will kill him.

"Good, and after that, I don't ever want to see you again," he said.

"Trust me, you will not even hear of her, let alone see her again," Ryland barked at him.

My dad glared at Ryland, and they stood staring each other down for the next few moments.

"She is dead to me, just like her mother," he said to Ryland with an evil smile on his face when he mentioned my mother. A wave of familiar anger took over me.

"No, you are dead to me, you pathetic excuse of a man," I said,

"I wish you were dead and she alive," I added not giving him a chance to reply seeing that I got into the car, and Ryland followed. I could feel my tears threatening again, but I wasn't letting him make me cry, not again. I wiped them away once again.

"You OK, beautiful?" Ryland asked, taking my hand in his.

"I will be. I will go get my things after school, and then I can be done with him, for good," I said, shaking my head.

"Yes, we can go by after school, and hopefully, he will not be there," Ryland said.

"Hopefully not," I said, "I just need to grab the rest of my clothes, my photos and my mom's box," I added.

"Your mom's box?" he asked.

"Yes, it is in my closet. It has photos, jewellery, the letter my mom left me before taking her own life, along with other things," I said, "I haven't been able to look at it since I lost her," I added.

I have tried a hundred times, but I wasn't ready.

"We can look at it later, together, if you would like?" Ryland said softly.

"I would like that, thank you, " I said, kissing his cheek.

"Anything for you, brown eyes," he smiled.

I smiled. He hasn't called me that for a while. I hated it at first, but that changed, my heart warms everytime he calls me that way. I rested my head on his shoulder as we got on the road to school.

"I love you, Ryland," I whisper.

"I love you too, Gracie," he replied.

It would be good to look at my moms' things again. It will make me an emotional mess, but I have to do it, and at least I will not be alone when I do it.

When we arrived at school, Lola and Ben were waiting for us. I smiled, getting out of the car and rushing to my best friend, hugging her. I hadn't seen her for a couple of days as she wasn't at school yesterday.

"Did you miss me?" Lola laughed.

"Always," I giggled, hugging her.

We pulled away, and she looked at me, a concerned look taking over her face.

"You have been crying. Are you alright?" she asked, "Or do I need to kill Ryland?" she was glaring at him.

"No, please do not kill my boyfriend," I laughed, "I am OK. I just had a run-in with my dad, that's all," I added.

"I apologise for the death stare," she said to Ryland.

"I will forgive you," Ryland chuckled.

"What happened with your dad?" Lola asked, turning back to me.

"It is all over, I don't want to talk about it," I said.

"OK, that is fine, but you know where I am if you need to talk," Lola smiled, hugging me again.

"I know you," I said, "Now let's head in," I added.

I didn't want to talk about it or have questions being asked anymore. I know I need to tell Lola the truth, and I will when I am ready. Ryland appeared next to me, wrapping his arm around me.

"You OK?" he whispered.

"Yes," I said, kissing him softly.

I already wanted today over with, and it's only the morning! I want to concentrate on school, get my things from the house, get on with my life, and pretend like my so-called father doesn't exist. I had better things to think about.

School, Ryland, finding a job, an apartment and College. I am not letting that coward take any of that from me. He has taken so much from me over the years, but not anymore. I was taking control of my life.

CHAPTER THIRTY-FOUR

Gracie

Ryland and I were at my house, getting the remainder of my things. My dad wasn't home, thankfully, as I wanted to get my stuff and get out before he came back. I had been dreading it all day but relaxed when I realized he wasn't here.

"Is that everything, babe?" Ryland asked softly.

"Just one more thing," I smiled.

I went into my closet, getting the box with my moms' things. I looked around and sighed. Although I was glad to be seeing the back of this place, I was sad too because this house is where I had all my mother's memories.

"Come on, my love," Ryland said, offering me his arm since he had bags in his hands, "I know you have your memories of your mom here, but right now getting away is for the best," he added softly.

I nodded, taking the memory box. We made our way downstairs, and just as we were leaving my father was coming in.

"What the fuck are you doing here?" he hissed.

"Getting my things," I said firmly.

I was not in the mood for him today. I planned to walk right past him and out of the door, but he had other ideas. He stood in front of Ryland and me, blocking our way out. I felt Ryland

E.L SHORTHOUSE

tense and his entire body language changed. He was angry.

"You better have everything because the moment you walk off that door, you aren't allowed back in here," he hissed.

"Trust me, I don't plan on coming back," I said.

"You better have everything from your damn mother as well," he said.

"What does mom have to do with any of this?" I said, feeling my anger build too.

"She was as worthless as you," he said, "It is because of her I have had to put up with you for this long, wish she would have just got rid of you like I asked," he added.

"How fucking dare you?" Ryland hissed, going to pounce at him.

I looked at Ryland, shaking my head. I needed to do this for myself.

"Don't you dare talk about mom like that," I growled, "You are the worthless piece of shit, not her," I added, my fists clenching at my sides.

I didn't care about what he said; that he wished mom would have gotten rid of me, because I have heard that a thousand times.

"No, she was nothing but a dirty hoe, just like you," my dad laughed.

Ryland dropped my things, lifting his arms to punch my dad.

"Let me do the honours," I said to Ryland.

He nodded, stepping behind my back.

"What are you going to do? You are too fucking weak to do anything, and you don't have the guts," my dad said, shaking his head in disgust.

"It would seem you don't know me after all," I said.

Before he had a chance to say anything, I flung my arm around, punching him hard in the face, so much so he fell to the ground like the damn coward he really is. His nose was gushing with blood, I could safely say that now he knows how I felt!

"I don't ever want to hear my mom's name coming from your lips ever again, you piece of shit," I barked at him, "You ever come anywhere near me again, it will be the last thing you do, and that is a promise," I added.

Ryland and I picked my things up and went to walk out the door.

"YOU HAVE NO FUCKING CLUE WHAT YOUR MOTHER WAS LIKE. SHE WAS A LYING, CHEATING SLUT," dad shouted.

I didn't respond because it wasn't true. My mother wasn't like that, but thinking about it, I wished she were. I wished she had found someone worthy of her love and would have left him, taking me with her. Life would have been so different right now, if that were the case.

"That was some punch, sweetness," Ryland said.

"Yes, who knew I had it in me," I giggled.

"I did. I am so proud of you, baby girl. So proud of you for deciding to walk out, standing up for yourself and for knocking that disgusting excuse of a human being to the floor," he said.

"It has been long time coming," I said, "But he does not get away with talking about my mom like that. She was incredible," I added.

"Gracie, I am sorry you have been through so much," Ryland said.

"It is OK. I have you now, and things will never be that bad again," I said.

"I am not going anywhere, beautiful, I promise," he said, kissing the top of my head.

"I love you," I cooed at him.

"I love you too," he replied, pecking my lips.

We headed inside, set my things down and only then I looked at my hand realizing it was swelling and red. I think I hit him harder than I thought, as it was starting to throb now. I guess when it happened, I had the adrenaline running through me, and I didn't feel it.

"Let me get some ice for your hand, gorgeous," Ryland said.

He took my other hand and led me through to the kitchen, making me sit down. He grabbed an ice pack from the freezer and placed it on my hand.

"It looks painful. Are you OK?" Ryland asked softly.

"It is, but I will be fine," I smiled.

"OK," he said, pressing his lips softly to mine.

I whimpered, kissing him back, and the pain soon faded from my mind. He pulled away after a moment.

"Hey, I was enjoying that," I huffed.

"And you can get more of it later," he chuckled, "But right now, rest your hand, and I will make us a snack." he added.

"Fine," I said, rolling my eyes out of habit whilst laughing.

Ryland made us both a sandwich and a coffee before sitting down next to me. I thanked him, kissing his cheek and resting my head on his shoulder. I was still trying to get my head around the fact that I punched my dad, but he deserved it. I just wish I had found the strength to stick up for myself before now.

The biggest difference, and probably the main reason this punch didn't happen before, is that I didn't have anywhere to go, and no one knew about what was going on. Now I have Ryland, Melissa, a house to stay in, and two people to talk to about it all. I had a support system in my life for the first time in a long time.

"Gracie, can I ask you something?" Ryland asked.

I looked up at him and nodded. You would think by now he would know he can ask me anything.

"Are you still hurting yourself?" he asked, pushing the hair away from my face.

"Not as often, no," I said, "I am not going to sit here and lie to you. I haven't recently, though, I did when I first came here to stay," I added.

"Thank you for being honest with me," he said, "Do you think you are ready to go and see someone? A doctor or a counsellor, someone like that?" he added.

"I am not quite ready yet, but I will," I said, "I promise," I added.

"When you are ready, let me know, and I will come with you, OK?" he replied.

"I will, thank you," I said, kissing him softly.

I will see someone, but not until I am ready, and I am grateful that he understands that.

"What do you want to do tonight?" he asked as we ate.

"Maybe we can look through my mom's box?" I said, "I don't think I am ready to go through it alone," I trailed off.

"Yes, I can do that with you," he replied.

I wasn't even sure what was in it. Yes, some of the things I put in, but there were things that my mother kept in, and I had no clue what those were. I had not ever been ready to look at them. I believed it would make it too final, but now was the time. I hope she will be proud of me. My mom always told me I could be whatever I want to be, and no one can get in the way of that.

I promised myself I would do everything I could to make her proud, even if she isn't around any longer. I felt tears brim in my eyes as I thought about her. I wiped them away quickly, I will save my tears for later when I am looking through her things because that will be hard.

"You OK, baby?" Ryland asked.

"Yeah. I was thinking about my mother," I said.

"I can't even imagine how you are feeling, but know I am right here," he replied.

"I know," I nodded.

Ryland and I finished up our food before grabbing my things and taking them upstairs. The pain on my hand had eased, so that was good. I unpacked most of it into my room, but the essential things would go in Ryland's room, since I stay in there anyway.

"Should we grab a shower, get changed and then we can look through it?" Ryland asked.

"Yes. I need to build myself up to it," I replied honestly.

"We got all night, sweetheart, just when you are ready," he said.

I nodded and sat the box on the bed. I can do this, it may not be until later I find the courage to do it, but I will, tonight, no matter what. I need to. It is time.

"Come on, handsome," I said, offering him my hand.

He smirked and took it. We headed to the bathroom for our shower. We shower together most of the time. It saves time and water, and it isn't like we haven't seen everything anyway. We stripped down, stepping into it.

I was facing the shower, my back to Ryland, and he was behind me with his front to my back. He pressed his lips over my naked shoulders, leaving a trail of butterfly kisses on my skin. It was enough to make me shudder and cause goosebumps to rise on my skin.

"You did amazing today, Gracie," he whispered, slipping his arms around me, "I honestly am so proud of you, my love,"

I rested back against him and closed my eyes as he stroked my side with his fingers.

"I couldn't have done any of this without you, Ryland," I breathed out.

"Yes, you could have," he said, "You have always had that strength in you, Gracie. You just needed a little encouragement," he added, kissing my neck.

"I am so grateful to you, Ryland. I hope you know that," I wanted him to know this beyond doubt.

"I do, and right back at you, beautiful, because if I hadn't met you I think things would be very different for me too," he said, "No one is ever going to hurt you again, not while I am around," he added.

And I believed those words as they fell from his lips. I have felt nothing but safe ever since I met him.

"I love you, Ryland, and I don't ever want to stop loving you," I said softly.

"I love you too, Gracie," he said, "And I don't plan on going anywhere. I am here for as long you want and need me," he added.

Anytime he says things like this my chest constricts, I really want him to know that he is it for me.

"You have told me that before, my love," I smile.

"I know, and I will continue to say it because I mean it," he replied.

"I know you do, just like I meant when I asked if forever was enough for you," I said, kissing him softly.

It hasn't been long, but we have been through a lot already. It has already become us against the world somehow, and I hope we can continue with that. Later tonight, I am going to need him more than ever before because my vulnerability is going to show, but then again, Ryland has seen every side of me, good and bad.

"I got you, brown eyes," he said, "I always will, no matter what," he added.

I smiled because I knew it was the truth.

CHAPTER THIRTY-FIVE

Gracie

Ryland and I were sitting on his bed, going through the box containing my mom's things. There were things such as jewellery, photos, my mom's perfume, along with some other odds and ends. It was nice to see all these things, but the tears were streaming down my face as I looked and recognized them.

"How are you doing, beautiful?" Ryland asked, wrapping his arm around me.

"I am OK, it's just all overwhelming," I replied.

"I can't even begin to imagine." he replied back, kissing the top of my head.

I sigh, resting my head on his shoulder, and continue to look through everything, missing the warmth of her smile; she had such a gentle smile, but she also had sadness in her eyes a lot of the time. I didn't notice that when I was a kid, but as I grew older, I noticed it because I became painfully aware of what she was going through.

"Who is that with your mom?" Ryland asked, "She looks smitten, and it doesn't look like the monster next door." He added, handing the picture to me.

I took it from him and looked at it. I had no clue who it was. I hadn't seen this particular photo before. My mom was looking at him like she was in love, and he was looking back at her the same way.

"It must be a boyfriend from before my dad," I said.

"Whoever he is, they both looked happy," Ryland said.

"She does, doesn't she?" I smiled, "I am glad she knew happiness at one point. I wonder when this was," I added.

"Let's see, some pictures have dates on them," Ryland said.

I looked for a date, but there was nothing. I turned it over, seeing my mom's handwriting.

Peter and I, August 2002.

"That date can't be right," I said, studying it.

"Why?" Ryland asks.

"Because my mother would have been at least three months pregnant with me." I said, confused.

"Maybe the date has faded or something with time," Ryland said.

I grabbed the last of the photos from the box, looking for more, and I found another two. One was from the same day, and the other was from June 2002. The one from June had the date printed on the photo.

"This doesn't make sense," I said, "She looks like she is utterly in love, but she must have been with my dad at the time. If she had someone else, why stay with my dad?" I added.

"Maybe she didn't know she was pregnant at the time," Ryland said.

"Even if she didn't, why stay with my dad when she had someone who clearly loved her?" I said, "Maybe it was my fault. Maybe he didn't want to raise another man's baby," I added, feeling the tears well in my eyes.

"I am sure that wasn't it. Your mother loved you," he smiled. There's gotta be another explanation for it!"

I know he was trying to make me feel better, but I was feeling guilty.

"We don't know that." I whimpered.

"Gracie, your mom loved you, and I am sure she wouldn't have blamed this on you!" he affirmed.

"Maybe," I sighed, "I don't think I can look at these things anymore." I added with a shake of my head.

"OK, we can put them away for now," he said.

We gathered everything up and put it back in the box. I still had a few more things to look at. I went to put the lid on, stealing another look at my mom and Peter's photo before I did. I studied the man closely. Not recognising him at all, I shook my head and put the lid on mom's treasure box.

"Can you put this away somewhere, just for now?" I asked.

I would look at it again, soon, just not tonight. I was too confused. Ryland nodded, taking the box from me and putting it away. I slipped under the covers, settling down in bed, and Ryland soon joined me.

"Come here, beautiful," he said, patting his chest.

I shift over and rest my head on his chest, his arm wrapping around me. I snuggled in close, telling him to put something on the TV, to try to distract my mind. Those photos kept coming back into my head, along with what my dad said about my mom.

"Ryland, what if Peter is my father?" I asked suddenly.

"Would your mom lie to you about something like that?" he asked, looking down at me.

"No, probably not, especially since my dad is a monster, surely if Peter were my father, she wouldn't have gone back to my dad," I said, "Sorry, I don't even know why I would think something like that." I added.

"You don't need to be sorry!" Ryland said.

It was a bad judgment call for a moment. My mother wouldn't have done that to me, to herself. I shake my head and push it all to the back of my mind.

"How are you doing, my love?" he asked.

"I am OK, I think," I said, looking up at him.

"Gracie, and I am here for anything you need!" he said.

"I know you are!" I said, kissing him

His lips were a good distraction for me. He went to pull away, but I wasn't ready for that. I pulled them back to mine, continuing to kiss him, only to pull away after a few minutes.

"You had enough now?" he chuckled.

"Hmm, for the moment." I giggled.

Ryland shook his head, laughing, and I snuggled back into him.

***

I woke up, reaching for Ryland, but he wasn't next to me. Where did he go? He was here when we went to sleep. I got out of bed, going to search for him. I found him in the kitchen, drinking what looked like tea. He doesn't usually drink tea.

"Ryland, are you OK?" I asked, going over.

"Yes, sorry, I had a bad dream that woke me up, and I didn't want to go straight back to sleep in case it continued." he sighed, running his fingers through his hair.

I went around to where he was, spinning the stool to face me, and stood between his legs.

"What happened, baby?" I asked, stroking his face.

"Honestly, it was a bit all over the place," he said, "I don't remember all of it, but it was about my sperm donor hurting someone, only I don't know who the woman was. I couldn't see the face." he added.

His nightmares weren't very bad, but he would still have them occasionally.

"I am sorry, love, you should have woken me up!" I said softly.

"I didn't want to. You have had enough to deal with!" he said.

"Ryland, it doesn't matter what I have going on. I am still here for you," I said, "We are in all of this together, no matter what!" I added, kissing him gently.

He pulled me into him, hugging me tightly. I wrapped my arms around him, hugging him back.

"Come back to bed!" I said, pulling away.

"OK, gorgeous." he said.

I offered him my hand, which he took, and I pulled him to his feet. He grabbed my hips, pulling me close, and kissed me.

"Mmm, easy, baby boy." I giggled in his lips.

He smirked, kissing me a little harder and swatting my ass before pulling away. Ryland slipped his hand around me, and we made our way back up to bed, making sure to be quiet since we didn't want to wake Melissa up.

"Hopefully, we can sleep for the rest of the night." Ryland said as we climbed back into bed.

"That would be good," I reply, "And if you get nightmares

again, please wake me up, OK?" I added.

Ryland nodded and pecked my lips. We got ourselves settled back down for the night. I turned my back to him and in response he shifted closer to me, pulling me back into him and draping his arm over me. I felt his warm lips on my shoulders and neck. I groaned, pushing back against him.

"Ryland, stop teasing," I huff, "Your mom is only down the hall, and you know I am not very good at being quiet!" I added, giggling.

It was the truth, that is why we need to behave a lot of the time when she is home.

"I know, but I have fun teasing you," he said, "The moment my mother walks out of the door in the morning, you are all mine!" he added.

"Yes, Sir!" I laughed.

Ryland reaches over, giving me a goodnight kiss.

"Goodnight, gorgeous, I love you!" he whispered in my ear.

"Goodnight, my love," I replied, "I love you more!" I added.

Ryland was quick to fall back asleep, but it wasn't as easy for me. My mind insisted on taking me back to my mom and those photos. There was something inside me, telling me I had to find out who Peter was. I don't know why, but the feeling was there. I may need to look through everything again tomorrow.

There is also a larger box with more of my mother's things in my house's attic, and I need to get that. My father didn't ever let me see what was inside of it, I tried to look at it once, and he beat me, so I didn't try again, and that's when he put it out of the way, but that would change. I will get it tomorrow when he is at work. I didn't think much about it at the time, but things are different now. There was a reason, and I want to know what it was.

Maybe that box will have some answers for me. I hope, or perhaps I am overthinking. There has been a lot happening recently, a lot of changes, and I think I need some answers. What is the worst that can happen if I look into things?

I tried pushing it all to the back of my head. I need to sleep if I want to think right since my to do list for tomorrow has grown considerably. I sighed loudly, taking hold of Ryland's hand in mine, and let my eyes close. It took a little while, but I finally felt the sleep beginning to take over me.

Tomorrow was a new day.

CHAPTER THIRTY-SIX

Ryland

I moaned, feeling a pair of soft lips on mine. It woke me up with a smile, that was for sure, and I heard a small giggle fall from Gracie's lips.

"Good morning to you too," I mumbled into the kiss, "I could get used to getting woken up like this," I added only for her to pull her lips from mine, and I huffed in disappointment.

"Oh, I am sure you could," she laughed.

"Lips back, now, please and thank you," I chuckled.

I slowly opened my eyes to look at her, and she was leaning over me, a smile playing on her perfect lips. Gracie playfully rolled her eyes at me before giving me what I asked from her, her lips. The moment they came into contact again, we both moaned in sync. I pulled away, only for a minute.

"What time is it?" I asked.

"Seven," Gracie said.

"Did you hear my mom leave?" I ask.

Gracie nodded and smirked. Oh, I know what was on her mind. I grabbed her hips and pulled her over me. She brought her lips down on mine, the kiss a little rougher than the previous one. I held her against me, and we lay there, only kissing to start with, but her kisses were enough to drive me a little crazy.

Gracie removed her lips from mine, sitting up on my stomach

and removing my tee that she had covering her body, tossing it aside, allowing me to take her in. She was so damn perfect, and I love how she doesn't try to hide from me anymore.

"Perfect," I groan, sitting up to kiss her flat stomach. Gracie laces her fingers in my hair, moaning softly and, rolling her hips onto me.

"You are ready for me, uh?" she smirked.

"Yes," I breathed out.

Gracie grabbed my boxers in her hands, and I lifted my hips so she could slip them off. They soon joined the tee on the floor. Gracie rested her naked body to mine, kissing me over and over. I let my fingers run down her back and over her ass, Gracie whimpering into the kiss as I touch her.

I reached into the drawer to grab a condom. Gracie takes it from me, opening and moving only enough to slip the condom on. She gently grazed her fingers along my length, and it was enough to make me hiss.

"Mmm, I am ready for you too," she breathed out.

Gracie took my hand in hers, guiding it between her thighs, letting me feel for myself that she was also ready for me.

"Yes, I can feel that", I smirked.

She let out a small giggle and shook her head at me. I grinned at her and placed my hand on the back of her neck, bringing her lips back to mine. The kiss was quick to become heated. Gracie lifted her hips, wrapping her hand around my length, gliding me inside of her. We called out in sync as I filled her up. After a little while, she sat back up, resting her hand on my chest and began working her hips back and forth.

"Fuck," I breathed out, gripping her hips and closing my eyes, enjoying every second of it, savouring it.

"You always feel so good," she moaned, picking up speed.

"Shit! So do you, baby girl," I grunted out.

I began moving my hips with hers, and as always we moved perfectly together. Everything we do together seems to be perfect. I opened my eyes to watch her.

"Ryland," she cried out while her head dipped back.

"Just like that, Gracie, baby, that feels good," I groaned.

Gracie began circling her hips, getting into a rhythm, then she found this back and forth motion with a swirl of her hips combining it all with a little more speed in every round. It felt incredible, and all I could think was if she kept that up, I would lose it a lot sooner than I would've liked.

"My turn," I announced.

I swiftly switch our positions. With Gracie below me, I pulled her leg around my waist, I thrusted back into her. She squealed out, gripping onto me while I pushed deep into her, my strokes quick and hard. It only took a few more minutes before I felt her walls clenching around me.

"Ryland, I am close, ahh, so close," she moaned.

I kissed her roughly, continuing to move into her until she couldn't handle it anymore. My name fell loudly from her lips as her body shook, and she released around me. The feel of all of this on me was enough for me to follow only seconds later, Gracie's name escaping my lips as my climax hit.

We fell still on the bed, catching our breaths. Gracie gently stroked my back and hair, making me smile as I nuzzled her neck.

"I love you," I whispered, kissing her neck.

"I love you too, Ryland," she replied.

I rolled off her, disposing of the condom before laying back down next to her, pulling her close to me. She rested her head on my chest, drawing circles on my stomach with her fingertips, while I did the same to her but on her lower back.

"I wish we could stay like this all day," she said.

"Me too, but we need to get ready for school soon, beautiful," I replied.

"I know," she sighed.

Comfortable silence filled the room, and I just held her close to me until we needed to make a move.

"I need a favour before we go to school," she asked, looking up at me.

"What do you need?" I responded with a question.

"There is a box in the attic of my house with my mom's things, my dad refused to let me near it. Can you come with me and get it before school, while he isn't home?"

"Yeah, of course, do you know what is in it?" I replied with yet another question.

Gracie shook her head. I think she is looking for answers, and hopes she can get them from that box.

"Thank you," she smiled, kissing me softly.

We lay there for another five minutes before going to get a shower and get ourselves ready for the day.

**

Gracie and I headed into her house, making sure there is no sign of her father anywhere. When we made sure he wasn't in, Gracie grabbed the ladder from the hall closet and set it up.

"Are you sure you don't want me to go up, Gracie?" I asked.

"Ryland, I will be fine," she laughed, shaking her head, "You worry too much," she added.

I couldn't help it, especially when it comes to Gracie. It was my instinct to worry about her, even with something as simple as this. I know I shouldn't worry this much, and I am sure that my worrying will calm down in time.

I held the ladder tightly as she climbed up it, opening the attic. I handed her the flashlight before she climbed into the space and I stood nervously below while I listened to her walking around.

"Got it," I heard her say.

She came back, handing it to me. It was quite a big box.

"There is another one, and I had no clue it was there," she said.

"Just be careful, Ok?" I said, setting it down.

Gracie went back to get the other one, passing it to me before coming down and making sure the hatch was properly closed, so her dad would have no clue she was up there.

"Come on, let's get out of here," she said.

We take a box each, heading out. She stopped for a moment, looking around. The place was a mess. She shook her head before heading for the front door.

"Can we just put these in your closet until after school?" she asked me, and I nodded.

We quickly got back to my house, we were running out of time and would be late for school if we didn't hurry. Who knew the day would come where I wouldn't want to be late to school? I know Gracie is a good influence on me, and because of her, I may be able to do more with my life than I initially thought, if I keep doing so well with school.

"What do you expect to find in those boxes?" I asked her.

"Answers. I used to believe my dad kept them from me just to be cruel, as part of his abuse, but now I am beginning to think there is more to it than that," Gracie replied.

"I hope you find what you are looking for, my love," I smiled.

We went to my room, putting the boxes into my closet out of the way.

"Ready for school?" Gracie asked, offering me her hand.

I nodded, taking and linking our fingers. We made sure that we had everything before heading out to get on our way to school. As I was driving, Gracie had put the music on. She was singing her heart out and dancing away, and at the same time I couldn't help the chuckle and the smile as I watched her out the corner of my eye. She was happy, and that's all I ever want. It was clear to notice a vast difference in her since she moved in with us.

"You are crazy, brown eyes, in the best way possible," I told her with a grin.

"I know," she giggled, "And luckily, you love my crazy ass," she added.

"I wouldn't have you any other way," I replied.

I reached over and gave her knee a squeeze, in return she smiled brightly at me. Gracie scooted over in her seat, resting her head on my shoulder. I wrapped my free arm around her, kissing the top of her head, and she snuggled in closer.

"We should do something this weekend, get everyone together and make a weekend of it," she suggested.

"Like what?" I asked.

"I still need to work on that plan," she laughed.

"I am sure between us all, we can come up with something," I responded.

Gracie nodded and kissed my cheek before placing her head back on my shoulder, keeping it there for the rest of the ride. I had an idea for the weekend. Ben's parents owned a beach house, a few hours from here. Maybe we could go there if his parents let that happen.

My mom would be fine with it, especially since she has let Gracie move into my room. Plus, it would give my mom a weekend to herself to do as she pleases.

I would keep the idea to myself until I can ask Ben. We got to the school, parked the car and went to meet Lola and Ben, just the person I needed. The girls soon got into conversation, and I pulled Ben aside.

"Everything alright?" he asked.

"I need to ask you something. Your parents' beach house, would they let you use it this weekend? Gracie wants the four of us to do something together, and I think it would be good for us all to get away from here," I concluded.

"Yes, they probably would. I will talk to them," he smiled, "It would be good for us to get away for a couple of days," he added.

"Thanks, buddy, but let's not say anything to the girls until we know for sure," I said.

"Good idea," he replied.

We went back to the girls, letting them finish their girly talk. Ben and I looked at each other, laughing and shaking our heads as they gibbered on.

"Hey! We saw that," Lola whined.

"Aww, I am sorry, baby," Ben replied, pulling her close to kiss her and she mumbled into his lips all too soon, forgiving him.

"Let's head in because they could be here a while," I chuckled, Gracie laughed and nodded in agreement and I wasted no time to slip my arm around her as we made our way in. It has been a good morning so far; hopefully, the rest of the day will be the same. And with some luck, later on, Gracie will get the answers she needs, I just hope there is nothing to upset her or turn her world upside down.

She has been through enough. She doesn't need to go through anything else.

CHAPTER THIRTY - SEVEN

Gracie

I was waiting for Ryland by his car as we didn't have our last class together. I was anxious to get back to look through the boxes and he should have been out by now, so I kept my eyes on the door, waiting for him. And soon enough I saw him coming out, the biggest smile came onto his lips when he looked up and saw me, I automatically smiled back.

"Hey, babe," he said, kissing me when he approached.

"Mmm, hello," I mumbled into the kiss.

The kiss was short and sweet, Ryland pulling away first.

"Ready to go home?" he asked.

"Yes. I need to know what is inside those boxes," I sighed, "Can we get a pizza on the way?" I added.

Pizza was my comfort food, and something tells me I will need it when I'm looking through those boxes.

"Yes, of course, and ice cream too?" Ryland smiled softly.

"That's a sure way to my heart, pizza and ice cream; you know me too well, baby boy," I replied, kissing his cheek.

We climbed into his car, heading to the diner to get what we wanted. Ryland's hand held mine the whole drive. I waited in the car as he went inside to get our order, being alone for those short minutes wasn't a great idea! As I had so much going around in my mind I got lost in thoughts and ideas of what could be in those boxes. Not all of the possibilities were good, though and I became worried in case, rather than getting answers, it could just bring more questions.

"You OK, sweetness?" Ryland asked, pulling me out of thought.

"Hmm, yeah, just getting lost in my head," I whispered softly.

"Let's get home, my love," he said, resting his hand on my knee.

I nodded, resting my head on his shoulder as we made our way back. We headed straight up to the bedroom and I took the boxes from the closest.

"Will you please eat at least a slice of pizza first?" Ryland asked.

"Honestly, I would rather look and then eat,"

He sighed and nodded while I made myself comfortable on the bed, with Ryland sitting next to me. The first box was mostly my mom's clothing and some of her favourite things. There were some old photo albums, and I took a look through them, but there was nothing in them that I was looking for. Maybe I won't get any answers after all.

I groaned in frustration, grabbing a slice of pizza to munch on before getting into the second box.

"What if this is a waste of time?" I sighed.

"You may not find anything, but it is best that you checked, rather than continue wondering," he responded, kissing me.

"I guess," I whispered.

I finished off my pizza and started on the second box, where we found some letters and a few more photos. I made my way through them, noticing more pictures of my mom and Peter. The dates span over a year; who was this man? I know she was in love with him because they look at each other the same way

Ryland and I look at each other.

"I need to find out who this man is, Ryland. He obviously made my mom happy, and I would like to thank him for that, especially because of the way my father treated her," I spoke, "I didn't think she ever felt real love, but looking at these," I said pointing to the photos, "I realize she did,"

I still have so many questions. If she was happy with him, and they loved each other, why did she stay with my father? I needed these questions answered.

"Maybe we can try to find him," Ryland suggested.

"I would like that, but I don't think it will be possible. We only know his first name, and I don't know anyone that my mom would have told about him," I replied.

"We will work something out," Ryland smiled.

I nodded, giving him a slight nod. I didn't know if that would be possible, but I know he is only trying to help me, so I left it at that and we continued to look through the photos. Ryland left to go downstairs and grab us a drink.

I lifted one of the photos. It was a photo of my mother and I. I must have been about four or five, and we weren't alone. There was another woman in the image with a little boy, who looked about my age. I had no clue who they were. I stared at the photo, but the more I did, the more I got confused.

I don't know who the woman was, but she looked very much like Melissa. It obviously wasn't her, but the similarities were uncanny.

"Everything OK? You look confused!?" Ryland asked.

"The photo I am looking at, I don't know who the other woman and little boy in it are, but the woman looks a lot like your mother, how strange is that?" I giggled.

"Really?" he asked.

I nodded and handed it to him. He took it from me, staring at it wide-eyed.

"It can't be," he said.

I was about to ask him what he meant, but he rushed out of the room before I could, taking the photo with him. Where was he going? I sat there, waiting for him to come back. He came back about ten minutes later, muttering to himself.

"This can't be right," he said, pacing the bedroom. "Did you say that it was you and your mother in this photo?" he asked.

I nodded, wishing he would tell me what was going on. He handed me the photo back and then gave me another one. It was of the same woman and the same little boy.

"Ryland, who are these?" I asked.

"It is my mother and I," he said.

Wait, what? How can that be? How can that be the four of us in one photo?

"But how can that be?" I asked, "Our mothers didn't meet, and we only met when you moved here," I added.

"Gracie, I have no clue, but it is," he said, running his fingers through his hair.

I tipped the rest of the photos out and rummaged through them. There were at least another half a dozen photos of us together.

"Do you remember any of this?" I asked him.

"I have slight memories of a little girl I used to play with, but nothing that can tell us anything," Ryland says, "I don't even know where this is, do you?" he added.

I also didn't recognise the place we were at. It looked like some beach with a park, but where, I don't know.

"No, I don't know," I replied, "Why don't we remember each other? Why hasn't your mom mentioned any of this?" I added.

Just as I predicted, now there were more questions than answers. Is there a chance Melissa just doesn't remember, the same way Ryland and I don't remember? Surely not. Ryland and I were only kids. Our mothers weren't. Why would Melissa lie to me like this? Where did she and Ryland disappear to?

"I don't know, sweetheart, but the moment she walks through the door, we will find out," he assured me, "I can't even think of a reason why my mom thought keeping this from you was alright," he added.

Ryland seemed upset with his mom, and I understand why. I didn't know what to feel right now. I don't want to get upset at her, not until I know the truth anyway.

"I can't believe we have known each other this long," I announced.

"I know, do you think maybe that is why we got so drawn to each other as swiftly as we did? Because we had met all those years ago?" Ryland pondered.

"Maybe, it would explain a lot," I whispered, "I don't understand where we met. I have stayed here my entire life. You haven't," I added.

"We moved around a lot, especially when I was a kid," Ryland said, "Maybe we were here at some point, and I just don't remember," he added.

All of this was very overwhelming and I needed a break from it all. I gathered everything up, placing it back in the box and setting it on the floor for now. I still needed to read the letters, but I don't think I can handle them right now.

"Come and lay with me?" I requested, laying down.

I was still letting all this sink in when Ryland managed a slight nod and came to lay down next to me, pulling me close. I rest my head on his chest, and he wraps his arms tightly around me.

"Maybe my mom knows about Peter," Ryland noted.

"Possibly, but before any of that, I need to know everything else," I responded.

"We will get your answers, Gracie, I promise," he smiled, stroking my hair.

I hoped he was right. All of these made me feel like there is a part of my life missing, part of me missing. It was a strange feeling. He kissed the top of my head. I just needed silence; for now, I needed thinking time. Our next findings would explain a lot.

***

Ryland and I had finished eating and snuggling for a bit, and soon I was feeling up to looking through the rest of the things. We had the letters on the bed.

"I will read one, and you can read one," I suggested.

There were two different handwritings on the envelopes, telling me the letters were from two different people. I began reading the one I had. It was a love letter from Peter, a beautiful one at that. He was telling her how much he loved her, how incredible and beautiful she was. I could feel the tears well in my eyes as I read it.

"Gracie, are you OK?" Ryland asked, concerned.

"Yes. This letter is beautiful. It is a love letter from Peter," I whispered.

"A love letter, can I see?" he smiled.

I nodded, handing it to him, he smiled as he read it.

"Oh wow, that is beautiful," he said.

"I know, right? He loved her so much," I gushed.

"I need to know why he left, or why my mom left him," I whispered, "I can't but think that If they stayed together she would still be here," I added in a whimper.

"I am sorry, my love," Ryland said, coming to hug me.

We read through the other letters from him. The last one was not long after I was born. So I was the reason she lost the love of her life? A feeling of guilt took over me. I know my mother would hate me for feeling like this. She would tell me it was not my fault and that sometimes life goes in a different direction than we hoped. I couldn't help it, though.

"Ryland, she lost him because of me," I sobbed, "I am the reason my mother had a life of hell," I added.

Ryland pulled me closer to him, hugging me tightly, and I broke down in his arms. He gently stroked my hair, trying to soothe me.

"Hey now, this isn't your fault," he whispered.

"You don't know that," I sobbed, clinging to him.

"Gracie, your mother loved you. You made her happy," he replied.

"I know she did, but she still lost Peter because and spent her life with a monster because of me," I breathed out.

Ryland just held me, doing his best to comfort me until I calmed down. It took a while, and all of it was still playing on my mind, but sadly I can't change what happened.

"I wonder who the other letters are from?" I asked curiously.

Ryland opened one of them, skimming through it.

"They are from my mother," he said.

We skimmed through a couple of them. We soon realized they wrote to each other for a while. They were supporting each other while apart. My mom and Melissa were going through pretty similar things, and by what they are saying in these letters, our fathers kept them apart. It is why Ryland's father took them away; he didn't want his wife around my mother.

"Bastard! How dare he? That is why he kept moving us around, so neither of us could get close to anyone, so no-one would know what was truly happening," Ryland hissed.

I saw a wave of anger rise in him that I haven't witnessed in a while.

"They could have helped each other if he hadn't taken us away," Ryland snarled.

He was right about that. If our mothers didn't get pulled apart from one another, both of them could have had a very different life. Ryland got up and began pacing. His fists clenched, he was cursing and mumbling under his breath. I could see him going to a bad and dangerous place in his mind.

I quickly got up to him, standing in front of him, making him stop. His eyes were full of anger when he looked at me.

"Ryland, please calm down. You are making me nervous," I whispered, taking his hand in mine.

I watched his eyes soften when I said that. He pulled me to his chest and hugged me tightly.

"Sorry, even the thought of the bastard makes me want to kill him, I am sorry I scared you," he said.

"I know, Ryland, but don't let him make you go there, he isn't worth it," I whispered, "And you don't need to be sorry," I added, lifting my head to kiss him softly, "We have each other now, babe. We can get through anything together," I spoke confidently.

"My mom will be home soon, and we can get to the bottom of all of this," he sighed.

"Yes," I agreed, kissing him again.

I hoped that was true. Surely, Melissa can give me answers, give us answers better than anyone else, but I don't want to upset her or put her on the spot. I wanted the three of us to sit down and have an adult, civilized conversation while looking through everything together.

"Please don't get angry with your mom, Ryland, OK? That won't help anything," I suggested, gently.

"I promise I won't," he said, kissing my forehead.

Melissa should be home in the next hour, and it could change everything.

CHAPTER THIRTY - EIGHT

—

Ryland

Gracie and I were in the living room along with all the photos and letters, sitting on the table simply waiting for my mother to get home. I was pacing the length of the living room as I was feeling mad at my mom, despite all my efforts not to be.

"Ryland, will you please come and sit down with me?" Gracie whispered, "You need to calm down"

"Sorry," I sighed, going to sit down next to her.

Gracie placed her hand on my knee, calming me down instantly. I was hoping I wouldn't lose it with my mom, since she doesn't really deserve it, but then again, Gracie and I didn't deserve to have been lied to either.

A few moments later, we heard the front door open.

"Hello, I am home," she called out.

"Mom, can you please come into the living room? We need to talk," I called back.

My mom came rushing through, a worried look on her face as she looked between us.

"Is everything OK? God, are you pregnant?" she asked.

"No, Gracie is not pregnant, mother" I said, shaking my head.

Her worried look was replaced with a confused one. She went

to speak, but before she could, her eyes fell on the table, seeing the things scattered out.

"You found out?" she stammers out.

"Yes, so can you sit? We need to talk," I said firmly.

You could hear in my voice that I was annoyed. My mom sighed, nodded, and sat on the chair across from us, reaching over to the table and grabbing one of the photos. It was one of her and Gracie's mom. She smiled as she looked at it.

"Katelyn and I were best friends. We met when you kids were two and stayed very close until we moved away, when you two were six," mom said, "Your mother was an incredible woman," she added.

"Why didn't you tell me, Melissa?" Gracie whimpered out.

"I was going to tell you, tell both of you, I promise," Mom whispered, "Even after we moved, your mother and I kept in touch for a little while until we sadly lost touch," she added.

"How did you lose touch?" I asked.

"Your father moved us around so much that I lost track of everything." she said looking at me, then she faced Gracie again, "He burned all the letters that Katelyn had ever sent me along with the details of the address," she explained, "I didn't know she had taken her own life until only a few months ago," she added.

I could see the tears welling in my mother's eyes as she spoke. I could tell by looking at her that Gracie's mom meant a lot to her.

"How did you find out?" Gracie questioned.

"I ran into an old friend, another woman that used to spend time with us, and she told me," she answered, "The moment I heard that I planned on finding a way to get to you because I knew your dad was a monster. I didn't even want to imagine what hell he had put you through," she added, sobbing, tears running down her cheeks.

We listened to my mom as she told us that this was the reason she went for this house; she knew Gracie was next door. It wasn't her original plan to move here, but then everything went down at school with me and that was when she decided to move us here.

"I still don't understand why you didn't tell us, mom, especially when we got together," I said, "If we knew, it would have explained why we were instantly drawn to each other," I added.

"Because I needed Gracie to find that strength within her, to leave that house, leave her dad. I didn't want to force her to. It was a decision she had to make, with just a little encouragement," mom replied.

I understood my mom wanting Gracie to make this choice, but even with that, she should still have told us this rather than letting us find out this way.

"I got the shock of my life when you showed up at the house with Ryland. I didn't expect that to happen. I was going to find a way to make contact with you, Gracie, without your father getting in the way," mom revealed.

"So, you came all this way just to help me?" Gracie asked.

"Yes. I didn't want you staying with that horrid man any longer," mom responded, "But I should have known you two would have found a way to each other," she added, smiling.

"Why?" Gracie and I questioned in sync.

"Because even at such a young age," she said pointing to one of the pictures, "The two of you had such a strong bond. I am surprised that you didn't realize you knew each other sooner,"

That was strange. You would think if we had developed such a strong bond at such a young age, we would remember each other. But then again, the two of us have been through a lot since then, and that said I am not surprised we block some of our life out.

"We did?" Gracie smiled, looking at me.

"Yes, trying to get you two to part from each other was not easy for us. The both of you would cry hysterically," mom laughed, "After we left, Ryland was miserable, and your mom said you were too," she added.

"Why didn't we come back here when that bastard left?" I hissed.

"Because I needed a fresh start for us, Ryland, and I didn't know that Gracie still stayed here, not until I ran into that old friend I told you about," mom stated, "Had I known, I would have come back here a long time ago. I would have taken both Gracie and her mother away from him," she added.

I could see the anger in my mom's eyes as she spoke of Gracie's dad. My mother continued to tell us about their friendship and what happened between them. She told us about all the days we used to spend together.

"Gracie, I am sorry, sweetie, that I didn't tell you sooner. I am sorry that I didn't come to you sooner. And I am sorry that Katelyn took her own life. You know she loved you, right? With her whole heart?" mom said.

"I know she did. My mom was the most incredible person in the world, but it all became too much for her. I know she didn't want to leave me, she just couldn't handle it anymore. I was angry with her for leaving me, but I soon realized why she did it," Gracie whimpered out.

My mom came over to the sofa, sitting next to Gracie and

wrapped her arm around her, hugging her. Gracie broke down as they hugged. I hated seeing Gracie this way. I stroked her back as my mom tried soothing her. It took a little while, but eventually she stopped crying.

"Thank you for coming here, Melissa, and getting me away from him. Thank you for bringing Ryland back into my life because I don't know where I would be right now without him, without you," Gracie said.

"Well, we are right here, sweetie, I promise," my mom told Gracie.

We knew the truth about what happened with our mothers, with us, but I know Gracie still needed to know one more thing, did my mother know who Peter was?

"Melissa, I need to ask you about something else," Gracie whispered.

"I know you do, darling. I can see the letters and photos," Mom said softly, "But first, I will make us all a coffee, and then we talk, OK? You need a little breather before we get into that," she added.

My mom did know who he was then. Gracie gave her a nod, and my mom went through to make us coffee and a snack.

"Gracie, are you sure you can take any more tonight?" I asked, stroking her cheek.

"I don't know, but I need to know, Ryland," Gracie replied.

Nodding, I kissed her softly. I didn't know if this would all be too much for one night, but I knew that Gracie needed to know. I just hoped it wasn't information that would break her all over again. All I could do was be there for her in any way I possibly could.

***

We had taken a break for half an hour, having our coffee and snacks, talking about other things. I could tell Gracie was getting anxious because she wanted to know about Peter.

"Melissa, I need to know about Peter now," Gracie announced, "Did you ever meet him?" she went straight to the point.

"No, I didn't meet him, but your mom told me about him," mom said.

"Who was he? I can tell by the photos she loved him, and he loved her," Gracie sighed.

"Yes. Katelyn loved him deeply," mom said.

"Then why did she stay with my dad? Was it because of me?" Gracie whimpered.

My mom took a deep breath.

"Your mother was planning to leave, even after she found out she was pregnant with you," Mom said, "But your dad found out she was pregnant before she had the chance," she added.

"What happened?" Gracie questioned.

"Your father threatened her, threatened you even before you were born," mom said, "He threatened to hurt both of you if your mom left. He said if she even tried, you wouldn't get a chance to be born," mom added, tears building in her eyes again.

"Meaning?" I asked.

"I would rather not say those words, but I am sure if you think about it, you will both know what he meant. And no, I don't mean he was going to force your mother to have an abortion,"

"He was going to make my mom lose me?" Gracie sobbed out.

My mom nodded. He was willing to do such a horrible thing. I had known long before now he was a complete monster, but that is something on a completely different level.

"I hope that bastard will rot in hell," I barked.

"You and me both, son," my mom said, shaking her head.

Gracie had fallen silent. She looked as white as a ghost. She was in complete shock. We didn't say anything because we knew she needed a moment.

"Is that why my mom stayed all those years, because he threatened her with me if she left?" Gracie breathed out.

"Yes, and your mother would do anything for you, Gracie," mom replied.

"Melissa, is Peter, my real fa-father?" Gracie stammered out.

I could tell by the look on my mother's face before she even said anything that he was.

"Yes, but Peter didn't know. Your father does, though," mom said.

"Wait, what? That monster next door knows I am not his?" Gracie snapped.

"Yes. He used you to keep control over your mother,"

I swear the more I heard, the more I wanted to go next door and kick the fuck out of that piece of shit!

"Then why keep me around once she was gone?" Gracie whimpered.

"I am guessing it is to do with money," mom pondered.

"Why didn't she tell me this?" Gracie cried.

"Because it was safer for both of you if she didn't. I know it seems cruel, but that was not it at all. She knew if she made one wrong move, said one wrong thing, she would be putting you in danger," mom replied.

Gracie started crying again, began pacing the living room, mumbling to herself as she did. She was trying to take it all in. We let her be because it was what she needed to do. I wanted to go over, wrap my arms around her and hold her close, but that wasn't what she needed at this moment.

"I need to find Peter. Do you know his full name? The letters don't have addresses or anything on them. Did Peter know my mom was married?" Gracie speaks.

"They used a P.O box, so your father didn't see them," mom said, "And yes, Peter knew. He wanted to take your mom away, but after everything that happened, your mother cut all contact with him," she added.

I can't even begin to imagine the emotions that Gracie was going through right now. She came back over, sitting down next to me. I pulled her close, holding her.

"Do you know his second name?" Gracie asked again.

"Yes, it is Peter Robertson, the last your mom heard he was staying in New York, but that was a long time ago,"

"Whatever it takes, I need to find him. I don't expect him to want me when he finds out the truth, but I want him to tell me about my mother, when she was with him because she looked happy when they were together," Gracie said.

"And we will do everything we can to help you, my love," I announced, kissing her forehead.

My mom nodded in agreement with me. Gracie needed this. She needed to find him, know him, and find a part of her that has been missing for all these years.

"Thank you, but right now I need to lay down. My head is spinning," Gracie said.

"I am sorry it took until now for you to find all of this out," mom said.

"It is OK, thank you for being honest with me, Melissa," Gracie smiled, "I understand why my mother liked you so much," she added, hugging her.

Gracie headed upstairs after that. I gave my mom a quick hug and sprinted up after my girl. She was curled up on the bed, crying. I went over, lay behind her and wrapped my arms around her protectively and let her cry.

"I have got you, " I whisper, stroking her hair.

Gracie turned around, curling into me and burying her face in my tee. I didn't know what to say to her, but I didn't think she needed words. I think she just needed me to hold her, and that I will, I will hold her for as long as she needs.
"I love you, Gracie, and no one is going to hurt you ever again," I cooed at her.

"I love you too," she sobbed out, clinging onto me tight.

She had overcome so much already, but she still has a long road ahead of her with everything she had learned tonight.

CHAPTER THIRTY - NINE

Gracie

I had been all over the place the last few days. I haven't been myself to be honest. I was spending most of my time locked in my bedroom when I wasn't at school. I had been trying everything to find Peter, but thus far I wasn't getting anywhere. I couldn't find him anywhere and it was frustrating the hell out of me! I was fighting with everything I had in me not to take it out on myself. I don't want to go down that road again.

Instead I had been taking my frustration out in Ryland, which isn't fair. I don't mean to, but I have just had so much going on. My emotions are all over the place, and I seriously needed to find Peter. I need answers, and I need to tell him the truth.

I don't even know if he will want anything to do with me. If he doesn't, that is his choice as long as he knows. I had tried everything I could think of. I don't know what my next step is going to be.

"Fuck!" I hissed, tossing my phone away, pulling at my hair.

I need to pull myself together. I don't like to be angry, and being like that isn't going to help with anything.

"Gracie, can I come in?" I heard Ryland's voice ask from the bedroom door.

"Yes," I called back.

Ryland came in, giving me a soft smile before coming over to sit on the bed with me. I moved into him as I needed the comfort of his arms wrapped around me.

"Any luck?" he asked softly.

"Nothing," I sighed.

"I am sorry, beautiful," he said, kissing the top of my head.

I snuggled tightly to him and he knew without me telling him that I needed him close right now. I hated myself for the way I have treated him recently, he doesn't deserve it, not after everything he has done for me.

"Ryland, I am sorry I have been such a bitch to you over the last few days. I didn't mean it," I whimpered.

"I know you didn't," he said, "You don't need to get upset," he added.

He placed his finger on my chin, using it to tilt my head back so that I was looking up at him, and pressed his lips to mine, giving me a soft kiss. On cue, I felt my entire body relax at his action, and I smiled into his lips.

"I need to stop getting myself angry and frustrated because it isn't helping," I stated.

"You will find what you are looking for, Gracie," he said, "It will just take some time," he added, pushing the hair behind my ear.

I knew he was right, but that doesn't make it any easier; right now I need to stop, even if it's just for a few hours before I drive myself insane.

"Can we get out of here for a little while? Go for a walk, and maybe grab some food? I haven't eaten all day," I said.

I was too preoccupied to think about food.

"Gracie, you need to eat," he said.

"I know, that's why I suggested it," I smiled.

He nodded, and we stole another kiss before making a move to head out. We decided to walk to where we were going for lunch, it was a lovely day, and I could do with the fresh air. Ryland linked his fingers with mine.

"I have been thinking about something," he announced as we walked.

"Do you want to share your thoughts?" I asked.

"The last known location for Peter was New York. Maybe we should take a trip to New York," he suggested, "We may get better answers there,"

He had a point. Maybe that would be better. We could even go take a look at some of the College campuses while we are there.

"How would we get there?" I questioned.

"We could drive. It will take about six hours, it could be fun," he smiled.

"Yes, good idea," I agreed, "Maybe we can go and look at some colleges too?" I added, hopeful.

I know Ryland still wasn't entirely sure what he wanted to do after high school. If he wanted to go to college, he could. He has been doing great at school. He is an intelligent guy, even if he will not admit it.

"We will need to go Friday and return Monday though," he said.

"It may be tight, money-wise, but I am sure we can work it out," I said.
"We will make it work," he said, "I think this is your way of trying to talk me into going to college," he added, chuckling.

I didn't say anything. Instead, I gave him my cheesiest smile. I wouldn't force it upon him, but I can try to encourage it. Ryland laughed loudly, wrapping his arm around my shoulder, he pulled me into him.

"You are lucky that I love you so much," he smiled.

"I know I am," I said proudly.

I was feeling better already. He always knew how to make me laugh and smile, sometimes without even trying. I would be completely lost without him, especially right now.

"You always have a way of making everything better, Ryland," I said, kissing his cheek.

"I try my best, my love," he grinned.

I hope he knows that I appreciate him, and everything that he does for me. I sometimes think that I don't show him that enough. Maybe I need to find a way to demonstrate to him. I will come up with something.

Right now, I just want to enjoy my day with him.

***

Ryland and I had a good afternoon. We had our walk, lunch, sex, and now we were relaxing in his bed, looking at hotels in New York. As long as it had a bed, a shower and was clean, that is all we need.

"Are you sure you are ready for this, Gracie? Because New York may be where you find your answers," he said.

"As ready as I'll ever be," I replied honestly.

We had concluded that we would go next weekend. We found a cheap hotel in the middle of the city which we were surprised about. Ryland double-checked that I wanted to do this before confirming our booking.

"No going back now," he smiled, kissing me.

"Yes. At least if I don't get my answers, it will still be worth the trip,"

I didn't want to go there with my hopes too high in case it was another letdown. I don't know if I can handle another big blow just yet. I have so many questions running through my head.

Will he want anything to do with me?

Does he have another family?

Does he remember my mom?

Is he a decent man?

It was some of many questions. I would understand if he doesn't want me in his life when I randomly show up seventeen years later. But, at the same time, I don't know how I will cope with another rejection. There I go again, getting lost in my head.

"Gracie, what are you thinking about?" Ryland asked, pulling me out of thought.

"I was just getting lost in my head, that's all, nothing to worry about," I responded.

I don't want to go into it all again because it is getting repetitive. The issues will still be there tomorrow.

"You want to go out tonight? See our friends? Distract me from everything else?" I suggested.

"Good idea!" he smiled.

I grabbed my phone to text Lola.

Hey, do you and Ben want to hang out tonight? X

I hadn't been spending time with Lola recently, only at school. I felt terrible about it. It made me want to tell her what was going on, but I will wait until Ryland and I have been to New York, and then maybe it will be time to tell her EVERYTHING!

Lola: Yes! I like that idea! We can work something out when we meet up?!

Gracie: Yes. Meet at Ben's about seven, if he is alright with that? X

Lola: He will be OK with it. You know he can't say no to me X

Gracie: Yes, that is very true! We will see you then X

Lola: OK. See you then, babe. Love you X

Gracie: Love you too X

"We have to go to Ben's for seven," I smiled.

"What are we doing?" he asked.

I answer with a shrug causing him to laugh. We will find something. We always do. It doesn't matter what, we always have fun when we are together. We could just stay in and watch movies or go out and find something to do, either way. It will be a good night.

"Well, we should get showered, dressed, have dinner and then head over," Ryland suggested.

"Good idea, wash all the sex and shame away," I giggled.

Ryland playfully rolls his eyes at me, laughing.

"No shame here, love," he smirked, kissing me.

"Mmm, no, not here either," I replied, smirking back, "Let's go, handsome," I added.

I got to my feet, offering him my hand, which he happily took. I pulled him to his feet, and we headed for a shower. I am sure we will probably be getting distracted in there too.

I wanted us to enjoy tonight. I needed it, Ryland needed it. It was going to be a busy week. We had to get organised given we are going to New York, school, and I would stop by and see my mother too. I haven't been to her graveside in a long time. I couldn't face it, but Ryland said he would come with me.

It would give me a chance to introduce him to my mother. I know that sounds crazy since she isn't here anymore, but I like to believe she is watching over me. She would have liked teenage Ryland. I smiled at the thought of my mom. She was so beautiful, intelligent and sweet.

I like thinking about her whenever I can, but only when she was happy, not sad.

"You OK, Gracie?" Ryland asked as we stepped into the shower.

"Yes, I am fine," I smiled, pulling him close to kiss him.

Right now, I want to concentrate on what I have right in front of me. I don't want to think about the past or the future, not at this moment.

Everything will work out the way it is supposed to. I hope.

CHAPTER FORTY

Gracie

Ryland and I arrived at my mom's headstone. It was strange being back here, it has been a while. After all, I couldn't face it, but now is the right time to do so. In fact, it has been too long, and she deserves better. I rest the lilies that I brought with me down; they were my mom's favourite flowers. I cleaned it up a little too, you could tell no one has been here for a considerable amount of time.

Ryland sat the blanket down on the grass that surrounds it, taking a seat, and once I finished, I joined him. I wish this weren't how Ryland and my mom had to meet, but it is, and I can't change that. Yes, they met a long time ago, so what I mean is meeting again when he is older and with me. I don't know, maybe some people find what I am about to do crazy; ultimately I don't care what they think.

"Hey mom, sorry it has been so long, but it was too hard," I said, "It doesn't mean I don't think of you every day, it's the opposite really, I miss you every day," I added, feeling the tears brim in my eyes.

Ryland rested his hand on my knee, smiling at me.

"Anyway, a lot has happened since we last spoke," I said, "I finally got away from him, mom," I added.

I knew she would be proud of me for that because she couldn't do it. I don't blame her for any of it, though. You can't change the past, right?

"I found out about Peter too. I wish you told me about him," I sigh, "And I am sorry you couldn't be with him because you were protecting me. I decided I am going to go find him," I added.

It was strange when I spoke these words to her; a gust of wind came over me, but everything else was still. It was like she was telling me she was sorry. I don't know, maybe I am just hopeful, either way, it was a comfort.

I told her about everything else that has been going on in my life, and by the time I was done, I was a sobbing mess. I felt my heartbreak all over again as I told her. I hate that she didn't have the chance to watch me grow, and for that, I will always blame that bastard.

"You got this, beautiful," Ryland smiled.

He wiped my tears away and kissed me softly, I instantly felt better. Nodding, I turned back to where I was.

"It isn't all bad, though I apologise for the tears," with a faint giggle.

I was feeling mixed emotions, to be honest. It was good to talk to her, tell her everything, even if it wasn't all good. I had saved one of the most important things until last.

"I would introduce you to Ryland, but as it turns out you already know him," I laughed, "Melissa came back mom, she came back to get me away from him. I understand why you two were close at one point," I added.

I honestly believed if they didn't lose contact, things might have been different for everyone. But, I was happy that my mom had someone like Melissa in her life, a true friend. I told her about what Melissa has done for me and how she told me about Peter.

"Anyway, back to Ryland," I smiled, "I am in love for the first time in my life. And for the first time since you, I have someone who loves me back, even though that monster tried to convince me I wasn't worthy of it," I added.

"Hello, Katelyn," Ryland announced, "I know you have been worrying about our Gracie here, and you don't have to anymore. I got her, I promise, and no one is ever going to hurt again, not while I am around," he added.

I sat and listened as Ryland chatted away to my mom like she was right here with us. It was making me fall even more in love with him, if that's possible. I giggled to myself as he rambled on. It was adorable to watch. I am sure she would approve of him. He was gushing over me and telling her how far I have come and the strength I have.

As I continued to listen to him, I suddenly shivered, and for a split second, it felt like there was a pair of arms wrapped around me, embracing me. It wasn't Ryland, he wasn't close enough. I closed my eyes, taking a deep breath, and I swear for a single moment I smelt my mother's perfume. It felt like she was right here with us, giving her approval. It was a strange feeling indeed, a feeling I have not ever felt before.

"I will stop talking now," he chuckled after about ten minutes.

"No, you are fine," I laughed, "I think she approves," I added, kissing him.

"You do? And what makes you think that?" he asked curiously.

"I can feel it," I smiled.

"Good, I am glad," he grinned widely.

"And to think at the start, mom, Ryland was a pain in my ass," I snicker, "Who knew he would become my saving grace?" I added.

"And you, mine, my love," Ryland smiled.

"I got lucky with this one," I stated proudly, "We are heading to New York this weekend. We are going to check out colleges and see if we can find anything about Peter," I added.

"Yes, your daughter is trying to talk me into going to college, something I didn't think I wanted, until Gracie," Ryland laughed.

I don't think his issue was he didn't want to. I believe he felt he wasn't good enough to go, which is bullshit! He is more intelligent than he gives himself credit for.

"Do or do not! There is no trying!" I announced, trying to impersonate the one and only Master Yoda. "I'll succeed." I informed both of them in my normal voice.

Ryland laughed loudly, shaking his head at me. He knew I was right. I would talk him into it, eventually. We still had a little time, so we stayed a little longer, it felt nice to be here talking with my mom.

"Ryland, thank you for doing this with me," I said, kissing his cheek.

"I would do anything for you, Gracie," he responded.

Breathing out, I silently thanked God for Ryland's life and willingness, as I don't think I could have done this alone.

***

Ryland and I stayed by my mom for another hour, mostly talking a lot of nonsense in the end, but that was alright. My mother was a patient woman, that was for sure. We gathered up our things and went to walk back to the car, but I stopped.

"I will catch up with you in a minute, baby boy"

Ryland nodded without asking any questions, kissed me softly and started making his way back to the car. I would follow in a few minutes. I just wanted a moment alone with her. I knelt in front of her headstone.

"Mom, I am going to be alright, aren't I? I am still scared," I whispered.

It was true I was still terrified of a lot of things. I didn't want to say that in front of Ryland.

"I need to know I am going to be OK," I whimpered.

I could feel the tears building in my eyes, but I didn't want to cry. A familiar embrace surrounds me, the same one I felt earlier. I see something fall next to me out of the corner of my eye.

I turned to find a large white feather next to my feet. I smiled, reaching down to pick it up. I stood for a moment, my eyes closed over and breathed in the fresh air—

a sense of relief taking over me.

"I get it, mom, loud and clear," I said.

It may sound odd, but it was the sign that I needed. My mom and I used to collect feathers when I was younger, and she always told me any time a feather falls, it is life's way of telling us everything will work out how it is supposed to.

It may only be a coincidence, but to me, it is my mother's way of telling me what I needed to know.

"Thank you, mom," I announced, "I love you, and I will see you soon," I added.

I slipped the feather into my pocket and ran to catch up with Ryland.

"Everything OK?" he asked, slipping his arm around me.

"Perfect," I gushed, resting my head on his shoulder.

I felt like a weight had been lifted off my shoulders, thanks to my mom. Freedom of sorts took over me, which I had not felt in a long time. I didn't need to be the broken girl, the one who knows nothing but hurt. I deserve better.

We made our way back to the car, Ryland letting me climb in first before getting in himself. I rested back on the seat, smiling to myself.

"It is good to see you smile like that, sweetheart," he said.

I rest my hand on his thigh and my head on his shoulder. Ryland wraps his free arm around me, kissing the top of my head.

"I love you, Gracie."

"I love you too, Ryland,"

We got on the road back home because we had a lot to get done before heading to New York. I don't know what New York will bring, but I need to find out either way. It is a step I need to take, something I need to do for myself.

"We are going to be OK, Ryland. I can feel it," I announced.

"Yes, yes we are. I don't doubt it for a second," he responded.

I still had a lot to deal with, and so did Ryland. He helped me, and now, it is my turn to help him in any way I can. I took the feather from my pocket and set it on the dashboard.

"Where did that come from?" he asked curiously.

"My mom, her way of telling me I was going to be OK," I said brightly.

"Sweet! We can keep it right there," he grinned.

I am glad he doesn't think I am crazy for saying something like that, believing in something like that.

"Next stop NYC, baby," I said excitedly.

"Yes! Bring it on," he replied, meeting my excitement, "No matter what happens, we will make it worth it," he added.

It was the next important thing for us, before graduating and everything that will follow; we have a lot ahead of us in the next months.

I just don't think that either of us realized just how much both of our lives are going to change.

TWO HEALING SOULS

Book two coming Agust 2021. Preview of chapter one, book two below.

BOOK TWO - CHAPTER ONE PREVIEW

Gracie

I sat in the passenger's seat wide-eyed as we drove through the streets of New York City. The place was incredible, the skyline beautiful. I was feeling a lot of emotions all at once right now. I was excited to be here and nervous because I have no clue what this city held for us.

"We made it, and in one piece," Ryland laughed.

"Yes, the long-assed drive was worth it," I smiled.

I nearly changed my mind about coming here at the last minute, but Ryland and Melissa talked me into it. I knew it was for the best. I wanted answers, scratch that, I needed them. We followed the directions to our hotel. It was close to Central Park, which surprised us with the price. We arrived, but it took some time to find a space to park; it was NYC, after all, and now I understand why not many people drive their own cars here.

I stepped out of the vehicle and took a better look around.

"I think I am in love," I gushed.

I don't think I have ever seen a place like that. I haven't seen many places in my life, but I am sure even when I do, NYC will still be up there. This place has always been at the top of my list for college, along with Oxford and Yale. Though Oxford doesn't have what I am looking for. I think that appealed more because it was the other side of the world, but through the course of the last year that choice got put on the back burner.

"Already?" Ryland chuckled, coming up behind me and wrapping his arms around my waist.

"Yes. How can you not love this incredible city?" I stated, looking over my shoulder at him.

"Hmm, am I going to have to drag you back home come Monday?" he laughed.

"I shouldn't think so, but I won't make any promises," I giggled.

Ryland shakes his head at me, chuckling before turning me around to face him. He steals a kiss before taking my hand and leading us inside.

"I can't wait to explore!" Ryland announces.

He was as excited as me. I couldn't wait either. We left at six a.m. this morning, so we would still have most of the day by the time we got here. We ditched school because if we didn't, we would not have gotten here until at ten p.m. tonight. The plan was to enjoy the rest of today, and then tomorrow we will be going to NYU for a tour of the campus in the morning, while in the afternoon we will be going to try to find something on Peter.

Ryland grabbed our bags from the back seat as we went in to get checked in. We had paid for everything, so it was only a case of letting them know we are here and get our key card.

"Good afternoon, welcome to New York," The receptionist smiled as we approached.

"Good afternoon," I replied, smiling back at her.

Ryland gave her our details, and we soon had our key. We thanked her and headed up to our room.

"I love how this weekend we can do as we please," I smirked.

"Mmm, yes we can," Ryland responded, smirking right back at me.

Yes, we had a lot planned for this weekend, but we still need to make time to be alone, because we don't get that often. We plan on making the most of everything this weekend!

"Shower and then food is what I need," I announced as we entered the room.

We have been on the road for hours, and I felt yucky. We grabbed a quick breakfast before we left, but any stops after that was just for coffee because we didn't want to add too much time to our travel time.

"Wonder if it is big enough for two, and I mean to save time," he said.

I raised my brow at him. I didn't know if I believed him. Ryland laughed and shrugged. That was what I thought. He went through to check the shower.

"What is the verdict?" I called out.

"Plenty of room, so get your sexy ass through here," he called back.

I made sure to take my time, so much so he came through and pouted at me. I gave him an innocent look, acting as if I didn't know why he was fretting.

"Fine! Be that way," he huffed.

He pretended to be mad, storming off towards the bathroom again, chuckling to himself the entire time. I laughed loudly, following him. I don't know why he was pouting. He knew I would follow eventually. I had a feeling a lot of this weekend was going to be like this, a lot of teasing, but that is always fun. I didn't plan on spending too long in the shower. We have things to do and say.

***

Ryland and I had finally got out of the hotel. It took longer than planned but it was worth it.

"Where to first? What should we do? Where shall we go?" I said quickly.

I think my excitement was getting the better of me. I was hyper suddenly. Ryland took hold of me and pressed his lips to mine. I knew that was his nice way of saying be quiet.

"And breathe," he stated, pulling away.

"Sorry, I can't help myself," I giggled.

I kept myself calm, and we made our plans. We found a café to grab lunch to take away. Ryland suggested sitting in, but my suggestion was better. Lunch and coffee in Central Park. What was the point in sitting inside when you can have lunch somewhere like that? It wasn't hard to convince Ryland to do that.

"Could you imagine staying here and coming to Central Park every weekend?" I smiled.

I would be moving here, and Lola too. Yes, Ryland said he would come with me, but we haven't really discussed it in detail. Maybe today would be a good time for that. I think it would be fun, maybe Lola, Ben, Ryland, and I can get an apartment, and none of us will have to pay for dorms. And I am sure between the four of us we could manage an apartment.

I took Ryland's hand in my free one as we got to the park and found somewhere to sit. It was not too busy because most people would be at work, school, or college, so we found the perfect spot. It gave us a great view, and the sun was hitting us. I snapped a couple of photos and sent them to Lola.

ME: Hey! Look where we are! Ahh! This could be our home soon! X

She asked me to send her photos. Lola and Ben were coming next month to get a campus tour. I would have invited them with us, but that would have meant I would have needed to tell her everything, and I didn't want to, not until I knew what this weekend will bring. She was quick to text back.

LOLA: I am so jealous! Could be? It will be. And maybe we can talk the guys into coming with us X

Great minds think alike, right?

ME: Hell yeah! My thoughts exactly! I am going to talk to Ryland about it right now. I will call you later X

LOLA: Talk later, Gracie. Enjoy your day X

I put my phone away and turned my attention back to Ryland.

"Ryland, if you end up not going to college, will you still come here with me? If you don't want to, that is OK," I said, "Just don't feel like you need to," I added.

We still had time before we graduated, but I would rather know in advance what was happening. If he doesn't come, I don't know what I will do. How many long-distance relationships work? I would miss him, and it would break my heart, but I wouldn't hold it against him.

"Gracie, if I decide not to attend college, I still plan on coming here with you," he smiled, "I couldn't deal with us being apart like that," he added.

"Are you sure? I don't want you to feel like you don't have a choice," I said.

I didn't want him to have any regrets or end up resenting me.

"I am positive, my love," he stated, kissing me.

I did feel better after hearing him saying that.

"Yay! Which takes me to the next thing," I said, "How would you feel about getting an apartment with Ben and Lola?"

"I think that would be great!" he beamed.

"Now, all we need is to talk Ben into it," I laughed, "The rest of us are up for it," I added.

I am sure we can convince Ben to join us. I was still hoping that Ryland would choose college, but it isn't something I will force on him. That is his choice. If he would rather instead go straight into work, I would support that.

I was happy we had that out in the open. I moved, resting between Ryland's legs, and we started on lunch. He kissed my neck for a moment, and that was enough to make me moan. I am glad he stopped because it doesn't take much for him to rev me up.

"How long is this tour tomorrow?" he questioned.

"It starts at ten and finishes about twelve," I reply.

"That is not so bad," he said.

I was ecstatic about seeing the campus, seeing where I would spend my time after high school. New York would be a fresh start for everyone, and I think we need that.

"What about your mom? Will she be OK if you move here?" I asked, turning myself around to face him.

"Yes, my mom will be fine, especially if she knows it is best for me," he said, "And as long as she can come visit and stay, she would be happy with that,"

After everything Melissa has done for me, the thought of leaving her behind weighed heavily on my heart. And it goes without saying I would miss her just as Ryland would too. Melissa can come to visit anytime she wants.

"Your mother will be welcome anytime," I said brightly.

"Not anytime, don't tell her that. She will be here every week-end," he laughed.

"Hmm, yes, maybe not anytime," I giggled.

"We will work it all out. It will be good for us, starting over somewhere different," he said, kissing me.

There would be a lot to plan before we move, but we have the time. And we will get there. The four of us can come before graduation and find an apartment.

I know I may not even get into NYU. I plan on applying for more than that. I will apply to other colleges here too, and if I don't get into any, I will come up with another plan. All I know is that, no matter what, I am coming to New York. Everything works out the way it is supposed to, right? I surely hope that is true.

"I don't know what is going to happen between now and when we graduate, but what I do know is as long as I have you, Lola and Ben, things will be fine," I said confidently.

Ryland agreed with a nod and stole another quick kiss. If I don't get into college, I will work and try the following year again, and if that doesn't work, I will consider somewhere else.

For now, I have other things I have to concentrate on, and I plan on doing just that.

———

Printed in Great Britain
by Amazon